Jesus in the Mist

Jesus in the Mist

STORIES

Paul Ruffin

The University of South Carolina Press

© 2007 University of South Carolina

Published by the University of South Carolina Press
Columbia, South Carolina 29208

www.sc.edu/uscpress

Manufactured in the United States of America

16 15 14 13 12 11 10 09 08 07   10 9 8 7 6 5 4 3 2 1

Library of Congress Cataloging-in-Publication Data

Ruffin, Paul.
    Jesus in the mist : stories / Paul Ruffin.
        p. cm.
    ISBN-13: 978-1-57003-699-6 (cloth : alk. paper)
    ISBN-10: 1-57003-699-3 (cloth : alk. paper)
    1. Short stories, American. 2. Southern States—Fiction. I. Title.
    PS3568.U362J47 2007
    813'.54—dc22   2006101063

This book was printed on Glatfelter Natures, a recycled sheet with 50 percent
postconsumer waste content.

For Amber

Contents

Acknowledgments

My gratitude goes to the following journals and anthologies where these
   stories initially appeared:

"Crows," *Louisiana Literature*
"The Day J.P. Saved the South," *New Mexico Humanities Review*
"The Hands of John Merchant," *New Texas II*
"Harvey Watson and the Angel," *Louisiana Literature*
"Hunters," *New Texas*
"In Search of the Tightrope Walker," *Connecticut Review*
"J.P. and the Water Tower," *Southern Review*
"Jesus in the Mist," *Louisiana Literature*
"The Natural Man," *Crescent Review*
"The Queen," *Pembroke Magazine* (originally published as "The Boat")
"Teaching Her about Catfish," *New Growth*
"Time of the Panther," *Cross-Timbers Review*
"The Well," *Kansas Quarterly*
"When Momma Came Home for Christmas and Talmidge Quoted
   Frost," *Idaho Review*

PART I

When Momma Came Home for Christmas and Talmidge Quoted Frost

"Talmidge," she said across the living room to her husband, who was stretched out on the couch with his camouflage clothes still on from a deer hunt earlier that Saturday morning—it wasn't quite eleven. He was in his socked feet, muddy boots just outside the kitchen door, where she asked that he always leave them. White shag did not clean up easily. He stirred at her voice but did not open his eyes.

"Tal-*midge!*"

Then he did open an eye and even turned his head a bit toward her.

She had been sitting a long time staring at the Christmas tree in general and at a great frosty blue ornament in particular, almost four inches across, hand blown and therefore not quite round but close enough that no one could tell without close inspection. It had been her mother's favorite over the years, passed down for four generations, probably the oldest one she had and the dearest to her. It even had its special velvet-lined box that a snow globe had come in.

"Whu-ut?" he finally said.

She slowly rotated her head in his direction until her eyes met the one that he had open.

"Talmidge, how far can you throw a softball?"

He turned his head back in alignment with his body, which looked all the world to her like a great mound of leaves raked up to haul off or burn.

The little ridge of hair he still had, with not so much as a trace of color left in it, resembled a horseshoe made out of dirty ice and wedged down on his head, the skin clamped between its prongs red as a blister. A front-end man at the local Ford place, he spent most of his weekends on that couch when he wasn't hunting or fishing, usually with the blaring television on, whether he was watching it or not, and flipping through the channels like it was a game and he was way behind. Such, Darlene had decided, was the general nature of the Southern male. If he had read more in his life than a stack of magazines, mostly having to do with guns and hunting and fishing, he never let it show. She had never seen him with a book in his hand, except for a tattered reloading guide he kept in the shop with all his man stuff.

He had been a good husband and provider for nearly twenty years, and she loved him, but, Lord, he was so rough around the edges, with not a dram of romance in him. Every time she thought she had him house-broken—in all the ways a woman would mean it—he reverted and went back to being the same man she met at the door every weekday evening: greasy and shopmouthed and smelling of beer and cigars. The mechanics had a daily ritual of meeting at a joint after work and drinking beer and smoking and griping about the owner of the dealership. She put up with it, since it kept him happy.

"Did you hear—"

"Two hundred and seventy-two feet, eight-and-a-half inches," he said. "If the ball ain't wet and it's a still day."

"That *far?*"

He rolled his head toward her again. "Hell, Darlene, get real here. I ain't thowed a softball in ten years, and I got no *idear* how far I can thowe one. Maybe from here to the road."

"Which is not all that far," she said.

"And then only if I had a ball and a reason to thowe it, and I ain't got either." He belched and rolled his head back and dropped his chin on his chest.

She saw no advantage in pushing, so she let him drift off to sleep. Before his lips had begun to puff and flutter, she had the blue ball off the tree and in its padded box. There was plenty of time, plenty of time.

For eight months now her mother had sat quietly on a bookshelf in the guest bedroom, six or seven pounds of gray bone ash in a plastic bag inside an urn made out of something just slightly cheaper than Tupperware and that inside the ordinary cardboard shipping box she came in, courtesy of the U.S. Post Office, which didn't even have the common decency to ask anybody to sign for it. They left her momma wedged in the mailbox like a carton of Mississippi State cheddar cheese, with the lid flopped open where any dog could have lifted on his hind legs and carried her off and maybe scattered her across the lawns of people she had never known and would have hated if she had. But Darlene didn't complain, just gave thanks that she got to her before the dogs did and brought her in from the weather.

Pitching cremation was not an easy thing with the old woman, since she had it fixed in her head from the time she was a little girl that on Judgment Day all the bones in the cemeteries would rise up and reassemble, knee bone to thigh bone to hip bone and all that, and walk forth to wherever it was they caught the freight that would take them off to Heaven. Darlene had a hard time making her understand that skeletons can't even get up out of the grave, much less walk, without tendons and muscles, which the worms would have taken care of, twenty-year gasket guarantee or not. And what were they going to do once they got off at the Pearly Gate Station and got their marching orders, sit around and clack their boney jaws together all day singing hymns of praise and gazing out on streets of gold, gold there was nothing to spend on, even if you could scoop some up?

She and her mother fought often about what the old woman called Darlene's lack of faith, but Darlene's final argument was always that faith, like anything else, occasionally runs into a wall it cannot penetrate, especially one that's built of scientific fact. She found it much easier to reason with her fifth-grade students, who carried their parents' beliefs on their shoulders like heavy baggage, than to deal with her mother and her notions of what happened to the body after death.

It wasn't until a family friend chose cremation and her momma heard about how sweet it was for the family to sprinkle her ashes in all the places she loved that she began to yield to the notion. It was like God had sent a messenger to help Darlene out. And *what* a messenger.

Old Miz Melvinson was the chosen one. She went to the same church as Darlene's folks before her father died and her mother withdrew into her shell, and they both belonged to a quilting group called the Stitch and Bitch Club, only her mother hadn't been to a meeting in months. She never attempted a stitch at home, but she fervently practiced her bitching. Miz Melvinson dropped by one Sunday morning to have some ice cream and whiskey with the old woman—what they called bourbon sundaes. They sipped on them and reviewed the rumors of the day until they just drifted off to sleep in the plantroom chairs and drooled and dreamed until well on over into the afternoon.

Darlene usually went over there on Sunday to spend a little time with her mother. It was that, or the old woman would insist on moving in with them, which Talmidge had already put his foot down about. "She moves in, I move out. It's that simple." That's what he had said.

They were all three seated there, the two old women snoring and Darlene flipping through a *Southern Living*, when Miz Melvinson rolled her rheumy eyes over at Darlene and started talking just as her mother stirred to life and started listening. It was odd how the subject came up, but come up it did, and Darlene was glad.

"You know, Myrell Atkins died last month." She wiped her mouth with the back of her hand. "I was just dreamin' about her. We was cousins, two or three times removed, maybe four. Had the cancer. By the time she died, they said she was just one big cancer. What the fambly done was to have her cremated, which was what she had ast for. The childern take'n her ashes out to ever place they ever lived at and sprankled part of her under azalea bushes and mimoser trees, in ditches and ponds, just all over everwhere that she lived at and loved. Big as she was, they was sprised and disappointed they didn't get a bushel basket of ashes so they coulda spread her futher."

Darlene tried to explain it, but Miz Melvinson could somehow not get it through her head that the size of a person did not determine the volume of ashes, since all you got back was ground bones and teeth, and in Miz Melvinson's case it would be just bones, only Darlene didn't tell *her* that. They removed anything artificial before incineration—or so Darlene had been told. She figured that meant gold fillings as well. She had been told that too.

The old woman took a snort of what was left of her BS and continued: "Gerald, her son, the dim one they call Dum-Dum, he take'n a good double handful of her for what he called agrigut or somethin' like that and mixed her with some ce-ment and water and poured a little square out by the road and made her initials in it with a pocketknife, only he got the letters backerds since he's dislectric, and put a pot of geraniums on it. Sweet is what it was."

She could still hear Mrs. Melvinson going on and on about it and would have gotten up out of her chair and hugged her out of gratitude but for the fact that the old lady had a goiter the size of an unshucked coconut on her neck and bristly with hair like a coconut and she wasn't sure how it would be touching something like that—warm and hairy and part of somebody's neck. So Darlene just smiled a lot and later, after the two old women had come out of their bourbon doze the second time, shook Miz Melvinson's hand as she left.

Talking with Talmidge about cremation was like talking to him about the economics of Tasmania. The first time she brought it up was essentially the last. He was sprawled on the couch, as always, firmly rooted in the wallow he had made for his butt in the middle cushion, thumbing through a magazine and looking at pictures of guns, when she just up and asked him what he thought about cremation. For a long time he didn't even bother to look over at her, but finally her insistence prompted him to raise his eyes from his *American Rifleman*.

"Well, this ain't the kind of thing I like to think about or talk about, so let me tell you just once and we 'll let it lay there forever after, if that's OK with you: I flat don't give a shit what you do with my body once the breath is gone. When I am thoo with it, as far as I am concerned you can have it cut up and barbecued and served in Ethiopia. Bury me in the ground or stuff me and prop me in a corner or have me cremated—I really do not give a hearty shit. Just make sure I'm dead first, whatever you decide to do with what is left after the spirit is gone."

So she said no more to him about it, though she went that very day and took her will out of the safety-deposit box down at the bank and retyped it completely, stipulating in language as plain as she could put it that she was to be cremated and her ashes were to be scattered. She named eight places dear enough to her that she wanted to be part of the rest of eternity and concluded with a paragraph that almost made her cry: "And I want what's left over to be kept safe and secure until such time as they can be mixed with Talmidge's ashes. And no matter what he says, he is for cremation too. If he goes first, he won't have a choice. If his ashes are already in the ground, I want them dug up and mine mixed with them and put back where he was. He may not be much of a husband, but he is all I have." She didn't know how to make it any plainer than that. Anybody who could not follow those instructions was a fool.

Disposing of her mother's ashes would have been a simple matter of driving down to Vaughan to the Old Home Place, just a few miles north of Jackson, walking back in the bushes to where the house had stood before fire took it one deep December, and scattering the ashes all about, especially under and around the azalea bushes her momma had so dearly loved. But where families are concerned, things are rarely simple. A hunting club bought the property—a sale agreed to by Darlene only when her three brothers outvoted her and told her she could sign or not but the place was sold—and threw up a game fence some twelve-feet high to keep in their cultivated many-pronged bucks, with locked gates and warning signs galore. And when Darlene asked permission to scatter her momma's ashes where the old house had stood, they advised her that no trespass would be permitted. Whatever their reason, they were staunch against the ashes being spread there. She even offered them fifty dollars, which they politely but resolutely refused. Like Momma would scare away the deer.

The notion that came to her that Saturday morning was the result of months and months of worrying about how to get it done: how to spread her momma's ashes where she promised that she would. The hardest part, then, was over. Convincing Talmidge was merely a matter of matching his wits against hers, which was like pitting a VW against a freight train.

That Sunday morning Talmidge was predictably out in the shop fiddling with his loading equipment. He had bought a big blue something-or-other machine, huge and complex as a chemical factory, that he referred to as a progressive loader. It would load two thousand rounds of pistol or rifle ammunition a minute, or something like that, without missing a beat, and the powder charges, he said, would be within something like an eyelash weight of each other through the whole run. That too made a big impression on her. He shot maybe five times a year out at the range and had never so much as drawn fur on a deer, though he hunted constantly. He did bring in a coyote once, but she refused to let him have it mounted —made him bury it in the backyard. So she couldn't see the need for anything that could crank out enough ammo in a day to equip most African nations, but he bought it with his own money, which he made on the side by rebuilding transmissions on the weekends with parts stolen at the dealership, so she didn't gripe about it. It kept him in the shop and out of her hair.

She walked in without knocking, which she wished she hadn't, since he had just passed some truly vile gas, so she just backed out and gave it time to clear, then knocked. He motioned for her to enter.

"Whussup, Baby? Sorry about the fart. More room for it out here than it was in there." He pointed to his belly.

"Talmidge, I have a problem, and I want your advice."

This was the way to handle him. Like most male animals, the way to get a man to do something is to let him think that he thought of it first. Actually, she was being a little unfair, since she had over the years subdued him to the useful and the good by methodically correcting his manners and language until she at least felt comfortable with him in Wal-Mart. But that was unfair too. He really was not such a bad sort, and he did love her, which no other man had done, or at least not long or properly. He would even go to church with her some Sundays, if she promised him fried chicken or a pot roast afterwards, or a quickie.

He had turned off the progressive part of his machine and sat looking at her while it whirred. "What can I help you with, lady? Your transmission slippin'?"

"Not a chance, with my man around," she said.

"Whut it is, then, Baby?"

"It's Momma, Talmidge."

He stared at her for a few seconds. Then: "She done come back from the dead, or whut?"

"Talmidge, I'm serious. Mother—"

"I'm serious too, Darlene. You talking about a *dead* woman, just ashes. Ain't no voices comin' from the box, is there? What the hell's she got to do with anything anymore anyhow? And how come you call her Mother with one breath and Momma the next?"

"She answered to both. I used *Momma* mostly when I wanted something. It sounded less formal. Now I just mix them up."

"OK, then what about her, whatever you want to call her?"

She cleared her throat. "We have not fulfilled her final directions. We have not scattered her ashes at the Old Home Place."

"And for a very good reason. We been told that if we go back in there we will be persecuted, without we got antlers and at least eight points."

"Prosecuted, not persecuted."

"Well, Darlene, I don't know about you, but I don't want either one done to me."

"Talmidge, where there's a will . . ." She stopped at that because it just didn't sound right, since her momma had not actually had a will, which caused all kinds of grief in settling the estate. Her sister had threatened to take her to court to get an antique German silver service, which Darlene didn't even want anyway, but it would have fetched a pretty penny at an auction. They fought half a year dividing up the paltry estate.

"There is a way to do it, which is why I am out here consulting you."

He reached and turned the loading machine off completely and spun around on his stool to face her. "And exactly how I can I help in *this* matter?"

Darlene looked over at the refrigerator in the corner of the shop. "Would you like a beer while we talk this over?"

"On Sunday morning? If I had of thought of that, you'd of said *no way, Hozay.* What you up to?"

"Call it a special occasion, Talmidge. Do you want a beer or not?"

"Does a frog have a water-tight asshole?"

"I take that to mean yes." Darlene walked over and took two beers out of the refrigerator and handed them to him. "You'll have to twist those caps off."

"You having one too?"

"This is some serious business, Talmidge. A beer will help."

He screwed the caps off and handed her one beer and threw back and downed half of his before he came up for air. He belched and winced.

"Arright, Darlene, tell me, whussup, girl."

"OK, Talmidge." She took a sip of beer and leveled her eyes at him. "If you wanted to get something through or over a game fence—like, say, a bunch of ashes—how would you go about it?"

He finished his beer and walked over and got out another one. It was clear that he was thinking but not that he was thinking clear. He sat back down on the stool and took a slug, then studied the condensation on the bottle.

"With shotgun shells. I would load shotgun shells with the ashes and shoot'm right over and thoo that fence, what I'd do."

"Unh-hunnnnnh," she said, "and exactly how long do you think it would take somebody from that damned hunting club to be all over you? Two minutes? Five? Ten? You have already told me that you can't mess with people like them."

"Thas the best way I can think of. You'd scatter'm all over creation with shotgun shells. Yer momma would blanket that place. Blast'r right outta the shotgun and then haul ass."

"Talmidge, you know how Momma hated guns. She'd come right back here and haunt both of us."

"Then what would *you* do, Darlene?"

Well, she had given him his chance to come up with a plan. Now she was ready to present hers. She sat down on the stool next to him and leaned forward and with her schoolteacher demeanor began: "Here's what. . . ."

When she had finished explaining her plan, Talmidge studied it a few seconds. Then he brightened: "Why don't we mix it two-thirds Bullseye and one third ashes and run a fuse down in there. It'd be like a grenade."

All she knew about Bullseye was that it was some kind of gunpowder or chewing tobacco.

"We are not going to turn Momma into a *bomb,* Talmidge. We are going to do it my way."

"Well, how about I blow it up with the shotgun once it's over the fence. I could do that, you know, fling it way high over the fence and blow that sucker to Kingdom Come."

"Either way, Talmidge, you would bring those hunting club people down on us in a flash, and besides, that is no way to treat Momma's remains. We are going to do it *my* way."

"OK," he said. "OK." He reached and flipped his big blue ammunition factory back on.

Two days before Christmas they drove to Vaughan from Tupelo, a four-hour pilgrimage under anyone else's dominion, a mere three hours with Talmidge's heavy foot hurtling the Dodge Ram south. He drove a Dodge to spite the owner of the Ford place where he worked.

Midafternoon they were there, alongside the road that had once been what everybody called the Main Drag in Vaughan but now witnessed an occasional passerby and that was all, except for the steady parade of vehicles going in and out through the gate on the road that led to the hunting lodge. The game fence, high and tight in its glory, glistened in the sun as they stood and tried to make out what tree was what on the Old Home Place, some thirty yards from the edge of the highway. She worked from memory, he from photographs he could recall.

Long they stood at the fence studying the line of trees and shrubs and low-growing plants as she named what she could of what she remembered. He merely nodded. A couple of trucks crept by, and men with orange caps studied them, but no one stopped and said anything. The two of them just acted like tourists, though Darlene could not imagine why anybody would believe that there were tourists in Vaughan. But it *was* where Casey Jones had his famous train wreck, after all. There was even a little museum in the depot at the site with lots of train stuff in it, including the bell from the *Cannonball.*

And then it was time. They walked back to the truck, and she took the cardboard box and carried it to the back of the truck, where Talmidge had lowered the tailgate. With a paring knife she pried loose the end of the container her momma's remains were in and lifted out the plastic bag, secured with a tie like one used for kitchen garbage. She undid the tie and opened the bag.

"Load her up," she said to her husband. "And be quick. There're too many of those damned trucks going by to suit me."

Talmidge, bless him, lost as he was at this unfamiliar enterprise, stared at her a few seconds, then snapped the hook ring from the big blue ornament Darlene had removed from its velvet box and inserted one of his reloading powder funnels and dipped a big hand into his mother-in-law's ashes and slowly dribbled her into the ornament until it was nearly full, probably a good pound. His lips said nothing. His eyes said nothing.

Then he snapped the hook ring back onto the ornament and hefted it for her.

"This is probably the craziest Goddamn thing I have ever done. Are you ready?"

"Yes," she said. "I am ready." She hesitated, then said, "But you have got to get it right. You have got just one shot."

"Yas'm."

"Wait," Darlene said. She went to the cab and got out their movie camera, then gave him a thumb's up.

A big man, in anybody's book, Talmidge nodded and removed his coat, slid up the sleeve of his sweatshirt, looked up and down the road, and dropped into a pitcher's stance. Then he rared back and cocked his arm, and when it went forward, the blue ornament arched high, far above the game fence, seemed to hesitate against the blue sky forever, then fell into the stark limbs of an oak and shattered into a great *poof* of silver and blue fragments and ashes, and as they stood watching, it all came down, easy and soft as snow.

"My God, my God," Darlene whispered as her mother's ashes lightly settled onto the ashes of what once had been her home.

Then a voice came, as if from the sky itself: "Such crystal shells, shattering and avalanching, you'd think the inner dome of heaven had fallen."

"Talmidge?" She stared at him for what to an onlooker might have seemed like a full minute.

"Sorry," he said. "It just come to me."

"It's from Frost," she said, "from Robert Frost. From a poem called 'Birches.'"

He shrugged and turned to get in the truck. She smiled and looked one more time toward the trees, then got in beside her husband and took his hand in hers and kissed him.

"My husband quoted Robert Frost, and I got a movie of it."

He looked at her and grinned. "Better not nobody see it. It wudn't nothing. I told you, it just come to me, something from junior high maybe."

They took their time going back, electing to travel the Natchez Trace, which Talmidge usually hated, since it held him to fifty. This time he seemed OK with it, even smiled now and then. What was left of her mother's ashes rode between them—they would return them to their shelf. As the remaining brilliant colors of late fall slid past them, Darlene's heart was hammering away—Momma had come home for Christmas, and Talmidge quoted Frost.

Harvey Watson and the Angel

Harvey Watson, last week laid to his rest with much pomp after a bout of circumstance, was one of the seven in ten Americans who in a recent survey conducted in something resembling a scientific poll professed to believe in angels.

Harvey was brought up in an Assembly of God church in rural Mississippi, where it was not unusual to witness on Wednesday nights and Sunday mornings and nights much weeping, wailing, and gnashing of teeth, real and artificial, and considerable talking in tongues. And whenever tent revivals came to town, usually twice a year—since it was judged by most deacons that their congregations needed an occasional break from the same singsong sermons preached by the resident pastor—it was time for the Greatest Show on Earth, as Harvey heard a friend's father put it once: faith healing. The roving evangelist would have a sawdust oval laid out and a circus tent erected over it, with folding chairs and an elevated platform with pulpit, and before the platform a clear spot for the healees to throw crutches or walkers or dark glasses and canes, ear horns, once the evangelist had laid a hand on their foreheads and yelled, "Heal, in the name of *Jesus-uh!*" The head would snap back and come forward again, and the cripple strode off the stage with the swagger of a teenage boy, the former blind man was dazzled by his sudden sight, and the deaf person started grooving to the music. He always found it strange that none of the healed people were folks he knew. Always strangers.

Harvey never got much into those mysteries and miracles of the church, though, because he knew that this one preacher took on his new trade to find something easier and cleaner than emptying septic tanks, which is what he did for three years after he got out of Parchman Penitentiary in the Delta for killing a mule and then the man who had been riding on it, simply because the guy was drunk and had had a falling out with his wife and crossed the future preacher's path and said something offensive. Word was out that he served more time for killing the mule than the man because the fellow who sassed him was known far and wide to be a homosexual.

Since Brother Simmons had mastered about half the material he was taught through the fourth grade and knew just enough decent English to get by, it always troubled Harvey when the preacher would listen to some instrument from God—usually a woman with a beehive hairdo in the congregation—spouting a strange tongue, presumably Hebrew, and then immediately interpret that language in very articulate English. Harvey didn't know a whole lot about good English, but he knew the difference there. He couldn't swear it had all been staged, but he believed that it was. He didn't have any reason to believe that the other preachers he was exposed to were any different.

And as for all the miracles and mysteries of the Bible, he rarely bought into them. The Burning Bush story and the three men making it alive out of a lion's den or furnace, a woman getting turned into a pillar of salt for just turning around and looking back at her hometown, some guy waving his arms and parting the Red Sea—Harvey just had a hard time believing them. And the Noah story. He kept trying to figure out how Noah could go to the four corners of the Earth and round up two of each creature, properly sexed, so that they could carry on when the waters receded, especially since it's almost impossible to tell the female equipment from the male on some creatures, even as big as an armadillo.

And he had trouble with the Jonah story too. He always thought that if a whale swallowed him and what was left of him after digestion was going to be a whale turd by morning, he might as well get out his pocket knife and make the big bastard suffer for swallowing him—give him a real dose of indigestion. Leave such a trail of bloody whale shit that every shark for miles around would home in on him and get their fill of blubber. Yessir, any whale that swallowed him would pay a hefty price.

Lots of those stories troubled him.

Further, he couldn't imagine how anybody could find Heaven enticing, given the way the preachers said it was going to be: standing around in choir robes all day singing hymns of praise. No mention of girls or dogs or fried chicken or watermelons or rivers to swim in. He never seriously considered choosing what they called the *Lake-uh-Fahr* over Heaven, but he kept hoping they were neglecting to mention some middle ground, like maybe Kingdom Come, which he heard a lot about. But, then, people got blown and knocked there all the time, so he figured that whatever the place might be like, the trip there would be painful. It was all so confusing.

When it came to angels, though, Harvey just flat out didn't believe in them. No way. No how. Fairy-like creatures with white robes and wings flitting around and sitting on your shoulder and all that. Nope.

But something changed Harvey Watson's mind about angels one Sunday morning when he was around eleven or twelve. He found his personal angel, one who stayed with him the rest of his life, through thick and thin. It is not necessary to go into all the wonderful things she did for and with him while he was growing up. It could get unsavory. So let us leap ahead to the period when he needed her most.

He led a charmed life, did Harvey—of this we may be sure, those of us who have heard the tales of his Army years in Yerp, as he pronounced the name of the land across the wide water to which so many of our soldier boys have gone in all seasons and for many reasons—and would have lasted another ten years at least, had a chain saw not taken personal interest in his right calf and helped itself to a serving of muscle and bone, in the process bleeding him quite beyond tolerance in a pine thicket on a hill above the Old Home Place in West Alabama. One of his grandsons found him wan and wasted, the saw still loping on at idle, awaiting further orders. They had to carry him down through thick brush and pine trees a quarter of a mile before sliding him into the back of his old blue pickup, the War Bitch, as he called her. Somewhere in there he lost his pulse and they never found it again. Nor did the doctors in Tuscaloosa.

Harvey served three years in the Army just after WWII, strictly occupation duty, but anyone who so served will tell you that hazards abound in any theater of war, even after the curtain's down. The falling of the curtain in that particular theater led to the raising of another one—longer, higher, and made of sterner stuff—which would not be razed for almost fifty years. But enough of this. Back to Harvey and his angel.

Within one calendar year—the only kind there is, Harvey once pointed out, fiscal to him meaning things involving the body—after his arrival in

Germany, he had heard more rounds snap past his head than many a dog-face who slogged ashore at Normandy, and the fire that came his way was what the media refers to as *friendly* fire. Harvey said there was nothing friendly about it—every damned one of them was trying to kill him.

A month or so after he assumed his duties as ambulance driver, he was hauling a German prisoner from one medical facility to another in Berlin and had to pass an American checkpoint, where they naturally enough asked for the papers on the prisoner. Having forgotten the documentation, late for the beer garden, and irritated with things in general, Harvey slammed the ambulance in reverse and tore out on his way back to get said papers when a volley of .45 rounds puckered the rear ambulance doors and a bullet blew out the back glass, traveling within an inch of Harvey's right ear before exiting the windshield. He hit the brakes, and the German prisoner, understandably bewildered, leapt from the vehicle even before it had fully stopped and was promptly clubbed to his knees by an MP armed with a carbine. The guards simply misread Harvey's intentions, and the prisoner wanted nothing more than to get out of the line of fire. What kind of hell would that be to survive the Battle of Berlin and die at the hands of crazy peace-time Americans?

Within a year Harvey heard the whiz of a bullet again—four of them, to be precise—while he was helping a buddy liberate two cases of beer from a storage shed at their base. The beer had every appearance of being unclaimed, and the boys at the barracks they were staying in, a converted country inn, elected to put a bid in on it. It all came right in the end, though. The guard who fired at them admitted that he had been a bit overzealous and agreed to split the haul, glad for the beer and gladder that he was not having to help load those old boys into an ambulance or a hearse and explain to a bunch of grave officers why he had killed his own kind. Harvey and companion were happy too and celebrated joyously and never got back to the inn with their beer.

In his subsequent years of service Harvey survived two truck wrecks with only minor injuries, four bar fights that involved a total of seventy-six stitches, and a medium-significant concussion from a crate of Spam that fell on his head in a warehouse. In 1949 he returned to the States a grateful man at having survived his tour of duty in Yerp. He had been in the line of fire twice and had suffered many wounds, but he wore no service medal.

Harvey always said that he survived his ordeals in Yerp because of his guardian angel, but his wife Martha wondered why, if that happened to be the case, would the angel let him get into such perilous circumstances to begin with, to which Harvey's answer was, quite simply, "She was a-testin' me."

"I don't see how bein' shot at by your own people and cut up with beer bottles and gettin' hit in the head with a crate of Spam is any kind of a test," was her reply, "except for stupidity."

"There's a lots that you don't know."

Over the years Harvey clung to his faith in the angel on his shoulder. She took him through double pneumonia twice, three truck wrecks, and one tractor inversion that left him hipcrippled on the left side so that he walked like a man who's lost a heel off one boot.

When people asked him why he didn't switch over to God and put his faith in Him and start going to church, Harvey said church wasn't where his angel was at and, furthermore, God had never so much as said a word to him, while his angel had spoken volumes, mostly when he was drunk. Said he started out on God when he was a boy, force fed by his parents and a string of fiery Assembly of God preachers, but no matter how diligently he minded his manners and behaved and how fervently he believed, no matter how hard he prayed to get new bicycles and footballs and Buck knives, He never seemed to deliver, even in conjunction with Santa Claus and the Easter Bunny. He blamed God for the family's poverty and the loss of his daddy's left eye to a trotline fishhook and never would accept the notion propounded from the pulpit that maybe poverty and accidents are tests of faith. When he found his angel in the fifth or sixth grade, about the time he really got interested in girls, he became a true believer.

Harvey's angel, as he described her, was a beautiful woman to begin with, maybe seventeen or eighteen the first time he saw her, he himself much younger and not even beginning to blush with body hair. He was rummaging around in a closet for a Monopoly set one Sunday morning after he'd played sick and got to stay home from church. He was all by himself, the house quiet as an Easter tomb, and when he bent over, the blood rushed to his head and he passed out—sort of, as he described it, not exactly out but enough out that he forgot who and where he was—and the next thing he knew the angel was in front of him, naked, and he saw for the first time what an undressed woman looked like.

He had no sister, and his mother was modest as a ghost about her body, so he had just about concluded that he would die before he'd see a woman without clothes on. The closest he had gotten was the lingerie section of the Sears catalog, but the formidable brassieres and girdles and high-rise, undelineated-crotch panties didn't tell him much. He learned from a boy at school that you could use a pencil eraser and remove panties completely from a woman in the catalog, but he had no idea what to draw in the spot after the panties were off. He usually just drew in a clump of hair, which he had been told all girls over twelve or so had a crop of. That always puzzled him. Like at eleven years and eleven months they were bald as a jug down there and then the minute they turned twelve that hair sprouted? There was so much he didn't know about girls but wanted to.

What stood before him in the closet that Sunday morning was a naked angel—she even had wings—and since everything else about her looked like a woman, he figured the secret parts did too.

He had what he described as rapture in the closet with his angel, for the first time feeling not simply the dry heaving of an unprimed pump in his hand—from his throbbing member an issue gathered and pooled and a drop of something warm and sticky fell between the great and second toe of his left foot. And it was good and glorious. And he knew that the angel had caused it.

So it was that he accepted her as his personal saviorette, and over the years he turned to her time and time again, not simply for *that,* you know, but for spiritual guidance and comfort as well.

The strange but beautiful thing was that his angel did not age the way he and his wife did. As the decades wore on, she changed scarcely at all, whereas his wife wrinkled and sagged and grew so vile tempered that at the slightest provocation she would first yell, then cry, then fall into a dark study for days on end. But after all those years the angel's face remained radiant and flawless, her skin smooth and white as untainted snow, her eyes a heavenly blue, and her body remained slender and shapely. Her voice was still soft and low, and she never lost patience with him. There were times her eyes looked tired, though, and she bent a bit at the shoulders. Harvey once summed it up this way: "It's like she ages one year to my seven, sort of like the human/dog thing." His wife accepted the analogy as fitting: "It makes *you* the dog, don't it?"

But Martha loved Harvey and tolerated his angel reasonably well over the years, and she intends to humor him, even in death, even when she halfway blames the angel for not being there to turn the chain saw off. The only thing she could figure was that angels aren't into mechanical things and wouldn't know a chain saw from a pair of scissors. She has directed that in the quiet little cedar grove where he's laid, behind a church near where he grew up, a smart looking plaster angel be erected, radiant of face, her wings curved in loving grace above his name and dates.

The Queen

Many a year Earl McManus stood and watched a ship he had had a hand in building slide down the ramp at the little shipyard he worked at in Pascagoula, splash into saltwater for the first time, rock gently, steady itself, and then move smoothly out to the Gulf for a trial run and then to wherever it was headed. He watched until it became a mere speck on its way to the pass between Petit Bois and Horn and nodded his head with both satisfaction and sadness—satisfaction that with his own hands he had once again helped build something so magnificent, so sleek and graceful, sadness in knowing that, as he might have to give up a beautiful woman, he had to let her go.

When finally it came time for him to retire, he tallied eighty-three boats and ships, wooden-hulled and steel, he had helped build, eighty-three launches of those beautiful ladies he so lovingly touched and then watched glide away. Most he never saw again. The morning he walked away from the shipyard for the last time, he ran his hand along the smooth side of a shrimper being readied for launch the following Sunday. He thought about going back to see her glide off to the south, but decided against it. He looked about to make certain no one was looking, then leaned and kissed the white-painted steel hull and left.

It was the Fourth of July, and they were crowded around the plate-glass doors leading to the patio in the little Mississippi coastal house the children had grown up in, and now they stood in silent awe watching their father work. There were the two sons, the daughter, their spouses, and seven grandchildren. It was the first time they had all been together in nearly ten years, time having scattered them across the country. And the reason they finally all came home was what was sitting in the backyard of their parents' home. When word came of it, there was no way not to come—this was serious family business.

John Turner was the oldest of the children and generally tried to take charge in such issues. He liked for people to use both his first and middle name, since his father's first name was John too, though he went by Earl. Finally he turned from the glass sliding doors that looked out onto the yard and spoke to Cora, his mother, who was hard at work in the kitchen and staying out of the mess the best she could.

"Momma, what possessed him to start this?"

"At's his binness, John Turner. We discussed it, but I left the decision up to him. It keeps him busy, at least. And happy. Lots of men can't handle retirement and just stay under the women's feet, lay on the couch and watch the TV or drink theirselves to death, so I figure I got lots to be glad about." She pushed the kitchen curtain aside and watched her husband a few seconds, then let the curtain fall back.

"Momma." The daughter spoke from the sliding door. Her voice had an urgent edge to it. "Why is it so big? Marvin says it looks to be more than thirty feet long."

Cora stirred her peas. "Exactly forty-two feet, not counting the figure-head."

"Forty-two feet?" The others turned their faces toward the kitchen, then back to the yard.

It was like they were watching something in an aquarium, with the children pressing their faces to the glass, the boat a derelict lying in the sand and gravel and any second a big fish would come swimming by.

"The figurehead will add another three. It's the head and bosom of an African queen. He got it—"

"Forty-five feet." John Turner squinted out at the scaffolding, where Earl was wrestling with a piece of timber. "That's a hell of a lot of boat."

Cora continued: "You better not call it a boat in front of him. To him, and to me, it is a *ship*. He got the figurehead from a sailor that brought it back from some little town on the coast of Africa."

"And let me guess," the daughter said, walking into the kitchen and lifting the lid off the rice, something she always did, much to Cora's irritation, "he's going to call the boat the *African Queen*, right?"

Cora shook her head. "Nope. Gon' call her *Cleo,* short for *Cleopatra*—she *was* a African queen. And it is a *ship,* not a boat."

The daughter snorted. "*Cleo?* Well, that is a dumb name for a boat, if you ask me," she said. "That sounds like the name of a colored girl that comes by to clean your house."

"Nobody ast you," Cora replied. "That's her name."

"It looks like to me," John Turner said, "that he could use some help with them timbers. How come he won't let us help him out?"

Cora, her head half in the maw of the oven, echoed back, "He won't let nobody help him but me, and he won't even let me come out there without it's something he knows full well he can't do on his own. Y'all know your daddy." She closed the oven door. "Or at least you used to."

She straightened up and brushed her apron front. "He had to call Floyd Robinson over last week to help him get part of some new scaffolding up, since we tried and tried and couldn't do it by ourselves. It liked to have killed him to call Floyd over, much as he's helped *him* with stuff over the years. John Turner, don't y'all *dare* go out there. He'll just yell at you and be in a bad mood the rest of the day and set to drinkin'. This is something he's bound and determined to do on his own. And if I was y'all, I'd get away from them doors before he throws a hammer at you. You look like a bunch of fools with your faces pressed to that glass."

John Turner muttered something to the others about "looking *at* a fool" and they all moved back to the living room.

The very day of his retirement from Crump Shipbuilding, Earl had called Cora out to his shop, where blueprints for a large vessel lay unrolled and taped together in five sections on a work table. In one corner was a profile sketch of the completed craft, its sails full of wind and two figures, a man and woman, sitting in deck chairs on the bow. He pointed to the sketch.

"Sam Buckley drawed the pitcher for me. What do you think?"

"Sam has drawed up enough boats that he ought to be able to do one right. Looks right nice."

"I am not asking how you like Sam's drawing. How do you like the ship? It is a *ship,* not a boat. It's a modified sloop. Diesel powered with optional sails, over forty feet long, can go anywhere in the world."

Cora studied the plans a while, the way she would go over a recipe. "It's a nice boat, Earl. *Ship.* But what are you doing with these plans? You ain't forgot already that you've retired?" She leaned forward and looked over the plans again.

"It's our *ship,* Cora, mine and yours. These are the plans for *Cleo,* which is what we are gon' call her, short for *Cleopatra.*" He put his battered right index finger on the couple in the deck chairs. "That's us."

Then he pointed to the figurehead, an ebony face and shoulders with a ribbon of red cloth covering the breasts. "I got a sailor getting me one of these from Nigerier. Hand carved. It's the real thing. Got a real nigger carving it out of a solid log. Teak or mahogany. Something like that."

Cora stood a long time looking at the sketch in the corner. "Somehow this is not what I figured you were going to do when you retired."

"You gotta dream big, girl. The world's our oysture now. Give me a few months, and I'll do what I been doing for most of my life: I'm gon' build us a *ship.*"

When she walked back into the house, she wasn't sure exactly what she was supposed to be thinking.

Nothing more was said about the *Cleo* until a few days later, when, just before noon on a Saturday, three heavily loaded City Lumber trucks pulled up to the curb out front. Cora stood behind the den drapes, her hand to her mouth, and watched as each truck backed in and unloaded. In a frenzy of excitement Earl dashed back and forth directing the unloading. When the trucks left, the corner of the lot that she had intended to be filled with rows of vegetables the next spring, now that Earl had time to garden seriously, was covered with stacks of timbers.

Earl was sitting on a mountain of beams figuring with a pencil when Cora walked out. "When you said you was building a boat, a ship, I really thought you meant some kind of big model, like for the mantle, three or four feet long." She stared at the piles of lumber. "But them stacks of lumber tells me I was wrong."

He stopped scribbling. "I told you it was a *ship,* a real ship. Forty feet long."

"Earl, you can't build a ship that big in the backyard. You ain't got a permit from the city. Who will you get to help you? Who'll buy it? How would you get it moved?"

"The hell with the city. I ain't read nowhere in the laws that a man can't build a ship in his backyard if he wants to. I bet you a dollar to a dog's ass that there ain't a rule wrote down nowhere that says a man can't build a ship in his yard. And I ain't going to *sell* it. I told you it's going to be ours."

"Earl, we ain't ever owned even a skiff. What would we do with a boat forty feet long?"

"Forty-five," he said, sliding down off the timbers and disappearing into the shop. "And it is a Goddamn *ship*."

That evening, after she had washed the supper dishes, Cora walked out into the dark yard, where she could vaguely see Earl, crouched on a stack of beams, silhouetted against the sky. He looked like some kind of big sea bird that had come in for the evening to roost.

"I don't guess I have to ast what you're thinking about," she said, resting her chin beside one of his feet.

"No, I reckon not. You want to come up here?"

In answer she raised her arms to him and he helped her onto the stack. They sat dangling their legs off, the way she remembered doing when they were first married, when all Earl wanted to do on his time off was sit at the boat dock watching the bright boats, all sizes, shapes, and colors, go out into the Gulf and then return. They would sit for hours with their legs dangling off the pier, sometimes talking quietly, sometimes just watching in silence as ripples from the boats washed across their feet. "Someday," Earl would say, looking out toward the Gulf, "I am going to have a boat of my own."

"I don't suppose," he broke into her reverie, "that this makes much sense to you."

"More than you think."

"It's just that, well, all my grown-up life I have worked at building boats and ships for other people—shrimpers, tugs, yachts, small freighters, fishing boats—and I have watched them one by one head off from the shipyard dock to places I've just *dreamed* about going. Oh, some of them are still right here in Pascagoula, but at least they get out into the Gulf. Do you realize, Cora, that I have never even touched the saltwater outside the islands?"

She patted his arm.

"Never been much out of the mouth of the river. Guys I've worked with for forty years have talked about fishing in the outside surf at Petit Bois and Horn Island, but I've never even been out there. And people having the ships built coming in and talking about all the places they were going to go in them. Jesus Christ, Cora, I've never been *anywhere*."

He pointed out toward the sky above the Gulf. "Even during the war, when other people got shipped off to Yerp or the South Pacific, I rode on a Goddamned train to Fort McClellan, Alabama, and I stayed at Fort

McClellan the whole two and a half years during the war. The only fightin'
I seen was in a bar. I wanted to be in the Navy. That's what I wanted. But
it never worked out."

"So you're going to try to do now what you wanted to do all along?"

"Yeah. I got the time now, we got the money—and this won't cost as
much as you think, me doing all the building, and there's all them boxes
of stainless steel screws and bolts and brass fittings in the shop, which I
ain't been stealin' all these years for nothing."

"You *stole* all that stuff? You told me you got it at the salvage yard."

"Well, I lied, but the statue of lamentations has run out on it now, so
they can't persecute me."

"You *stole* all that stuff?"

"Most of it would of been wasted anyhow, Cora. You wouldn't believe
what them people thowe away."

She laughed. "I guess I ort to be mad at you, but now I just think it's
funny. If you'd worked a few years longer, you could have stole a whole
ship. Kinda like that Johnny Cash song, where he steals all them car parts
and puts him together a Cadillac."

"Might near could," he said. "Might near."

They were quiet for a few minutes.

"I got the know-how. Cora, Honey, this is our one chance to break out,
to . . . you understand."

"I wondered. . . . "

He pulled her close to him. "We have always had something come
between us and what I think we've both wanted to do—I mean, admit it,
Cora, you've wanted to break away and leave all this behind us, ain't you?
Kids and yards and cooking and keeping house?"

"Well, I don't know about—"

"Ain't you ever thought about being out on the sea, free, the wind in
your face, going places, seeing things we've never seen before? Cora, think
how few times we have been out of Missippi. None, except for trips to
Atlanter and Birminham to visit family. We ain't never been anywhere
because we just wanted to *go* there."

"Not really. There was that one time we take'n the kids and drove over
to AstroWorld in Houston. That's all."

"Hell, girl, think about all the countries out there we could visit by sea.
Just think of it! A ship the size this one's gon' be will be able to go just
about anywhere."

And think of it she did as the *Cleo* rose from the backyard like something coming up out of the earth itself. She found herself more and more drawn to the smudged and dog-eared volumes in the bookcase beside their bed: *Robinson Crusoe, Mutiny on the Bounty, Two Years Before the Mast,* books on sailing and ships and navigation, maps of the world's seas, magical dreamlands that Earl had lost himself in all those years when work and the kids and subsistence income had kept him landlocked, had not even allowed him into the waters of the deeper Gulf, which he could see from the seat of a crane at Crump's.

After that July the 4th, when the kids first saw the beginnings of the *Cleo,* there were persistent phone calls and letters asking about the project.

"Oh, it's coming right along," Cora would answer. "Your daddy's not the fastest shipbuilder in the world, but he's real good at it. He's doin' it right is whut."

One evening while Earl was stretched out on the couch after a particularly exhausting day of beam wrestling, the phone rang and Cora answered. It was the daughter.

"Oh, it's coming along all right," he heard Cora say. "You know how your daddy works—slow but sure." After a few seconds she lowered her voice. "Now Ruth Ann, y'all don't worry about what he's spending—"

"You tell her," Earl yelled down the hallway, "that I am going to spend ever red-ass cent I got saved on that ship and when I die at the wheel somewhere off the coast of India or Africa, they can pack up and come help you sail'r home! Then it'll be up to you to decide how to satisfy them."

Cora laughed when she came back to the den. "Lord, Earl, she *heard* you."

"Good." After that there were fewer letters and phone calls inquiring about the *Cleo.*

Over the weeks the bottom beam fleshened into bright ribs. Then came heavy planks, which Earl sometimes had to steam over washpots to get the wood to bend and fit properly, and caulking shone like veins along the deep sweep of the sides. Neighbors leaned over fences and talked and pointed, cars drove slowly past, and sometimes people would stop and stare from the street. One afternoon two little boys ran and hoisted themselves onto the wooden fence surrounding the yard and clung with their chins on their hands shouting, "Noah, Noah!" until Earl crawled over the edge of the boat and threw a hammer toward them.

One Sunday, just as Earl and Cora were sitting down for a noon meal of fried chicken and creamed potatoes and gravy and all the other things that go well with them, John Turner and his wife and children dropped in.

"What brings y'all by?" Earl asked, poised over a drumstick.

John Turner was holding back the den curtains. "Just wanted to see how your boat's coming. We were driving over to Mobile to hear the Blackwood Brothers in concert. Thought we'd drop by."

"Real sweet of you, Son," Cora answered. "It does a heart good to see your folks and then go listen to gospel music."

Earl had continued with his chicken, but he paused long enough to say, "It is a *ship*."

"We don't get over this way much, New Orleans being so far away," John Turner's wife said.

Earl wiped his mouth on the sleeve of his khaki workshirt. "We noticed. At least a hour and a half." He rose from the table and reached for his hat. "Well, I got to get back at it. Y'all enjoy your visit."

"Daddy." John Turner cleared his throat. "Could we talk a few minutes?"

Earl hung his hat back. "If it can be quick. I got lots to do today." He sat down beside Cora on the couch, but she got up and went into the kitchen.

"You boys go on outside," John Turner told his sons. "Ruby, you go read something in the bedroom." The little girl started down the hall, and the boys walked toward the back door.

"Naw, not out back," Earl said, pointing toward the front door. "Go out that way. Y'all stay out of the backyard."

"But we want to see the boat," one of them whined.

"It is a Goddamned *ship*. Just stay away from the *Cleo*. Go out front. Play in the traffic."

"Daddy!" John Turner started.

"Earl," Cora cautioned from the kitchen, "try not to talk that way around the kids."

"Then somebody ort to teach'm the difference between a boat and a ship."

When the children had disappeared, John Turner and his wife sat down on either side of the old couple.

"Now, Daddy," he began, laying his hand on Earl's knee, "I am representing the family here today—they have elected me their spokesman."

"The family, huh?" Earl shook his head and lifted his son's hand off his knee and dropped it like a piece of concrete. "Since when did the family not include me and your momma? Or are you in on this too, Cora?"

"I got nothing to do with it, Earl. I don't know nothing about what John Turner's talking about."

"So the family, whoever that is, elected you spokesman, boy?"

"Yessir," said John Turner, looking over at his wife, who, it was apparent, had just as soon been somewhere else. She was gnawing at her lips. "Henry and Ruth Ann and I decided that somebody had to talk to you, and they chose me to talk for the family, for us."

"Now that we got it straight who the family is, what are you supposed to talk to me about?"

John Turner rose, walked to the picture window, and pulled back the curtains. "About that." He pointed to the backyard.

"About the *Cleo?*"

"Yessir, about that monstrosity, that *boat* out there."

"It is a *ship,* a Goddamned fucking *ship,* and—"

"Earl," Cora cautioned, "your language . . ."

"The next one of you that calls it a boat can just get the hell out of this house and *stay* the hell out. You tryin' to make it sound like a toy, and it ain't. And it ain't got nothing to do with y'all, but since you've been elected family representative and all, go ahead and say what you got to say."

John Turner sat back down. "Well, we have decided that it is unfair for you to squander family money on foolishness like that b-b-b—that *ship.* We know it's your money, your retirement and social security, but that money's supposed to see you through, to make life comfortable until, you know, until. . . ."

Earl stared at him. "Until I'm dead."

"Well, yessir. If you waste all your money on that big old barge, you know who'll have to come up with the money if you get sick and have to go to an old folks' home or get in bad debt or whatever."

At that Earl stood up and reached for his hat. "Why don't you come with me, John Turner? I got a few things I want to say to you by yourself, since you are the *spokesman.*"

The spokesman for the family looked at his wife, then stood up and followed the old man into the backyard. Earl motioned for him to climb up the ladder behind him and onto the deck of the *Cleo*. He motioned to a nail keg. "Just set down right there, Son, and let *me* talk for a minute."

John Turner sat down, and his eyes swept over the interior of the boat, out of interest perhaps, perhaps out of dread.

"You just listen, now. I ain't going to say this but once, because to say it more than once would mean that I got some doubts about the truth of it, which I ain't, or that you ain't listened, which is your problem, not mine."

John Turner watched and listened without blinking.

"Hey, Grandpa." It was one of the boys, just over five. He had climbed the ladder and hoisted himself up onto the gunwale.

"Hi, Justin," the old man said. "Me'n your daddy've got some talking to do. Maybe I can bring you up here later. . ."

"Aw, Daddy, let him see the boat."

"John Turner, it is not a . . ." But he just let it slide. Nobody understood the difference.

The boy slipped between them and stumbled down some makeshift stairs into the cabin.

"You OK, Justin?" Earl asked him, just as he poked his head out of the doorway and grinned.

"I fine. Bumped my head is all."

"Maybe you ort to go on back to the house, where everbody else is. Me'n your daddy have got to talk."

The boy came up the steps and stood between the two. He looked seriously at his grandfather.

"What is it, Son?" the old man asked.

"What does see-nile mean?"

John Turner snapped forward. "Now, Justin, you'd better do as Grandpa says and go—"

"Naw, naw, let him talk. Where'd you hear that word?"

"Well, Momma'nem was talking, and they said that you are see-nile. What does that mean?"

John Turner turned his head away from Earl and looked somewhere far off.

"Aw, Justin," the old man said, reaching out and stroking the boy's hair. "They was talking about how me and your grandmomma are gonna go *see the Nile*. We gon' sail out of the Gulf of Mexico and across the Atlantic, that big ocean, and on into the Mediterranean and *see the Nile*. That's a river in Egypt. Weird one—it runs north."

The boy wasn't at all interested in the Nile and which way it flowed. When he looked through the kitchen window and saw his grandmother holding up a piece of cake, he scrambled over the side and down the ladder and they heard no more from him.

Earl turned back to his son. "Senile, huh? Y'all are gonna *think* senile before all this is over."

"Before what is over? This damned *ship* building business? Aren't you proud? I got it right."

"John Turner, you and the others ain't been much like family to us in quite a while. Y'all made it clear a long time ago that you wasn't exactly proud to have people know that your daddy was a laborer in a shipyard. That's all right—I understand. And I can understand you not writing or calling or coming by except when you just had to, and not letting us be real grandparents to your kids. That has hurt like hell, especially your momma, but I can understand it. What I flat-ass *cannot* understand is what right you got to tell me how to spend the money I have worked my whole life accumulating. Me and your momma sacrificed to raise y'all, sent two of you to college, bought you cars, give you the money for the down payment on your house. We done all for you that it was our duty to do."

He narrowed his eyes and stared at John Turner.

"Now we got to do our own thing, as the saying goes. I got some good years left in me, and the money I been spending is mine, so you and the others are from this point on not to mess with me and your momma about the *Cleo*. I'm going to get'r done, and me and Cora are going to see the world in her. And if we spend every damned penny I have saved up over the years, that's all right too. I expect we'll sell the house, furniture, and everything else before we go, so that whatever y'all, the family, got coming will be in this ship."

The old man stood, rubbed his hand along the rail, which even before final sanding was smooth to the touch, and looked out toward the Gulf. "When our time comes, y'all can come claim the *Cleo* and tug her back home, if you can find her and if you figure it's worth the effort."

John Turner, who had been leaning forward on the nail keg, hands on his knees, finally spoke: "Daddy, this is crazy. The neighbors think you're daft. Everybody in this town talks about Old Man McManus and his *ark*, and when they talk about you, they twirl a finger at their temples. The whole damned thing is embarrassing—it's ridiculous for a sensible man to be doing what you're doing."

"That may be, John Turner, but it's *my* backyard, *my* money, *my* time, and *my* Goddamned ship. So you let folks talk all they want to. Since you're the family representative, maybe you can explain it to them. Now let's get back to the house."

"I don't want to go back in there yet. There is more talking to do."

"Then stay your ass out here and talk to yourself. I am thoo talking." He swung over onto the ladder and went into the house.

John Turner just sat there a few minutes staring at nothing in particular, then got up and climbed down the ladder and went inside. In no time at all he had his family loaded.

As John Turner was driving away, he stopped, backed the car up, and got out at the curb. He turned to face Cora, who was still waving on the driveway. "You can tell him," he yelled, "that even if he *does* get that big piece of junk built, he'll never move it out of that yard! Momma, you just call me when you need us to come and tear it down and haul it off."

Except for occasional thinly disguised references to the *Cleo* by letter and by phone, the kids had little else to say about the project. John Turner told Cora on the phone one evening that they had decided to let the old man burn himself out on the boat. He assured her that they would look out for her if Earl "wasted all the family savings on that junk of a boat." Cora told him that was real nice to know, then pointed out that it was a *ship*, and hung up.

Day after day, month after month, Cora watched Earl disappear over the rail of the boat and descend into the depths, the hammering and sawing and banging punctuating her waking hours until whatever she did—whether cooking, sewing, or housecleaning—was done to the beat of the *Cleo*. She went out only when Earl called her for help, preferring not to think about when the boat would be finished, if ever, and what changes would come into their lives if Earl did fulfill his dream. She still thought of it as a boat, though she never said so to Earl. A boat was something that never went anywhere much—a ship took to the high seas and went to exotic places. Except for the shifting around of scaffolding and the gradual disappearance of stacks of lumber, she could not tell that he was making any progress at all.

Then one morning, almost two years after the first stacks of timbers arrived, Cora looked out the kitchen window before breakfast to see Earl applying a brilliant coat of white paint, and before the sun had set the next day, the ship was trimmed out in green and gold, as lovely and delicate looking as any ship she had ever seen. In another week the masts were up, the figurehead was mounted, and the name *Cleo* was painted on either side of the bow and across the stern. Earl said it wasn't necessary to name her the *African Queen,* since any damned fool could tell from the figurehead that she was a queen and not a local one. And *Cleo* seemed so personal, so part of the family, like the name of a dog.

As the days progressed, there came plumbing fixtures, lights, portholes, lines, bits of teak and mahogany trim, and, then, lo and behold, one morning they walked out and stood before her in her resplendent glory: the *Cleo* was a ship, a beautiful little ship, anchored high and dry in a suburban sea.

After Cora's official tour, which left her breathless with admiration for such extraordinary craftsmanship in a man whose life work had been done for someone else and in the dingy dark beyond her sight, the two of them sat in lawn chairs Earl had moved onto the deck.

"Reckon we look like the couple in the picture?" he asked her.

"I guess we *do.*"

"It's finally finished. *Cleo* is real, she's ours."

"But what do we do now, Earl? You're over seventy years old, and this ship is a long way from water. What do we do now, just look at her?"

"Let me worry about that. A little bit more varnishin' below and some riggin' to do, a lot of layin' in supplies and then. . . . " He sighed. "The world is ours."

Cora stared off toward the Gulf, where the sun was just losing itself to dusk.

"We don't know what in the world come of 'm, John Turner." Mr. Bogart, a next-door neighbor, pointed to the sign in Earl's front yard. "All we seen was they had a FOR SALE sign in the yard for a couple of weeks, and had two big garage sales. Somebody brought in a big truck with a trailer and hoist behind it."

He pointed to the fence, where a large section was missing.

"Then we woke up yesterday morning and seen that the SOLD sign and the boat was gone. He hauled it out of here at night—you can see where the ruts cut up the yard along the driveway—and they was gone. I called you soon as I could. Maybe if you had of come yesterday, you could of stopped him."

John Turner just stared at the tire ruts and gap in the fence.

"Mr. Bogart, how could they haul a boat that big across the yard and down the street?"

"I don't know how he got that damned thing under the wires and all, without he lowered them masts, which is what he must of done."

John Turner still did not speak. He swept his eyes from the fence to the street, which led off toward the Gulf.

"Me and Molly drove down to the dock this morning, early, but that boat wasn't there. They done gone, John Turner. Furniture's gone, tools, cars. He sold everything and they done gone. He was sly about it too: Here one day, gone the next. But you know how your daddy is."

John Turner nodded and got in his car and drove off toward the landing, near the Coast Guard station, where they probably launched it. He parked and got out and walked to the end of the pier. He stood a long time and stared wordless out toward the Gulf, where, far beyond his sight, the grand ship *Cleo* sliced elegantly through water deep and green, while Earl steered a steady course to the southeast and Cora sat in a lawn chair on the forward deck, a chart across her lap, studying the African coast.

Jesus in the Mist

The night I found him, I might not of, except that I had been on the road so long looking, nearly three months—like it had become some sort of quest for me, almost religious—that I sensed it was him even before I had waded through the crowd of whispering and mumbling onlookers that gathered around his truck, which I recognized right off, and I found myself staring up onto the tailgate at the man that might have once been Grover Johnson and the husband of Alvarine but now looked like anybody but him—bad scrawny and wearing a toga of some sort and weaving on unsteady legs, pointing at the Goddamned mirror, which had already started to gather fog in spite of the warm night air, like it had any choice with that humidifier belching steam like a locomotive. And there was beer on his breath.

I knew that it was him. And that was enough for the time being. I could find out later what I come for. I eased back through the crowd and found myself a convenience store and bought two six-packs of the cheapest bottled beer they had—I hate drinking beer out of cans—and set down across the street from that bunch of whatever the hell they were and just watched and listened and sucked my beer, my mind on Alva, way back in Mississippi. Of course I kept my eye out for cops, since I didn't want my ass run in for public drinking, which some places in the South are real strict about. Midway through the second bottle somebody over there yelled, "I see him, I see him," and then they drew tight around the truck like starving Biafrans around a load of rice.

And shit, the noise they made. Couldn't have been more than fifteen or twenty people, but it looked and sounded like a whole herd, pushing and bellering, and I thought that for a minute they was going to turn the truck over. Finally I saw him hold his hands out toward'm like he was holding back the tide, and whatever he said must've worked.

They didn't turn the truck over. Two sips into my third beer they broke up like a July thunderstorm with the energy thunderclapped out of it and started drifting away, one by one and two by two, serious and quiet, until there wasn't nobody left but Grover hisself, hunched over on the tailgate like he was the loneliest man in the world and wore out by what he'd just been through, only then I noticed that what he was doing was counting money. I could see both sides of him, since the mirror was slid out of the camper shell onto the tailgate beside him and the steam was gone off of it and the lights were still on—the Grover I was actually seeing and the Grover reflected in the mirror, one plain as the other. Then he pulled a sheet over the mirror. I wasn't sure whether it was the beer or what, but I had the strangest feeling. I shook my head and it went away. So I got up and started across the street, real slow.

But I need to go back a little ways here for this to make any sense.

Picture it now: a pickup truck caravan of grown-up men—well, big and haired over anyway, since when you say grown you have to factor in more than meat and bones and a deep voice—arriving in the big city of Jackson and being turned aloose there for three days, like animals out of a zoo, and most of them never been outside Lowndes County, or one of the other three Mississippi counties that Four-County keeps the juice flowing to. Junior high or high school dropouts mostly, but some with diplomas, which they didn't mention, since to that bunch if you marked the importance of education on a light pole, you'd have to dig down below ground level to find the notch. A good-looking wife or a new truck or shotgun was to brag about—not a high school diploma. What the hell good does a little bit of math and history and English do a guy that hangs on poles all day stretching wire but rattle around in his head like a ball bearing, if it ever gets in there at all. All smart in their own way, I guess, like me, but not real big on formal learning. We knew electricity, backwards and forwards, and that's what counted. At least we knew it well enough not to get killed or turned into a quad by it more than once.

So there we were in the Big City to participate in the state softball play-offs, a dozen wide-eyed rednecks and a manager, one back-up utility player, and a supervisor's son that handled the equipment, which wasn't much to handle, since we had our own gloves and favorite bats that we wouldn't have let Jesus Hisself lay down the cross and tote for us. You don't let that stuff out of your sight, not with luck being involved the way it is in sports. You keep it locked up at home, and you sleep with it if you just happen to go to bed somewhere away from the house or trailer or whatever you live in, especially when you're on the road. The kid carried the ball bag that also had the catcher's stuff in it, since it was too cumbersome for Charlie Williams, the catcher, to have to keep up with. Charlie could barely keep up with Charlie.

Middle of the afternoon on a Saturday we all strung into the Holiday Inn there just off I-55 like we was the New York Yankees coming to town for the World Series, wearing our uniforms and clacking across the tiles, but some scrawny ass little clerk come running out of an office behind the counter, squawking like a chicken, and said we couldn't go down the hallway with cleats on because they'd tear up the carpet. So we snatched'm off and tied the strings together and slung'm over our shoulder, the same one that most of us had our bats on, with the gloves slid down on the barrel. Like I say, you don't lay your bat or glove down. Most of us just had a gym bag for our other stuff, except for three that was in the National Guard, or had been, and they carried duffel bags, like that was a status thing or something. I never even knew what a fucking duffel was, much less why they needed a bag that big to tote one in.

For almost all of us it was the first time to go to the Big City, being young and mostly poor and not prone to travel anyhow. I mean, once every few years a storm would mow down half of Birmingham or Tuscaloosa, not far over the state line from Columbus, and a couple of trucks would be dispatched over there to saw up trees and get the lines back in the air, but you sure as hell don't see much on them trips—like as not you sleep and eat in the trucks and go to the bathroom behind piles of limbs. Got to go to Tupelo once too and a place call Ranchland, not far from there, when a ice storm went through and sheared the limbs off nearly every pine in a five-mile stretch.

So we dug the trip to Jackson. Ate good food in the dining room of the Holiday Inn that Friday evening, which Four-County paid for, and slept two to a room, which Four-County paid for too. Well, the customers paid for it, but they didn't know it. Everybody talked about having a beer bust, but Billy Pounds, the manager, who was also a damned supervisor, said that if we went and screwed ourselves up and got picked off early in the round-robin that got started the next morning, then we would find ourselves stringing wire on somebody else's poles. So we went to bed fairly early, after we finished off the little bit of hootch that Teddy Billingsley smuggled in in the bottom of his duffel bag.

Wasn't nobody in the mood to screw things up for the team. Everybody there was tried and true and had been on the roster for three or four years, all but Sammy Criswell, that played centerfield, and he was a office clerk pick-up at the last minute to replace fat-ass Raymond Shelton, that we all knew wasn't worth a shit from the first swing he took at batting practice the day he tried out, letting the bat go flying farther than the ball he hit. He was a pick-up hisself, to stand in for Lester Plummer, that let his lawnmower roll back over his right foot and whack off all but his little toe, however the hell anybody can do that, and slow him up real bad. Let's just say that Raymond lived down to our expectations, and we got rid of him quick as dogshit off a shoe.

Matter of fact, Raymond never would have been put on the team to begin with if Old Man Sheffield hadn't of just insisted on it, since they was cousins. Sheffield, who used to run a electric supply place before he retired, filthy rich, footed the bill for the uniforms and balls and stuff and acted like he owned the team—you know, like we was a professional team that might bring him millions down the line. Any time we had an expense that Four-County wouldn't cover, Old Man Sheffield would. He tried to turn us into a football team once, but we sprained and broke so many legs and arms and shit that he give up on that. Problem was, he regarded his big-shot self as a hands-on owner too and got involved in everything we did. I just kept hoping he'd come out on the field with us so one of us could knock his ass off. If he'd had any sense, baseball or bidness or otherwise, that wouldn't have been so bad, but ever since I'd known him he was, as Sally the Secretary in the head office put it, severely mature. Still is, the last I noticed, and it ain't reversible. We just called him a old fart. Still do. At any rate. . . .

Before we knew it, it was morning. We got up and dressed in our uniforms and walked down to the dining room in our socks and ate a big breakfast, cleaned out the buffet completely. Had them people in the kitchen peeping through the doors to find out just what it was that had descended on the place. Scrambled eggs, soft and light, and rashers of bacon, grits and toast and biscuits and jelly and fruit and coffee and all the juice we could put down—a buffet might turn a profit most of the time, but that morning it didn't. The thing about a buffet is that you can't eat it all up, not without they run out of stuff, which can happen. A softball team made up of power-company linemen can flat skew the odds.

But then the fun was over and we had to get serious about working out in the parking lot, which was still a little foggy, before we went on over to the three-field complex where the playoffs was scheduled. We took some towels from the room for bases and laid out an infield and got in position for some serious grounders, which move about three times as fast on concrete, only they are more predictable, when somebody up and asked, "Where in the hell is Grover at?"

Then we all looked at where a white towel had been folded up for first base, and there wasn't a first baseman. That'd be Grover, see, Grover Johnson, from Caledonia, not far from Columbus, the best damned first baseman I ever seen, and he could hit a softball half a mile, seemed like—best hitter on the team, especially the long balls. Tall and lean and ropey with muscles and veins, hands the size of garbage can lids. He could lean and stretch out and a ball that come within ten feet of the bag was like as not to end up in his mitt, and my God, he could rare back and throw a man out from first to third or home quick as a teenage hard-on. He was something. And he was missing.

Everybody turned and looked at Buddy Stevens, that roomed with Grover, but Buddy said Grover was in the bathroom taking a shower when he left for breakfast. Then nobody could remember seeing Grover at breakfast either, which was real odd, since where there was food, there was Grover, almost always. So we went in to see could we find him.

"Well, he's not here." The hotel clerk shrugged his skinny shoulders and pointed. "He's done gone." He screwed up his mouth and shook his head from side to side, like his word alone was not quite enough to emphasize the fact that Grover Johnson was indeed gone from the motel —gone where, the clerk didn't know, doubtless didn't care, but decidedly gone. His bag with an aluminum bat sticking out of it slung on a strap across his shoulder and something flat and rectangular wrapped in a sheet and tucked under his arm, Four-County's first baseman and premier hitter had checked out earlier that morning, put his stuff into the back of his green Ford pickup, and drove off into the mist toward the interstate.

"Well, that bag was all he brought with him." Floyd Adams, the rangy second baseman, was standing at the desk with the manager and catcher. He shook his head and stared off at the parking lot. "So what you reckon he had wropped up?"

The clerk shrugged again. "Beats me." The phone rang and he turned away to answer it. The three men looked at each other and shook their heads again. I just set off to the side and wondered. The others were up looking through all the rooms, with Buddy.

"What the hell is going on here?" the squat, square catcher asked. Charlie was built like a damned World War I concrete bunker. "Ain't like Grover to take off without saying something. He was here last night."

"Hell, he'll be back," Pounds said. "You watch. Grover ain't never let us down."

Adams lowered his early-morning Falstaff, which he kept in a brown paper sack, and stared back toward the parking lot. "Grover's never been nowhere like this before."

"Grover's never been *nowhere* before," Pounds answered. "Period. *But* here."

Charlie pulled off his cap and scratched his head. "What the hell you rekkin he had wrapped up under his arm?"

"I done asked that," Floyd said.

"Did you get a answer?" Charlie shot back.

The clerk, who had just finished on the phone, turned back to them. "Well, they got one of them starved-artist sales going on in the hallway on the second floor—y'all musta saw it. You can figger out *why* they are starving. My bet is your friend bought a pitcher and take'n it home, only it was a lot bigger than your average pitcher. . . . "

"Naw." Pounds shook his head vigorously. "Naw. Not Grover. For one thing, he don't know shit about art. Second, he ain't got money for a pot to piss in, much less a pitcher. Naw. Not a pitcher. Not Grover."

"He wouldn't buy nothing for the trailer without Alva knew about it," Charlie said. "And Alva ain't here."

"He might of called her," Pounds said.

"I bet it wudn't no pitcher," Charlie said.

"Then what the hell do you think it coulda been that he had wrapped up?" Adams asked.

"Would you quit sayin' *wrapped*, Goddamn it?" Charlie rolled his eyes. "That word went out a hunderd years go, you fuckin' redneck. The word is *wrapped*."

"You say it your way, I'll say it mine. That's the way my daddy always said it."

"Fuck you *and* your daddy, you fuckin' redneck." Charlie reached and slapped Adams on the shoulder, but it was all in fun. Everybody knew how far you could push Adams, which wasn't far. It's just that Charlie knew within a millimeter how far he could go without getting his head knocked off. But, come to think of it, anybody who took a swing at Charlie had better land the knock-out blow or his ass was grass. Hell, these were all bad-ass people in their own way. Me too. Didn't nobody mess with me much neither. Nobody in their right mind fucked with linemen—people that played with electricity all day just wasn't to be fucked with.

"In one of our sheets too." The clerk was leaning out over the desk with his nose as far into our bidness as he could get it. I half expected Adams to knock all his teeth out. He had a bad temper, which is why Pounds didn't try to stop him from drinking the beer. He was the kind that one minute you could be talking to him about anything from pickup trucks to guns and the next he'd have you on the ground begging to be let up.

"We'll pay for the damned sheet if he don't come back," Pounds said. "Quit worryin' about the fuckin' sheet. We got ballgames to win, and we need Grover. I don't give a rat's ass about no sheet or no pitcher. What I do give a rat's ass about is winning softball games."

We milled around in the lobby for a little bit, waiting till the room search was complete. It was like a crime scene, with everybody serious as cancer. Then we all gathered around Pounds, who just happened to ask again what Grover might have had wrapped up in that sheet.

"What you rekkin, Buddy?" somebody asked him. "You's the last one to see him."

"No rekknin' to it." He had kept his mouth shut to that point, wondering, I guess, whether he ought to say anything. "What he done was, he take'n the mirror out of the bathroom. It ain't nothin' but wall there now, with holes in the plaster where the screws was."

Well, of course that snoopy-ass clerk was leaning close and heard that and he come out from behind the counter like he had had a Louisiana hot sauce enema and wanted to know just why the hell Grover would take a mirror out of the room, and then he started in on how *somebody*'d have to pay for it *and* the sheet, whereupon Adams set his beer on the counter and grabbed the clerk by his lapels and set *him* on the counter too, but Pounds pulled Adams off of him and announced that we'd come up with the money for the sheet and the mirror, which meant that Old Man Sheffield was about to get another bill to wonder about. But he was pretty easy. He'd just say, "I swear, y'all can tear up more shit." Then Pounds said it was time to load up and get on to the field, that maybe Grover would meet us there.

But he didn't. And we flat-ass needed that long-ball hitting of his. We lost the first game 7–3 to a bunch of firemen and policemen from Grenada, of all the little popcorn-fart towns, then faced a determined church group, Assembly of Godders from Corinth, who spent twenty Goddamned minutes praying that they would whip our asses and take the trophy home for Jehovah. They coulda saved fifteen of them minutes and still won—tore us a new one middle of the afternoon, 13–2, with a damned *preacher* hammering a grand slam in the fifth inning, like God really *was* on his team, and the round-robin was over for us. You talking about humble. Before it was good dark we was in the Four-County parking lot in Columbus drinking beer and cussing ourselves for the way we played, but mostly cussing Grover.

Old Man Sheffield showed up in his big fine Lincoln Town Car and set in on Pounds for letting it happen, but Pounds wasn't in the mood for anything but beer, so he handed him the bill for the sheet and mirror and told him to get the fuck out of his face, that it wasn't his fault.

"Are you telling me this team can't cut it without Grover Johnson?"

"That is exactly what I am telling you," Pounds said. And that was that. We left.

Grover Johnson had never stayed in a motel before—had not, in fact, ever been more than fifty miles from Caledonia, where he was born and schooled to maybe the ninth grade, or Columbus, less than twenty miles away, where he worked stringing wire. Four-County Electric Power Company hired him right out of junior high school, when he couldn't have been more than fifteen, and after about a decade of ordinary young American male foolishness he settled right down and became a proper husband and finally father. This is what Alva, his wife, told me that evening when I dropped by the trailer to find out where he had got off to.

Alva—her whole name was Alvarine—wasn't what you'd call a raving beauty, but she was real young, some five or six years younger than Grover, and had damned fine legs, what I had seen of them on company picnics, up to where her short shorts started interfering with where my eyes was going, and her face looked good enough, even without makeup, which I'd never seen her with. I'd never seen her but a few times anyhow. Mostly Grover kept her in the trailer and out of the sun.

"And you got no idea where he's at?" I asked her after I'd told her about what he did. "I'd really like to know."

"Lord, no. It ain't like Grover just to disappear. He don't never go nowhere." She tilted back the beer she'd been nursing. And she glanced a couple of times at a pack of cigarettes on an end table, but she didn't go for one, not that I would have minded. I like to watch women handle a cigarette. It tells you a lot. "Not like Grover at all."

I asked her what she was going to do if Grover didn't come back, and she said she wasn't too worried about that, that he never knew anything but Caledonia and Columbus and Four-County, and sooner or later he'd get hungry for her cooking or run out of what little money he had with him and come home with his tail tucked between his legs.

"Or he'll get hungry for *me*," she said. I didn't like the way she looked at me when she said that or the way she ran her tongue over her lips, or maybe the problem was that I *did* like it, but there were two kids bouncing on a bed back at the end of the trailer, so I guess she didn't mean a whole lot by it. "He will," she said. I kept wanting her to light up. Wanted to see how she held it, how she handled it with her lips. Like I say. . . .

There was something in the way she set on the edge of that little couch with her eyes leveled at me that made me think that maybe she was right, that he would come back. And something that reminded me of a birddog on point: every muscle tense, eyes fixed straight ahead, just quivering with excitement and quick energy and waiting for the word. Which I didn't give and couldn't, not with them two kids back there mattress dancing. She let me know without saying a word about it that Grover wasn't taking care of things at home. I guess I shoulda asked her when the kids wouldn't be there and if it would be all right for me to drop by again—you know, if Grover didn't show back up and all. My you-know-what was starting to feel like a quail ready to flush, come bird dog or shotgun. But I couldn't dwell on it.

"Alva, what if he don't?"

"He will," she said. "He will." She smiled. "Give him a week anyhow."

Then she broke point and told me she had to get the kids ready for bed, and she thanked me for coming by. She brushed past me to open the door, and the hair rose up on my arm nearest to her like she was full of electricity. I hoped she didn't notice what else was rising. Then she closed it again and my heart started triple timing.

She brushed past me again and went into the kitchen and took a piece of notebook paper and a pencil out of a drawer and wrote something on it. Then she tore off the part she had written on and handed it to me.

"That's his daddy's address in Greenwood. If y'all really want to find him and beat him up for losing the tournament, he might be there. Or his folks'll know where he's at."

I studied the piece of paper.

"But don't hurt him bad. I ain't got time to nurse him. Just try to talk him into comin' back home."

I nodded and folded the little piece of paper and put it in my billfold. She opened the door again.

When I was backing out of the drive, she stood there in the doorway looking down at me, and I swear I could see her legs right up to you-know-where, which is how thin her dress was and that light at the end of the couch burning right through it like it was nothing, like she was standing astraddle a light beam that was out to blind me. I told myself then and there that I wasn't going back without Grover was there, much as I'd like to do a little mattress dancing on that bed with *her.* Felt like I'd dodged a bullet. I shook all the way home.

Under a thin moon that had wedged itself like a thorn in the night sky, his face seemed almost a stranger's to me, no more the chin, cheeks, and forehead of Grover Johnson than what he said he conjured out of his mirror, his eyes way back in their shadowy caves, his hair and beard the color of the camper shell, which looked white because it had been once and in contrast to the dingy truck was still considerably lighter. But, shit, he might of dyed his hair for effect. Looked like a skinny Moses in that toga. Or at least I'm led to believe from Sunday School pictures that's what Moses wore when he parted the sea and all, like anybody was around to paint the pictures, but he damned sure didn't do it off the tailgate of a pickup.

Less than three months since I last seen him, and I wouldn't of known him except for the truck, which looked the same as it always had, like something you wouldn't steal if somebody left the keys in it and the motor running and you had just robbed a bank. Hadn't been washed in years, if ever, with road grime thick enough to grow peanuts in.

"Y'ain't the first one not to believe," he said after we'd done our hellos and he invited me to crawl back in the shell and we'd talked a while. I mean, I hadn't said shit about believing or not believing, but he read it in my eyes. He unplugged the lights and we set down across from each other, behind the mirror frame, which was still slid out on the tailgate, and got into the beer. He'd shoved my beer in with some of his in a ice chest. But I noticed that it was mine he started in on.

"Not many folks do, before they see it for theyselves." He nodded toward the mirror, which he had mounted in a simple pine frame padlocked to the cab end of the shell with a plastic-dipped chain. "Not the first, and you won't be the last. It's natural."

I let him do the talking. I didn't have anything worth saying. Except finally: "I didn't say that I don't believe it. It's just that I ain't seen anything yet to *make* me believe. I couldn't see shit from where I was over there on the curb. But that crowd must of seen something."

"Let the steam hit it, fog it over, and the face comes out, plain as day, with hair, even the eyes—man, it's the eyes that gets people, like they looking d'rectly at you, no matter where you're standing. Like they foller you. Folks gasp. You can hear'm suck breath and then they gasp, like they seen a ghost or come in their britches, which maybe they have—both or either, I mean."

He was holding his beer but not drinking it. He was making points with it and sloshing it all over his toga. I just set there and sipped and listened, because he looked like he'd rather do the talking. I never was much for talking anyhow. What the fuck's the point, since most people ain't gon' change their minds about anything you got to say. Of course, if you got a mirror with Jesus's face on it, it sure gives you a edge.

"I pull into a town, usually on a Friday, and park somewhere where I know people bound to walk, and I set there for hours studyin' the place to make sure where my truck ought to be at the next morning. If they got a Wal-Mart, then there ain't no studyin' to it—that's where I'm gon' be at, bet your sweet ass. That's always the place. Right there next to the people that has them puppies and kittens and shit out to give away because they tired of fuckin' with'm. You ever seen what shows up in their parking lots? And they wouldn't dare try to run you off if you got a religious agenda. They'd lose all kinds of customers if they was to do that.

"If they ain't got a Wal-Mart, and they got a downtown with a courthouse, which is the case here, I find the best corner. Nearest Wal-Mart is thirty miles off. I'll hit it tomorrow night prolly.

I prefer the county seats, of course, because they tend to pull lots of country people in. Soon's I can, I park my truck in the spot I want and go to what looks like the hot-spot café to get something to eat and use the bathroom, talk around a little bit, let'm know I'm in town and what I'm all about, and then I crawl up in the back here and sleep until dawn."

He leaned and patted a sleeping bag that was rolled up and stashed in a corner. I looked around at all the crap back there with us, which I could just barely make out in the light from the streetlamps: the sleeping bag, the mirror, a vaporizer/humidifier—whatever the hell you want to call it —a couple of spotlights mounted on pieces of 2x6, a few hanging clothes and two plastic leaf bags filled with something bulky, a metal tool box, and long, narrow pieces of plywood painted white. Some other shit that I couldn't make out at all.

"It ain't half bad, except in cold weather. But even that has its good side—it's easier to fog in cold weather."

I guess there's a Goddamned bright side to everything, hunh?

The signs come out first thing, he said, one that attached to the grill of the truck, one for each side of the shell, up high, and one that hung from the open tailgate. Said he had some small ones made up at a Kinko's to put in the windows of stores when they let him do that. They all read the same thing—*See the Face of Jesus*—in letters eight inches high printed in black paint over a white background on plywood strips so that somebody of average eyesight could read them from two blocks away, or all the way across a Wal-Mart parking lot. He wired the signs to little brass loops he had bolted onto the truck so that people wouldn't steal'm.

"You'd be s'prised how many people will walk off with one if they ain't wired on good. Like they was pieces of the cross or something. Must of lost eight or ten before I put them rings on. What for, do you rekkin? Can't be meanness. Just something to take away I guess, something to remind them of the time they seen the face of Jesus."

I asked him why they didn't try to take the mirror.

"Because of the shotgun I got in here is how come. Don't think they ain't tried."

"You are shitting me."

"Ain't either. Folks're real serious about religion. They'll walk in the shadder of death to touch the robe of Jesus."

"That mirror ain't exactly. . . ." Then I shut up about it.

"Grover, how do you work it? I mean, how do you hook'm?"

"Well, the signs do their work, you know, and they start milling around. Then I get up on the tailgate and start talking to'm. This damn robe helps, of course, since you don't see that many people with one on."

I shook my head. "Naw, not these days you don't. Not unless you're where faggots hang out." Then: "What do you say? I mean, how do you start it?"

"I start with simple stuff, stuff they've heard a thousand times in Church and Sunday School: how God so loved the world that he give up His son Jesus to be nailed on the cross and murdered for their sins and all."

He drug the word *murdered* out like *murrrrrrderrrrred-uh*. Don't ask me why. I guess it made it sound more important. I never did understand preachers.

"It's the same story, the very same one they've heard all their lives, only they act like they hearing it for the first time, mainly because I am a new voice saying it, like it's just another version of the same story, only it's the same thing, the very same thing. You might remember them damned tent revival evangelists when we was little, how they'd blow in for a week and rack up all the change they could from the pore bastards that believed their bullshit—faith healin' and all that crap—but they told the same fuckin' stories them people heard in church ever Sunday. It was just somebody different tellin'm. The tent and sawdust floor and a new voice, but they ate up the same damn stories.

"I mean, don't people go to see movies about World War II over and over? Hell, like they think it's gon' turn out different this time, like maybe the Japs are gon' take over California and move east and conquer the whole United States or the Germans are gon' develop the atom bomb first and take over the world? They *know* how it's gon' turn out. It ain't the story they come for, but the pitcher show. It's how it's *told* that makes it differnt. That's how come they'd have them revivals—it's a differnt person tellin' it.

"They're standing there pretending to listen to me telling them that same old story, and ever damn one of 'm is craning to see past me into the back of the truck, trying to see the mirror."

He reached into the ice chest and took out another beer, opened it, chugged it, eased the bottle down to eye level. "You know I *always* wanted to be a preacher."

"I *didn't* know that."

"Well, I did. Only I couldn't imagine what I'd say to a bunch of people that they hadn't heard before. I mean, how do you tell the same story but tell it different? You gotta have something that gives you a edge. Noah and Jonah and David and Goliath and all that shit. How you gon' tell that differnt? Or the Christmas story. I always wanted to hear a preacher say that two wise men and a dumbass showed up on camels, carrying candy and silver rattles and shit like that, stuff a baby would like. People done heard all that so many times that they got it memorized. That's where the mirror comes in. It's my edge. They don't give a hoot in hell what I'm *sayin'*—what they want is to see Jesus in the mist."

I nodded and watched him.

"Then I ask how many of them has seen Jesus's face, and they'll be two or three hands shoot up out of the little bunch that's gathered, and I'll say, no, how many has *really* seen the face of Jesus in person, and there might be one hand, usually none, because they get to thinking about what they're saying and they know they're lying, so the person that belongs to the one hand that's up gets to lookin' around and thinking about it some more and soon there ain't no hands, so I say to'm that just after dark I'm am going to show them the real face of Christ."

Along about sundown, when a pretty good crowd had gathered, he'd slide the mirror out onto the tailgate and hook up the lights and vaporizer, which he run off his truck batteries.

"When the sun's hotter'n a sonofabitch on the mirror, it's hard to get it to fog, but sooner or later it'll do it. I just found it better to wait till dark, when it's cooler and there's more humidity, and the effect is better with lights on it.

"Your average vaporizer won't generate enough steam out in the open like this. I souped one up with a double coil, though, and that mother will boil out a gallon of water in thirty minutes. They's times, when it's cool and the humidity's high, that I can't even see the side of the truck by the time I'm through. You could hide Robert E. Lee's army in that fog.

"After a while the steam gets so heavy on the mirror that condensation sets in and big tears start rollin' down His face, and across His forehead, and in that red spotlight it looks like blood, man, like blood pouring right outta that crown of thorns on His head and running down into His eyebrows and beard, and tears just streaming down His face. Hell, it gets'm. They weep and say *Praise the Law-erd,* and sometimes they talk in tongues. It can get spooky, is what.

"People reach and touch it, man, touch and say they feel the power of Jesus. One man swore he come away seeing better'n he seen in years and years. Another one throwed his crutches in the bushes and walked away just like he'd never been crippled."

He went on and on a while, and then I just broke in and asked him how come he fucked up our tournament when he walked out that day. If

I was ever going to get to where I wanted to get to, I had to get him off that damned mirror.

"I hated to do it. I Goddamn well hated to do it. Y'all was counting on me. I was the best long-ball hitter you had, and we had a good shot at the trophy, but a man's gotta do—well, you know, without me saying it.

"We beat everbody in town, everbody in Aberdeen and Tupelo and West Point and Starkville, and if Macon had of had a team, we'd of beat them too. We was good. Red-hot fielders and hitters, the best team Columbus ever had, bar none. Strong and fast on the bases, quick in the field. Bad is what. And I went and messed up y'all's one big chanch to take the state."

Brother Grover relaxed at that and took a long swig of his beer, belched, and stared quietly at the big hand that held the bottle. "I got the call is all." His voice was a little dreamy.

"I been lookin' at pitchers of Jesus all my life long in stuff from the church. And the face in that mirror is *His* face.

"And I'll tell you something else: That bit about it being impossible for Jesus to be anything but black and brown-eyed is deadass wrong. He is almost blond, and His eyes are as blue as they'd be if the mirror had holes where His eyes are and I held it up to the sky."

I just nodded.

"And He's crying."

"Cryin'?"

"Yeah, bawling His eyes out is what."

"He would be, I guess."

"Yeah," Grover said, "He would be."

"So you just take'n the mirror off the wall? Which we had to pay for, I might point out. Well, Old Man Sheffield did." I hesitated. "The mirror, not the wall."

"Yeah, Buddy'd already went down to breakfast and I was in the shower. When I slid the curtain back and stepped out, the bathroom was foggy as hell. Then I looked at the mirror. I stood there looking at where my face had been before I got in the shower. Jesus's face was where mine had been." He sipped his beer.

"Then I wiped the mirror off with a towel, and there I was, nekkid as a jaybird and my hair all wet and slicked back, drops of water in my beard, and I turned the hot water on in the sink and shower and steamed the place up till I couldn't see much more than the light over my head, and it looked like the moon on a foggy night, and when it had cleared enough for me to make out anything in the mirror, there the face was again.

"What I done was, I dried off and went out and set down on the bed and tried to make some fucking sense out of what I seen, but I couldn't. I peeped back around the door and the face was still there, and His eyes was right on mine, staring at me, and He had them damned big old tears just rolling off His face."

"So you just take'n it off the wall?"

"Well, hell yeah, I take'n it. I sure as shit wasn't gon' leave it there. Not with what I seen in it. Man, that'd be like walking off and leaving a gold mine, with streaks of gold showing. Hell naw I wasn't gon' leave it there. I got my Leatherman and take'n the screws out of it and wrapped it up in a sheet and got dressed and put my stuff in the duffel bag and slipped out."

"Abandoned us."

He sighed. "Yeah, I guess so."

After he left Jackson, he took I-55 toward Memphis, detoured over to his daddy's place in Greenwood, where he borrowed some tools, then went on to Memphis and didn't stop until he'd cleared the traffic there, and then he hit I-40 and drove until he came to Jackson, Tennessee, which was where his old hero, the train engineer Casey Jones, was from and which therefore he figured was a reasonable enough place to stop for the night. From Jackson to Jackson, you know. And that he did. His granddaddy was from Vaughan, Mississippi, where Casey had his big wreck and got killed—he's the one that started the Casey Jones museum there, but that's another story. Grover parked in the far corner of a Wal-Mart parking lot and crawled into the truck bed and got bad drunk on a bottle of Jim Beam he kept under the seat and passed out beside the mirror.

When the fog had cleared from his head and the parking lot on up in the morning, he unwrapped the mirror and sat on the edge of the bed studying it. All it threw back was sky and a couple of passing clouds, but he knew the face was there, and he knew how to coax it out, so he hatched a plan and within three or four hours he had a camper shell on the truck, a vaporizer and spotlights in the back, and, as he put it, a song in his heart and a vision in his head.

He spent the rest of the afternoon building a frame for the mirror and wiring the truck so that he could get the lights and vaporizer to work off the twelve-volt circuit, then slept in the Wal-Mart lot again in a sleeping bag alongside the mirror, which was now up on its side the way it was in the motel.

Late the next day he set up the first time in a parking lot near the house that Casey Jones lived in when he wrecked, using a crude sign on a posterboard: SEE JESUS! Only six people showed up, but Grover drove away with twenty-seven dollars and some change more in his pocket than he had when he parked there.

"And that was the beginning of my service," he said, laying his empty bottle down and reaching for another beer. "Ain't been what I'd call a intrapanoorial genius, but it ain't a bad living." He hesitated. "And I have give a whole lot of people hope that didn't have much before."

I nodded and sipped on my beer.

"How'd you find me?"

"I went by your folks' place, and they told me you said something about goin' to Jackson, Tennessee. It wudn't all that hard to track you down from there—just take'n some time. It's not like people don't remember a guy with Jesus's face in the back of his truck."

"So my folks give me up."

"I told'm I had a termination check for you."

"Bastard."

Traffic on the street had died down to almost nothing, but I noticed that a cop cruised past a couple of times to make sure we wasn't planning to walk off and leave a few washtubs of fertilizer and diesel fuel in the truck and blow up the courthouse. And things got quiet while we worked on our beer, which also started working on me, but I just pissed in a can that he handed me—looked like one pork-and-beans had come in and he had cut the top off of—then leaned and poured it out over the edge of the tailgate, which he said was standard procedure.

When I'd taken care of that bidness I just up and asked him what he did for pussy. I know that sounds kinda blunt, but when you've just pissed in a can in front of a man and poured the piss out into the street with him watching, it's not like there are too many things that can't be said between you. Besides, I'd known Grover a long time.

He smiled. All I could see of him was his dark face between the light hair and the toga, couldn't see his mouth move at all when he said, "I get by."

He said that when the need come on him too fierce, he would start working on some woman that take'n his fancy, giving her a private showing of the face and all, and it usually worked. "We crawl back in here and have a religious experience, a lot of laying on of hands, you might say, and a whole lot of speaking in tongues and *with* tongues. Keep one eye open for a husband or boyfriend, you know."

And then I got bold. I had to. Hell, I hadn't been thinking of much of anything else for months.

"What about Alva? Do you ever miss her?"

He got quiet about the women then, and for a long time he sat in the dark and didn't say anything.

"Grover, I ast you about Alva."

"I know you did."

Everything got quiet again and stayed that way a long time.

"Grover, Goddamn it, I ast you about *Alva*."

Finally: "Hell, I miss her bad. Of course I do."

"Then how come . . ."

"I got the call." He sighed. "When that comes, you can't just turn your back on it."

"*I* could."

"Naw, you could not. Without you been there, you don't know what it's like. If you had of stepped out of the shower that morning and seen what I seen, them big old blue eyes full of pain and suffering and tears and love, you would have did what I did and take'n that mirror off the wall and be where I'm at."

I shook my head, but in the dim light of the streetlamps I doubt that he could see it. "Naw, I *could*. It'd be Alva's eyes I would remember."

He give me a look. I could tell even in the little light in the back of that truck. "You don't know shit about Alva's eyes."

"And you don't know shit about what *I* know." I knew I was getting in dangerous territory, but I wasn't backing down. Then I decided I'd better soften it a little. "I know that I'd rather be looking into a woman's eyes, that can at least look back, than in something I imagined in a fucking mirror."

"Have you been messing with Alva?" His voice was low but hard.

"No I have not. I have not touched Alva."

He was quiet a few seconds. Then, "I have seen both sides, man, and I got to tell you that the spirit side is what matters."

"You don't think Alva's got spirit."

"Alva is the *flesh*." He reached and tapped the sheet-shrouded mirror. "*He* is the *spirit*."

"Grover, are you going back to Alva?"

"What the hell is that to you?"

"I just want to know."

He lifted his hands above his head and made some sort of sign.

"Know what I call myself?"

I told him no. How the hell would I know something like that? I'da figured *Grover* if I got that question on a multiple-choice test somewhere. Or maybe *looney*.

"Omega."

"Omega?"

"Yeah, like in the Bible."

"Where in the Bible—"

"Got Alva back there in Caledonia. And me, Omega, out here."

"I don't get it."

"Alva and Omega, fool. Ain't you ever read the Bible?"

"Yeah, but not much. That's just something you heard some preacher say is all."

"Christ said, 'I am Alva and Omega.' The beginning and the end. Alva was the beginnin'. Alva was the *flesh*. I have *excaped* from the flesh. I am the *spirit*."

"So you chose a Goddamned quarter-inch-thick mirror that when it's fogged up you *think* you can see the face of Jesus in when you got a whole *real* woman back in that trailer in Caledonia that you know Goddamned well you can see more than the face of, and she ain't thin and hard and cold as a sheet of glass, and all you gotta do is love her and she'll love you back! Seems like to me *you* the one that's fogged up."

I was getting agitated, but I didn't really give a shit. I needed to know where Alva fit into his plans. Hell, we'd been sneaking around mattress dancing for months, and I was just about ready to ask her to move in with me, into a real house, where the kids could have a room apiece. I'd been divorced for four years, and I was ready for a live-in woman again. But if there's a husband out there somewhere, you gotta be careful or end up either bad hurt or dead.

"What you don't know about the spirit would fill that courthouse out there from the basement to the attic and spill over into the streets like that piss you just poured in the gutter. You don't—"

"You don't know what the *fuck* I know about the spirit." I hesitated. "*Or* the flesh." I leaned forward and stared into the dark of his face. He had his hands flattened against the side of the bed like he was trying to retreat, but he didn't say anything.

"Grover, that is a fucking *mirror*. It is glass with some kind of silver shit on the back of it to reflect things."

I yanked the sheet off of it and threw it at him. He flung it aside.

"You might see yourself and all kinds of other stuff in it, but the *face of Christ* ain't in there. Did you ever ask yourself *why it would be?* Why would the face of Christ show up in a mirror in a bathroom in a *Holiday Inn* in *Jackson* fucking *Mississippi?*" I slapped the frame with my hand. "It is *glass! Glass!* With some kinda Goddamn silver shit—"

"Don't *do* that! Don't *hit* it!" He pulled his hands up into what looked like fists, but I couldn't tell for sure. Goddamn, it is dark in a camper shell at night. Y'ever notice?

"*Why?* I'll tell you why. Because it is your *living* is why. Not because the face of Christ is in that Goddamned mirror! You ain't no better than them TV evangelists that rip people's asses off right and left. Money is all they are interested in." I slapped the frame again, this time harder. "A mirror is all that it is—glass and . . ."

"I told you not to *hit* it!"

Hell, you'da thought I had hit Jesus in the flesh.

He got up on his knees and towered over me since I was still slumped back against the side of the bed. "You are afraid to look at it is what. You know the face is in there. I will *show* you. You are scared of what you'll see. You—"

Then he set to fumbling around with that damned vaporizer and spotlight so that I could get my personal viewing.

"I would see what I *wanted* to see, which is what them dumbasses flocked around this truck earlier was seeing. If you told'm it was Hitler in the mirror, they would see Hitler. Or the Virgin Mary or Martin Luther King or Elvis or the Pope or whoever the hell it was they wanted to see. What you've got is a fucking blemish that looks like something you want it to look like. It's like kids seeing the shapes of animals in the clouds. You can see what you want to see, what you *need* to see.

"You are a weak man, Grover, and maybe it's *you* that needs to see Jesus so bad. But His face ain't in that Goddamned mirror, not any more than it's in one of them courthouse windows out there." I pointed. "It is a fucking *mir-ror*. You are what the preachers used to call an *idolator*, worshipin' a *mirror!*" I reached and slapped the frame even harder. It rocked on its base.

"You hit it again and I will have to kill you, in the name of Jesus-uh."
He already had the vaporizer going and had the red spotlight turned on,
but he was on the other side of the mirror, so I couldn't see him. The water
must have still been pretty warm, because I could hear it rumbling and
beginning to hiss.

"I mean it," the voice came from the other side. "You better not hit it
again."

So I did. I slapped the shit out of the mirror itself—the back side,
which was toward me. He didn't even have it backed with plywood, just
mounted in the frame. I felt the glass flex and heard a *spang* like ice way
out on a pond in deep winter, and then it just exploded toward him, with
pieces of mirror bouncing off the bottom and side of the bed and going
everywhere and picking up the glare of that spotlight and I swear he was
showered with little pinpoints of light like red stars, and while I was
scrambling to get through the open end of that camper shell, what I was
thinking, crazy as it was, was *Where do you rekkin Jesus is in all that?*

The last I saw of Grover was through the frame where the mirror had
been. Steam was everywhere, and in the red glow of the spotlight it was
plumb weird, like something out of a horror movie, like looking back in
some kind of witch's cave. I could hear him fumbling around in the front
corner of the bed, where I bet the shotgun was.

But I didn't hang around to see. I bailed out the end of the truck and
hit the pavement hauling ass and didn't stop running until I was two blocks
away and wouldn't have stopped then except I ran right out of a shoe and
had to stop and go back and get it, which was stupid if somebody's chas-
ing you but not so stupid if you got a long way to run, and when I looked
up I saw a deep, dark alley between a couple of buildings, so I made sure
he wasn't in sight and slipped up in there and flattened myself against a
wall and waited. I'm telling you that my heart was flouncing like a big old
catfish in the bottom of a boat.

I waited for, hell, I don't know, maybe two hours or so, didn't so much
as fart or clear my throat, but Lord, I could have used one of them beers—
I'd of swilled it. Then I crept out to the end of the alley and looked every
way there was to look and didn't see a living soul. So I eased up the sidewalk till I could see his truck, only it wasn't there. There was a couple of
cars and a truck parked across from the courthouse, and the truck was
mine. Since I had had that truck just a couple of months, there wasn't any
way he could have known what I was driving, unless he just happened
to pay attention to the tag, so I figured I was OK there. I hung around

another few minutes to make sure he wasn't gonna come gunning around the corner spraying buckshot, then walked over to where his truck had been parked. It was almost like I had to convince myself that the whole evening had happened the way I remembered it. But when the smell of that piss hit me and I saw a jillion pieces of that mirror where the truck had been, reality set in bigtime and I knew for sure that the experience I had had wasn't imaginary, religious or otherwise.

The drive back home take'n me the rest of the night and most of the early morning. I wasn't in any hurry, to be sure, since I didn't know whether with his mirror broke and all he would decide to go back to Alva. Hell, I didn't mean to break the thing. I was just making a point. And I guess I did.

I damned sure wasn't going to feel bad about it any longer than I had to. I mean, he stole the mirror to start with. I got to thinking that me, if I was him, I'd just set up in Wal-Mart parking lots and sell slivers of that glass, call'm sacred or something. I mean, if Jesus was in there, He still would be, and there'd be lots of Him to go around because that mirror flat-ass grenaded. I didn't have time to count, but I had it figured at somewhere around three and a half jillion pieces of Jesus in the back of that truck and another jillion or so on the street behind it.

Along about two or three in the A.M.—not like I paid any attention to the clock or my watch—I happened to look up and to my right and saw the moon, and I had to force my eyes to get back on the road. I kept wanting to see the face of Jesus in it, like He'd migrated, you know. Not that you can see a face when you got nothing much more than a fingernail moon. Besides, you couldn't do anything with that, the moon being public property and all and not the kind of thing you can haul around in the back of your pickup to show people. But all I really saw was the face of Alva, even with the moon as thin as it was—I mean her face filled out the dark place where I knew the rest of the moon was but couldn't see, the penumbrella, or whatever it's called—and that got me to thinking about things other than the spirit.

I crept into Caledonia just after sunrise and circled past her trailer four times before I decided to light—I just said *fuck it* and went on and nosed my truck up beside Alva's Camry and killed the motor and set there a long time. Jesus, God, I must have looked and smelled like roadkill. Something caught my eye on my shirt sleeve, and damned if it wasn't two little slivers of that mirror imbedded in it. I picked'm off and put'm in the ashtray for safekeeping—why, I don't know, but it seemed reasonable. Then I just set there with my chin on the steering wheel staring at what now was a splinter of day moon, wondering what the hell to do.

Then I saw her face in the little window of the door. And I knew.

In Search of the Tightrope Walker

On the rutted road, with cotton plants growing right up to and leaning out over the edges so that a man walking down it with his hands outstretched, as if trying to balance, might almost touch them on either side, the car sat idling a few feet from the mailbox that marked the end of a driveway. He rested his chin on the steering wheel as he studied the trailer across the green rows from him. This he did for a very long time, noting how the rows looked like little waves—and wondering whether to go on or not. Here the road that he had so long been on might end, perhaps for good, perhaps undone, a thing of dust and old dreams. Beside him on the seat lay a crude map an old woman in Corinth had with labored hand drawn in pencil on part of a grocery sack for him two days ago. He folded it and slipped it into his shirt pocket. Soon he would know whether this would be the end or yet another beginning. He lifted his head and put the car in gear.

Past miles and miles of Delta flats he had driven that morning, on asphalt for a very long way, then at a crossroads he turned south onto what amounted to little more than a trail that wound off through broad fields toward a stand of trees at the edge of which he could see for miles the trailer that floated, small and white, on a vast sea of green, a set of power lines strung out to it on a lone picket of crosslike poles. At first he didn't know what he was seeing, just a white speck that in time assumed its shape against the fields and the swatch of trees behind it. But there were no trees near it. It was as if the trailer had simply bobbed up out of the sea of cotton that grew right to the edge of the small yard split by a gravel drive.

He inched up the drive, passed an old white El Camino that looked like it might have made it that far and simply died, and stopped a few feet out from the wooden landing at the front door, which was open. Behind a screen door, matted by dust and lint pulled into the mesh by a window fan, he presumed, stood a woman in a thin white robe watching.

She did not move, did not speak as he got out of the car and with hesitation approached the landing and lifted a foot to the lower step.

"Who are you?" she asked before his foot settled on the next step. She had a hand clutched at her collar, holding the robe tight about her. "And what do you want here?"

"I am looking for Mary Anne Hollis. Are you Mary Anne Hollis?"

"No," she said. "I would like to know who you are before you come up those steps. And what you want here. I have a bad dog with me."

"Do you *know* her?"

"I might."

He looked about him and saw nothing but green in all directions. And then the feeling came back, the helplessness that descends on a man when he accepts his insignificance in the great scheme of things, tiny speck that he is, inflated only in his mind by his mad dreams that in all the universe mean nothing at all to anyone but him. But he knew it was fleeting. It came and went like weather or like the euphoria he sometimes felt when he believed he actually might find her.

"I was told that she lived here. Someone even drew me a map."

"You can't always trust maps. And people lie. If I knew where you might find her, why should I tell you? I don't know who you are or why you might want to see her."

To either side of the trailer there was nothing but a monstrous green smear of acre upon acre of cotton, which had just begun to break into bloom, giving the undulating surface the appearance of little glitters of sky and sun off waves, and beyond it the line of trees, a darker green than the cotton. It was like a painting, a study in green, with the intrusion of the ghostly white trailer and myriad sprinkles of white and gold.

"My name is Davis. Davis Wilson. And I have searched for Mary Anne Hollis for years, for nearly ten years, over half this country."

He had still not moved his foot from the first step, as if it had all come down to this one frozen moment when he either had found her or had not, and he was afraid to know, but down deep he felt belief well up, an almost palpable knot in his chest, already heard the music coming back, saw her far back in his mind's eye as she glided effortlessly across the wire.

Oh, Lord, how he remembered her skinny little body so tightly bound by the silken silver outfit she wore that every bone stood out, ribs and pelvis and vertebrae and high on her back the nubs of her sprouting wings. She walked within touching distance, as untouchable as the angels, her eyes fixed straight ahead, and all he could do was stare and try to quell his hammering heart. That blond hair and pale, celestial face, those thin arms and legs, every line of muscle and bone, chest flat as a boy's, and about her the faint scent of spices. She didn't look at him, didn't have to. It was enough that he was permitted by the gods to see her.

Septembers the carnival came to the little Mississippi town near where he lived, as surely as football seasons, welcomed with an almost frenzy by the kids who were still too young to be swept up in the sweat and agony and glory of the gridiron. And even more by the country kids who rode their bikes down dusty backroads to the glitter and the glare, then back out under the eery light of the moon or simple stars, penniless, with the sticky sweet of cotton candy still clinging to their faces and the throb of the midway dancing from ear to ear.

It was September and he was there. Midafternoon, sweaty from the long ride, he leaned his old green bicycle against an oak at the edge of the fairgrounds and secured it with a double-knotted rope, then booth by booth frittered away the hours and precious coins: flung softballs at concrete bottles squatting like stone soldiers, threw darts at balloons that dodged and weaved with every ribbon of air, and slammed around the oval bumper-car court. He kept deep down in his pocket a quarter, sacred and assigned for the Big Top, and waited for the night to come.

Finally the afternoon waned, the sun relented, and he joined a chattering band who for all their fervor might well be going that very night to some great stirring revival meeting where angels would be witnessed and miracles and maybe even the Holy Face Itself. For what they were going to see could not be seen elsewhere in their little lives: the magic of the Big Top, as fascinating for him as what went on under the revival tents, where the lame threw down their crutches and the blind were blessed with dazzling sight. On impulse—he could never have told anyone why, for most of his life in those days was mystery and whim—he broke from the ranks and slipped around behind the tent, in his pocket his only prize for the day, a fuzzy rabbit foot strung on a chain. He rubbed it for luck as he stood at a back flap, hoping no one would discover him and chase him away. And luck it brought him: that shining girl, the tightrope walker.

With a man who might have been her father—a burly chap with heavy dark hair on his shoulders and back and arms—she descended from a trailer, a burnished aluminum loaf that squatted behind the tent, and followed him through the flap, disappearing into the shadows from which muffled music came. He stood a long time looking at the slit through which she had entered, until applause and children's shrieks brought him back and he hurried around to the front, paid his quarter, and went inside.

What a delight were the elephant and two tigers and one lone, crippled lion who in another tent, under evangelist Thelma Bentley's curing hands, would have sprung whole again, king of jungle, proud and nimble. They gamboled about the single sawdust ring, spurred by two men with whips, until his hands stung from battering applause and his throat ached from yelling.

And then from behind a curtain came the man and little girl, mounting the pole as if gravity no longer mattered. One smooth step off the circular platform, four or five silken strides, and he was across to the other platform, followed by the girl, a nimbus of motion. Back and forth they went, back and forth, until his uplifted head reeled with her silver sheen. His eyes never left her. For a finale she threw herself into the man's arms, whereupon he swept her to the side and up onto his shoulders, and she stood balanced, arms outstretched, as he crossed the wire again.

On his ride home that night he could feel the first lilt of fall coming on even before he had dipped into the night-cool hollow of the low-water crossing on McBee Creek. But it was not fall he was thinking of, not the grinding of his wheels through heavy gravel or their whir through foot-deep water, not the notion that he still had over two hard miles to home and to bed. On that moon-bathed lonesome road he thought of nothing but the silver girl suspended against a canvas sky, defying all that we fear.

Often over the years he thought of her, when an uncertain mood settled on him, like the feeling you get in early spring when the earth rekindles with tongueless and indefinable longing, and the music of that September night came back and echoed in his head, that night when gravity was a minor force and tugged no more than death, when a shining angel balanced above the sawdust earth and their upturned faces saw in the insect-stirred air nothing but light, light, light.

And when he thought of her there was an ache, an emptiness, that nothing could really satisfy or fill, and he would wonder what might have happened to her, where she was, what perilous balance she kept, whether time had been gentle or cruel.

As he grew old, retiring from his university teaching job and divorcing his wife of almost forty years, finding her became an obsession, as if his life had at long last come down to that.

"Ma'am, please, if you know her . . ."

"You have two last names. That is odd."

"Uh, ma'am," he tried. The knot had risen and his voice almost failed him. Something told him, something said, *You are here.* But he had heard the voice before. "I just need to find Mary Anne Hollis. That's all. I was told she lived out here. Somewhere." He turned and again ran his eyes across the great expanse of cotton fields that shimmered in the noonday heat. "Somewhere out here."

"What do you want with her? I might be able to help you out, but you have to tell me why you want to see her."

He drew his foot back from the first step and leaned against the railing. "I saw her . . . I saw her perform once. On a wire. A long time ago. She was a tightrope walker and I watched her once. When I was a boy. Probably no older than she was. Ages ago."

She dropped her hand from the collar and crossed her arms. "How in the name of God did you find this place?"

He looked up at her, vague behind the furry screen. "Are you—"

She hesitated and leaned her head against the screen door. "No, I am not Mary Anne." Then she unlatched and opened the door and reached out a hand. "I am her sister, Margaret."

"Her sister." He ascended the steps and stood before her, his heart in his throat. "At least I have found *you.*" He held his hands wide, as if to embrace the fields that the little trailer sat in. "Finally I am getting close. After all these years, all the false leads, the hopes. . . ."

Then his hand touched hers and he interlaced his fingers in hers and for a very long time they simply stared into each other's eyes.

"Before I let you in, I want to know just how in the name of God you found *me.* And what you want with Mary Anne . . . "

"Does it matter?" he asked. "I mean, I pretty well told you why. . . . "

"All right, then, maybe it doesn't. You're old enough to be entitled to be a little crazy—like me. Come on in. You look like you've been on the road a while. You've got something stuck in your head that you've got to deal with, and maybe I can help." She released his hand.

He leaned and looked behind her. "Where's the dog?"

"There's no dog. That was just to make you nervous."

"It did," he said as he stepped past her. He was suddenly aware of the pale dust that coated his arms and clothes and had surely settled over his face and what was left of his thin gray hair. He must have looked like a ghost too, the way she did to him when he first saw her through the matted screen.

When he was in the room, in the light from the doorway and what came through the curtains, he saw a dining room table in the little kitchen area, with three chairs, and in the room in which he was standing a small couch and end table and in the corner a miniature television set. The paneled walls were filled with pictures of a girl walking across a wire, sometimes with a man, sometimes alone, and in some there was fire beneath, the flames appearing only a few feet from the wire, in others clowns frolicking just below where she walked. In one a great lion stood immediately beneath her, his head up and mouth open, eyes on the girl, as if waiting for her to fall into that gaping maw.

She stood in silence as he moved from photograph to photograph, studying the girl on the wire.

"These are all pictures of her?" he said finally. "Or of *you?*"

"They are pictures of Mary Anne, and they cover about a four-year period, from the time she was maybe twelve until sixteen."

"But she looks the same—the same age—in all of them." He continued to run his eyes over the photographs, lingering on first one, then another.

"That's just perspective and costume. The costumes never changed much. They just made them bigger as she grew. Study the chest and you'll see changes." She laughed. "Very minor ones, but changes."

He laughed then. "Yes. I noticed that. But she never did seem to change much at all. In size. In height."

"It's genetic," she said. "For both of us. I doubt that I grew five inches in height between ten and now. Neither of us ever had a problem with weight. Our breasts just never seemed to catch onto the idea that *they* were supposed to grow."

He turned from the pictures and studied the robe, trying to discern what shape might be beneath it. It was obvious that she was not wearing a bra. He could see the outline of her tiny left nipple.

"Why are you staring at me?"

"I'm sorry. Sorry. It's just that—"

"We could have passed for twins," she said. "It's OK."

"Where *is* she?" he asked.

The woman eased down into a chair and motioned for him to sit on the couch. She fished a pack of cigarettes from the pocket of her robe. "Do you mind if I smoke?"

"No," he said. "It's your house."

"Trailer. There's a difference. Trailers are not really part of where they are. They move. Not like a house. It's hard to call a trailer home." She lit a cigarette, drew deep, then let the smoke ease out through her nostrils. "Would you like a beer or something? Whiskey? I have a little whiskey here, and some beer."

He shook his head.

"Water?"

"No. I'm fine. Really. What I want—"

"What you want to know about is Mary Anne."

"Yes."

"Just what do you want with her? Why did you go to the trouble of trying to track her down? I could understand it if you were in your twenties or thirties, maybe. But now?" She shook her head. "Why did you do it? Jesus, why would you want to track down an old woman? Hell, look at me, man. We were one year apart in age. Like I said, we could have passed for twins. Why in the name of God . . ."

"I—I don't know that I can explain it. I always wanted to *know* her." He stared at a picture in which the girl was standing on the wire with one foot, her legs and arms spread like something taking flight. "I mean, from that very night that I saw her. She was the first girl to really capture my imagination, the first girl . . ."

"Where did you see her at? That show went everywhere, all over the South, from St. Louis down to Key West, from Charleston over to East Texas."

"Columbus, over on the other side of the state."

She smiled. "Columbus. Yeah, I remember being there myself, at least twice. The whole family traveled with that carnival in those days. Our parents were jugglers. What year?"

"I don't know. I just know that I was a boy and she was a girl, and she wedged in my memory brighter than anyone I have ever known."

He pointed to a picture. "She performed with that man. He had hair all over his back. I remember thinking that he looked like a gorilla. Was he your father?"

"Father?" She laughed. "Hardly. That was Billy. And he pretty much *was* a gorilla."

He pointed to another photograph, one in which she stood on the shoulders of the man he remembered.

"The hairy man. Billy? Who was he?"

She laid the cigarette in an ashtray and stared at the picture.

"If you'll pardon me for saying so, he was just a typical male sonofabitch. He *kept* her."

"*Kept* her?"

"Yes. One morning our parents just up and left us. We were in a little town not far from Memphis. But across the state line, in Missippi. I woke up in the trailer we were living in and went in to get some breakfast, and there was Mary Anne at the kitchen table holding a little piece of paper telling us that they were sorry but they couldn't afford to keep us anymore, that they had accepted jobs with another show that was going to Kansas or Oklahoma, somewhere way off west. And that was that. They were gone."

"They just left you in the trailer?"

"Yes. It belonged to the carnival. Wasn't theirs." She picked the cigarette up and brought it back to life.

"And the hairy man?"

"Well, he had been working with Mary Anne for a couple of years, training her, teaching her the wire, and she was getting pretty good at it, so he just told her that he would take care of her, that she could move in with him. Which she did."

"And she was how old?"

"Somewhere around eleven, I guess. At least over ten." She pointed to one of the photographs. "That was her first professional walk." The girl in the picture looked exactly like the one he remembered, everything about her: hair, lithe body, the shiny outfit. "*I* was just over eleven then, maybe twelve. I don't know for sure."

"Then he became your father?"

She laughed a throaty laugh. "Oh no, no, not father." She coughed, cleared her throat. "Lover."

"What?" He shifted forward on the couch and studied her face.

"Hers, not *ours*. Somebody called our aunt in Birmingham, who came and got me the day our folks left, and I grew up with her. Billy talked her into leaving Mary Anne with him. I didn't have any skills the carnival could use except for doing laundry, and I was plenty tired of that. They could get anybody to wash those damned outfits."

"And he just *kept* her?"

"Yes. *Kept* her. Within two weeks after he took her in, he was beginning to do things to her. You know. Kissing and touching. Nothing really —no penetration or anything. But there wasn't but one bed in that little trailer, and they shared it, so in a matter of months it was everything. She told me all this much later."

"How could she stand it?"

"You stand what you *have* to, especially when you don't know any better. He was gentle with her, she said, and she thought that he really loved her. But he let her know that he could run her off from that job anytime he pleased. He had made her, and he could break her. I mean, the owners and managers thought the world of him. And he did bring in the crowds."

"Still . . ."

"Still nothing. Lord, she was making pretty good money for a kid in those days, and she loved being on the wire with him, and she sure didn't have anywhere else to go. And, confused as she was, she said that she loved him as much as he loved her. So she stayed. She didn't know any better."

He shook his head and continued to stare at her. "Oh, my God."

She snorted. "Come on, man. You have to live under those conditions to know what it's like. It's easy enough to think of how horrible it looks to somebody living in what you might call the real world of normal people with families and regular jobs and church and all, but she didn't know any better. And she said it wasn't horrible. It becomes horrible when someone points it out to you or when you learn what it means to *really* be loved by a man. At times it was uncomfortable for her, confusing, but that is all. I told you—she didn't *know* any better."

"How long did she stay with him?"

"Years. Until she fell."

"Fell?"

"Yes. She shattered her hip and several vertebrae one night." She pointed to one of the pictures. "That was her last professional walk. She fell the very next night after that shot was taken."

"There was no net?"

"They never walked over nets. That's part of the attraction for the crowd, knowing that if you slip and fall, they're going to get to see you hit the sawdust like a sack of sand or fall into the mouth of a lion. The sonsofbitches—excuse the language—haven't changed in three thousand years. They are still there to see blood. Or a girl laying there with her hip and back broken and blood seeping out of her mouth and nose. I can still remember the sound they made as she fell past him, reached for the wire and missed—it was like they thought at first that it was part of the show, *ooh*ing and *ah*ing and shrieking—and then the awful silence when she landed on that platform, one they had had lions running across, like everybody in the place had sucked in their breath in disbelief. And I can remember the sound when she hit and the sounds of her bones breaking. I was sitting right in the front row—I always went to see her when the carnival was close—and she landed not more than a dozen feet from me. And the sound of the crowd as she laid there staring up at the wire, where he still stood, balanced, like he was waiting for her to climb back up there. They were screaming and yelling and some of them were even clapping, like they still thought it was part of the show, with her laying there mangled like a doll a dog's been hold of."

He was watching her intently as she played with her fingers, doing a little dance with her fingers, weaving them in and out of each other.

"She was on his shoulders, balanced on one foot, when he did something odd. I mean, the man was steady as a rock on that wire, but she said he done some sort of twitch with his shoulders that pitched her off to the side before she could adjust, and she fell. She grabbed for the wire but couldn't get a hand on it and down she went." She slapped her hands together. "It would have been all right if she had landed in the sawdust—maybe sprained something and been bad bruised, but it wouldn't have been so bad. But she landed on the steps of that damned platform and it almost killed her."

"Oh Jesus."

"That was it. She spent several weeks in the hospital in Memphis, where a surgeon did the best he could to put her back together, and months doing physical therapy. Had operations galore. Lord, you should have seen her scars. One ran the entire length of her back."

He shook his head.

"There was no going back to the wire for her. She missed too much time, for one thing, and she never could regain her confidence. She didn't even try to go back up there."

"And the man?"

"Oh, the *man*. You know, *man* ought to be a four-letter word. Yes, Mr. Billy. Mr. Billy, he took care of himself. He had already been messing around with an older woman. By the time Mary Anne got out of the hospital the first time, he had thrown all her stuff into a corner of a property trailer, which is where we found it when me and my aunt went looking. He was shacking with the other woman."

"God, that must have hurt her."

"Sure, it hurt her. But what hurt more was realizing that he probably tossed her that night."

"You mean—"

"I think he literally wanted her off his back and he made that move to throw her. He got bored with her. Or he got scared that somebody would figure out that he was screwing a minor. I don't think he intended to hurt her that much, just bang her up a little so that she would lose her confidence and not go back on the wire, which would give him an excuse for throwing her out of the trailer."

"Sonofabitch," he seethed.

"Indeed." She leveled her eyes at him. "Most men are. I been trying to tell you that."

"So what happened?"

"Billy made the mistake of messing with the wrong woman one night, and a farmer up in Corinth blew his head off with a shotgun behind one of the tents."

"Actually, I meant *her*."

"Well, in time she got to the point to where she could get around OK and after living a year with me and our aunt she ended up working in a garment plant in Memphis, then met a man from the Delta who brought her over here. I was already living over here with a carpenter, another sorry sonofabitch, if I may say so. Me and Mary Anne both did all kinds of jobs, including several years with Wal-Mart. Her husband died ten or twelve years ago, and mine just ran off, but he didn't run far—got killed in a beer joint parking lot screwing this married woman in the bed of his pickup. Her husband caved his head in with the blunt side of an axe blade. Shoulda happened sooner. Shoulda used the blade side to make sure. *I* shoulda been there to see it. Eventually me and Mary Anne just lived out here on Social Security and what little money we had put away."

She stood and walked to the door, looked out. "Thought I heard the mailman. He don't come much."

"What a sad story." He glanced toward the door. "Will she be here soon?"

"Mister, most stories about people are sad. The ones about animals sometimes turn out all right, but not them about people. Exactly what were you brought up to believe that this life is all *about?*"

"I don't know," he said. "It's just that I have never—"

"Then count yourself among the lucky ones. Her story's no worse than most. At least she had them years on the wire. She had a whole lot to be proud of. She excaped gravity a long time."

He shifted on the couch and swept his gaze across the panorama of photographs. "I guess there are times she really misses it, huh? The exhilaration of being up there, above all those people, just sliding effortlessly along . . ."

"Oh, Sweet Jesus. Some nights she would lie back there on that bed, and I would hear her humming the music and I knew her head was full of the lights and noise, that it had all come back to her and she was there again, afraid of nothing, slender and young and pretty, balanced, every muscle and every nerve in tune with that wire. Oh yeah, she missed it."

"*Missed?*"

"What?"

"You said *missed.* You used past tense. Where is she? Where is Mary Anne? Will she be here soon?"

There were tears in her eyes now, and he felt them edging into his as the gravity of that awful word *missed* tugged at him. He stood and reached a hand out to her and pulled her to her feet.

She leaned her head into his chest. "No, she won't be here soon. That girl on the wire died years ago."

"Oh, Lord," he whispered into her hair. "I missed her. I came too late."

She nodded, then managed, "I kept her alive with the photographs." She waved her hand toward them.

"Oh, my God. Oh, my God. I have looked for so long."

She kept her head against his chest. She was crying.

"When? When did she die?"

"Does it matter?"

He held her, felt her thin body shudder against his. "I guess not. I just wondered when."

She pulled away from him and waved her arm again toward the pictures. "You may take some of them, if you like."

"I am so glad that I found *you,* the closest thing to her," he said, and then he gathered her into his arms and held her in the quiet of the little trailer. He kissed her lightly on the forehead, and she held her head to his chest while he stroked her back. "She was the first girl I ever loved." And then the tears came, hard, for both of them. For a very long time they clung, like a man and a woman holding each other on a small planet with just the two of them on it, with neither knowing what to make of it all, while outside the world spun on and the sun bore down as it had to on the little white trailer in all that ocean of green.

"So many years I looked for her. Every summer, when I wasn't teaching. During spring breaks. Off and on for a decade I have looked. Finally, with the help of the internet—thank God for the internet. . . . " He still clung to her.

"Yes," she said quietly, "I see."

"Can you tell me where she's buried? I would like to go there. I would like to visit her."

"You are already there," she said.

He held her out from him. "What do you mean?"

"I mean that her *spirit* is here." She waved her arm toward the fields and circled it above her head. "All out here. The body is nothing but bones and meat. Just atoms. That girl on the wire aged in body, but her spirit will always be on that wire, above everything."

"Oh," he said. "Oh."

He held her another few seconds, then released her and returned to the couch, and she sat back down in the chair.

"I guess it is time that I left," he said finally, after long minutes had passed with neither of them speaking. "I am supposed to meet my daughter in Greenville tonight. She has two lovely children, a nice husband."

"Neither of us ever had children," she said. "I've wondered whether it was a mistake."

"They are a mixed blessing." He rose and stood before her again, then pulled her back to her feet and embraced her. "I am so glad that I found *you.* It was almost like finding *her.*"

"I'm glad too," she said into his chest.

He released her and turned toward the door. It was his intention not to look back, but he couldn't help himself. She was crying, and he was crying.

"I hope I'll see you again," he said.

"Me too."

"I'll go now."

She took his hand. "Take any of the photographs you would like. I would be honored for you to have some of them."

He walked over and studied the rows of pictures for a few seconds, then reached and took down the one of the girl standing balanced on one foot, her face tilted up, her legs and arms spread wide. The hairy man was not in it.

"This one, if you don't mind. This one will do. This is the way I remember her, the way I *want* to remember her."

She nodded and reached and touched his face with her fingers. "Good-bye," she whispered.

He opened the screen door and stepped out into the full sun and descended the steps. He walked quickly to his car and got in and started the engine.

She came down the steps and toward him but stopped halfway. He rolled down the window.

"I don't want you to get out of the car," she said. "But I have something to show you."

"To *show* me?"

"Yes. Drive up the road until you can see behind the trailer and stop and watch. It will be a few minutes." She hesitated and smiled. Then: "And when you have seen it, promise me that you will drive off and not come back."

"Ever?"

"I would never say that."

"Then I promise."

She returned to the trailer and he did as she directed, stopping his car a few yards up the road. He could see in the small backyard two sturdy clothesline posts with guy wires bracing them and a single heavy wire running between them. He had not noticed them before.

"Oh, my God," he breathed.

In a bit he saw a thin form move across from the trailer to the wire, at first stiffly and slightly tilted from the waist as if she had been snapped in two and pieced back together by someone who did the best he could but did not quite get it right, then with silken grace. She was wearing a silver outfit that blazed in the sun, so bright that it almost burned his eyes. A few strides and then she leapt, and her arms shot up, and she grabbed the wire and swung effortlessly around and flipped and landed on her feet, crouched an instant, then rose and turned toward him, her face tilted to the sky, one foot on the wire, her legs and arms spread like an angel suspended above that ocean of green, ready to take flight.

"Oh, my God. Oh my dear God . . ."

He turned and drove away then, as he had promised that he would. His eyes did not cease to shimmer until the car settled onto asphalt and he drove west toward the sun, brighter now than he had ever known it.

Teaching Her about Catfish

To her, he is reasonably certain, he is a man of mystery and imponderable depths, and to him she is a lovely young wife, a former student of his, with still much to be taught, so on a sultry July morning they roll free of each other and before the sun has moved its blade of brightness another inch across the bed, she agrees to go with him to their little farm in the country for a late afternoon picnic and for a lesson on sex.

This is all about catfish, how to tell whether they are male or female. He has on many occasions told her that the matter is quite simple, requiring only a sense of sight and delicate touch. Experience helps, of course, as he is forever pointing out, and he has never failed to declare the maleness of every fish he has ever brought in and cleaned for her to fry.

"One does not cook the females," he insists, "because they carry eggs."

"Considerate," she answers every time he says it.

She has never quizzed him at length about any assertion he has made about this and that—and he has made plenty over the two years they have been married—though he has sensed somehow a moderate skepticism now and again. Professor at a local university and in possession of a Ph.D., he fancies himself a logical purveyor of knowledge and his innocent young wife a logical recipient, so this surmised skepticism has prompted him to invite her to go with him to the country for a lesson.

Then, again, perhaps all this is simply about, well, *sex*. At least this is his intention.

In a few hours they are standing on the levee of the pond. Down by the creek, in a neat semicircle, lies camping equipment—an ice chest, a bag of odds and ends for cleaning fish and cooking, a sleeping bag for a picnic blanket and whatever else it might be used for, a frying pan and some dishes, a thermos, and a small basket of fruit and bread.

The plan is simple. He will check the fish traps, which always have five or six catfish in them, and if there is a male of sufficient size there will be catfish for dinner, fried in a skillet over an open fire down by the creek. If there are no males, he is uncertain what they will do, though they have brought along canned tuna, which she can transform into a salad in minutes. He has little doubt that there will be several males to choose from.

In the process of selecting their fish for their dinner he will carefully and memorably explain to her the difference between a male and female.

"Somehow I fail to see the sport in this," she observes as he hoists the chicken-wire trap onto the dam, pleased that five fish have fallen for the cloth sack of chicken entrails, whose foul smell she has the good sense to stand upwind of.

"Sport fishing is for those of leisure," he answers, certain there will be a retort.

She bends and squints in at the fish, straightens up, and says cutely, "For the money, time, and energy you spend fooling with these things, you might as well be sport fishing. I'm certain that on a per-pound cost basis—"

"They taste better if they're raised on commercial food. That's the expense of it."

". . . they would run us," she continues, "about four dollars a pound. We could buy them—farm raised on *truffles*—for less than that." She taps the wire with her foot as he pries the cage open.

"I prefer to raise them myself. I know where they have been and what they have been eating." He sorts the fish, throws back the two smallest ones.

She runs her eyes around the perimeter of the small pond, dotted with dollops of cow manure. "At least you know where they've *been*."

"I've been thinking about raising some chickens, for the eggs. Home-grown eggs—"

"I hope you are kidding." She searches his face for that little giveaway glint of eye or corner-of-the-mouth twitch, but he stonewalls it. It is better to let their pretty little heads wonder. He knows how much mystique counts in a marriage.

"I will assume you are teasing," she says as he lays the three catfish side by side.

"I'm considering it. But forget it for now. Look here." He points to the fish, whose gills heave and flutter in the awful air. She kneels down beside him. He picks up a male in one hand, female in the other, and holds them inverted for her to examine. Their pale bellies, speckled with grass and dirt from the dam, seem dreadfully vulnerable, designed to hug the safe mud of pond and river bottoms, never to be exposed to sun and air. Whether it is the unnatural paleness and softness of their bellies or simply her discomfort at seeing the desperate creatures gasping, she winces and steps back.

"Girls never quite come to terms with cold-blooded things, do they?"

In defiance she leans forward and probes the underside of the larger fish. "This the male?"

"Do you think so?"

"Yes, because he has the fattest head."

He shakes his head, his large, well-educated head: "Can't go just by the size and shape of their heads. Look here." He lays the fish down on their backs and points to the fleshy genitalia of the male, then to the corresponding spot on the female. He moves his finger back to the male and with his fingernail lifts the delicate papilla. "This is the male—his, shall we say, penis? And the female . . ." He moves his finger to point again.

She squints and leans closer. "Not very extraordinary, is he? Neither one of them, for that matter. I can't even see that there *is* a difference."

He patiently points again. "Look, the male." Then to the other fish. "The female. Just think what happens because of that difference. Think of what just these two catfish could do."

"I cannot see a difference. Isn't there an easier way?" She has tentatively touched each of the fish where he has pointed.

"It's the only dependable way."

"They look the same to me. Now, why don't you put them back into the water? They're getting dry as leather."

"No problem. Catfish can live an hour or longer out of water. As a matter of fact, there are some, called walking catfish, that can actually crawl overland from pond to pond."

"Right. On the same farm where the cows fly in for milking."

"That's no lie, Honey. There *are* walking catfish. *National Geographic* had an article on them one time, with actual pictures of the fish crawling along the edge of a field."

"Yeah, I remember that. Same issue with the unicorns and basilisks."

"All right, damn it, don't believe me."

"Throw the female back, please. She's getting awfully dry."

He eases her back into the water, drops the male into a five-gallon bucket, and picks up the other, a female, to show her once again.

"Forget it. I'll take your word. She's getting leathery. Please put her back. The one in the bucket's plenty big for us to eat tonight."

So he slips the fish back into the pond and, with her right behind him, takes the catfish in the bucket down to the edge of the creek. While she arranges their gear and she flattens out the sleeping bag, he clears a spot for a fire and starts gathering branches and logs.

While he starts the fire, clearly a male calling, she separates utensils and begins mixing batter. The recent dry spell has seasoned the wood well, so the fire catches quickly and brightens up the campsite. The sun is just dropping away.

"Damn, this is gratifying," he observes, as much to himself as to her, "a man bringing his own meat in for the evening, building his own fire on land he has claimed for his own."

"Claimed?" she breaks in. "Not exactly. If you handled the budget, you'd call it something else."

"Come on, Woman! Look at us: a couple facing the dark and starvation —surviving, happy, content. We could start civilization over right here, you and I, launch the human race right here."

"Yeah." She grins, mixing cornmeal, pepper, and salt in a bowl. "Kids and catfish just pouring off this twenty acres. The beginning of the Western World all over."

Laying the catfish onto newspapers, he looks over at her. "Sometimes it seems that there's not a dram of romanticism left in you."

"Well," she says, brushing a strand of long blond hair from her face, "men live in dream worlds most of the time. You ought to be thankful that their wives are capable of maintaining a grasp on reality." She holds up a batter-coated spoon and waves it at him.

"Still, it would be nice if you could see how—how symbolic all this is here: you, me, with a fire, fresh-caught fish. It's so primitive, so elementary. I just feel good, self-sufficient."

Her smile, lit by the still-bright sky and the glow of the fire, reassures him that she understands, though he knows that she won't say so. "I think you'd better get that fish cleaned. I'm ready for him."

She walks back to the batter, and he takes the fish out of the bucket, removes a hammer from the bag, holds the fish against the trunk of a nearby oak, and strikes its head sharply. The catfish quivers, and he takes a sixteen-penny nail, grips it with the thumb and finger of the hand that pins the fish to the tree, and in three strokes drives the nail through the head and into the trunk. He lays the hammer down and with a fillet knife slices through the skin in a ring just behind the pulsing gills. Then he grasps the skin with pliers and pulls briskly toward the tail. The pink body springs out of its dark skin like a new-born child, twitching, throbbing. Even he would admit its grossness: the broad, flat, skin-covered head contrasting with its delicate pink body.

"Oh, God, doesn't it hurt him?" She is leaning over his shoulder.

"Probably. But this is the way it is done." He cuts the body from head as she grimaces behind him, fascinated and abhorred, and lays it on a flattened paper sack. With the hammer he pulls the nail loose and flings the whiskered head, wrapped with body skin, down through the trees into the creek. The turtles will feast tonight.

He kneels and picks up the fish and slices open the belly.

"And now for a lesson on internal anatomy," he begins, turning the belly flaps aside with the tip of the knife. She moves close, perhaps out of deference, perhaps from curiosity, perhaps because in his self-appointed role as Explainer of Great Mysteries he has summoned her so many times that she is looking and listening from habit.

It is then, just as he feels her breath at his ear—it is then that he sees in the last light of day, among the pinks, purples, and reds of the entrails, the two sacs of roe, lying side by side like red-veined yellow sausages. It is too late to hide them, to fling them off into the darkening creek. He can only hope that she will ask no questions. "This," he points out, pushing the roe aside and lifting the swim bladder with the tip of the knife, "is his swim blad—"

"What are those yellow things, the long finger-like things?"

A man of nobility knows when lying to his wife will be futile. He knows when he's been caught. So he says simply, but not without some difficulty, keeping his reddening face turned away from her, "Those are, uh, eggs."

In the seconds that follow, he becomes intensely aware of the awesome silence of the woods, the heat and crackling of the fire, the darkening of the sky. For what seems like minutes he squats there, knife tip under the bladder, waiting for her to speak. He turns and looks up into her eyes. He can see the campfire reflected in them.

"He has eggs," she says in an emotionless voice. He does not respond, so she says, reaching and flicking drops of water into the oil in the skillet, which sits on a rebar rack low over the fire, "My, that is extraordinary of *him*. Are you going to half *him* or fillet *him* and cut *him* into sections or what?"

"Whichever you like."

"Oh no, you are the catfish expert here. *You* decide. And do it quick— this oil is almost ready."

"Come on, damn it. I made a little mistake. The chances of finding eggs in a catfish this time of year are practically nil." He slices off the large fillets on each side of the backbone, then cuts them into three pieces each. "Roll him well in that batter and we'll fry him up."

She takes the fillets and drops them into a large glass bowl filled with cornmeal. "Even if there hadn't been eggs, she would still have been a female, and you still would have made a mistake, a big one."

"Yeah, but if she hadn't had eggs, you wouldn't have known."

She rolls a piece of fillet in batter and holds it out over the shimmering oil. Little bubbles are beginning to string up to the surface. "That worries me even more. I just wonder how often you're wrong and get away with it. What if we really did have to start things over right here, just you and me and a couple of catfish? You would have blown it for the catfish."

"Ease up, please. Let's get this fish cooked while we've still got a little light left."

"Fry *her* up, you mean." She is obviously enjoying it.

"Yeah, *her*."

On the way back to the truck with the last of the camping equipment, she walks beside him, her right hand in his left. It has been a good evening, and nothing else has been said about the catfish mistake. The sleeping bag was not used for anything else—he just wasn't in the mood, and besides, once a day should be plenty for a couple married over two years.

As he crosses the fence, she looks up into the night sky and says, innocently enough, "The stars are so bright I feel like I could touch them if I really tried."

"Yeah, they do seem closer out here."

"I was just wondering," she continues as he reaches to open the door for her, "whether the stars are male and female, like everything else.

"You won't forget it, will you?"

"I'll bet you'd say the bright ones are male."

"They probably are.

"If they were male and female and you knew how to tell the difference, would you show me sometime?" She is smiling.

"Yeah," he says, pulling her close, "I'd show you if I could."

The Natural Man

What awoke Dottie that morning was not the usual growling and clanging of the garbage truck emptying the dumpster down the street but the marvelous music of a man peeing in her commode.

There was heavy bumping about in the shower stall and a baritone voice singing a bit off-tune. So unlike the delicate sounds of the girls twittering about before breakfast.

Her eyes fixed on the colorless ceiling, from which hung a ceiling fan whose blades at long last had a chance to turn, with a hot-blooded male beneath them.

God, how long it had been. . . .

And it could so easily not have happened. One aisle over, two minutes later at Kroger's, no need for Chinese cabbage—and she would have awakened in her cold, celibate bed again, the squeak of little girls pulling her back into the known world. That reach for the Chinese cabbage, her hand falling absently on his, was all it took to turn her world around and bring a man back into her life.

She could still hear him in the shower as she slipped out of bed and into the old robe she'd worn for God only knew how long. Like her life, she mused as she pulled it tightly about her shoulders: worn-out, shapeless, wearing thinner and thinner each year, almost all the color gone. For a divorcee of thirty-three she was not quite over the proverbial hill yet. Hell yes, there were wrinkles. Nobody could have endured the last few years with Teddy and not walked away without a few wrinkles, but she looked a damned sight better than a couple of friends in similar circumstances. In the bedside mirror, with the morning light just beginning to add color to the room and his shower still going, she felt even attractive, not really beautiful maybe, but attractive. Any woman felt better about herself and things in general after a night of lovemaking. Her cheeks had a high point of pink in them, the first time she'd noticed that in years. "God," she breathed as she brushed through her hair, "if only he will stay."

Five years with two girls and no man was . . . well, Goddamn it, not fair, for one thing. Teddy walked out of the marriage into another one: younger woman (a virgin, he'd bragged), no kids to complicate things, same amount of money coming in, minus the three hundred he had to send her each month—lucky bastard he was to get off that light, but her attorney was young and a wimp at that. Jesus, no wonder the sonofabitch was able to say that he'd never been happier. And there she was with eight- and ten-year-old girls, no permanent man, a half-assed secretarial job, and little prospect of brighter times ahead. A total of fourteen love tosses with nine different men in five years did little to boost her ego. She had just about decided that if she had to be the one to carry on the tradition of sex in the Western World, the race was doomed.

And then, right there with their collective grip on the Chinese cabbage, a man and woman came together and started doing the things that men and women *do* together, as if they'd rehearsed for it—as natural as the sun coming up. An "I'm sorry, you take it" both ways, the meeting of two pairs of eyes, and nature took right over with Her magic. She smiled and winked at herself in the mirror as she heard the bathroom door close and his bare feet start down the hall.

"My God!" she shrieked as quietly as one can shriek, when he came through the door into the bedroom. "Get under the covers, quick, or put something on. The girls'll be up any second." He was nude, totally, not even a towel pulled across his loins, and, she noticed with no small delight, he was partially erect. Dottie forced him onto the bed, spread her robe, and fell onto him. She had not even given him time to speak.

They made love again, no matter about the girls. They'd seen her in bed with men before, at least twice, and if she had her way, they'd see her tossing with—oh, shit, she'd forgotten his name. Gene, *Gene,* Goddamn it. She kept wanting to call him Jim. With him beside her, on his stomach and sleeping again, she clenched the old robe across her middle and stared at the water-ringed yellow ceiling above the bed—not in the crush of loneliness she usually felt staring up there, not in the desperation of an unmarried woman approaching middle age, but in that euphoric uncertainty she always felt as a girl when she sat on the front steps with her father and watched the first days of spring greening up the lawns and trees along their street. It was a longing, but also an indefinable promise, tongueless, and it tightened her throat with expectation and brought tears to her eyes. She turned over and laid an arm across his back and studied the details of his boyish head and neck, the long, easy hair that flowed past his ears. The column of air from the ceiling fan was no longer chilling—she needed it to cool her off.

It was not just that Gene was young and well-built and handsome. All that was fine, of course—but those were not the things that she would look for first in a man, not by a long shot, and certainly not the things she would ever seriously dream of finding. And the fact that he satisfied her in bed, something most of the men she had made love to had not done, was good, but again not essential. God, she recalled, rolling back over and staring at the ceiling again, the nights she had spent sleeping alone, nights when loneliness lay like a cold white stone in her stomach, nights when she wanted so desperately to go into the girls' room and crawl in between them and crush them to her, night after night of flinging an arm out in half sleep and waking as it fell onto cold sheets. *Cold.* The bedroom, the house—everything was so damned *cold.* There was something so primal about it. A woman without a man lives in a barren world of *cold,* a tundra, where nothing matters but mere survival: sleep, work, food, sleep, work, food. Even the children were at times a mere abstraction, as much as she loved them. God, how a woman needs a man! How easy to understand why a woman will put up with a sonofabitch of a man, forgive his cruelty and his selfishness and take him back time and time again, just to keep away the *cold.*

It was that Gene was *there,* not simply an adult body she could wrap herself around but someone she could talk to on her level, another adult whose attentions could, for however short a while, be turned to her as hers could be turned to him, someone her arm could fall on in the night and remain on in sheer animal comfort of warmth and closeness and someone she could awake with and talk to. Perhaps any man would have done— she had thought that before. Or, she regretted having to admit it, any *woman.* She needed someone to cling to.

And then there was his manner. Jesus, how could anyone resist him? In the dim parking lot just outside Kroger's as she was trying to balance her two sacks of groceries across a knee and unlock the car door, she heard that smooth voice ask, "May I help you with that?" Then he was holding the two sacks and smiling at her. She got into the car, leaned and unlocked the back door, and he set the groceries on the seat. "Thanks," she returned, and reached to start the engine.

His voice stopped her: "You're not married, are you?"

She looked at him a few seconds, then moved her hand from the key. "Not for some time. Does it show?"

"Yes. It declares itself. Mostly in your eyes." God, what a smooth voice. She couldn't see much of his face in the lighting of the parking lot, but she could remember pretty well what he looked like. There was a period of silence as she tried to decide what to say. Nothing would come, so she thanked him again and started the car.

"Dottie." He raised his voice over the sound of the engine.

"How—"

"I saw it on your check at the counter. Please stop the engine. I want to tell you something." So, for no reason that she could think of, she turned the key off and stared straight ahead into the dark at the edge of the parking lot. He laid his forearms across the sill of her door and, with the assurance of a physician administering to a frightened child, said, "I would like very much to go home with you and make love to you the rest of the night."

Dottie stared harder at the ceiling and tried to recall what her response to his line had been. "Line, hell," she said to herself, "that was no line. That was a plain, straightforward statement, as natural as saying, 'Hello, my name is Gene.'" All she could remember was the slow drive so that he could follow her home on his bicycle, the two or three times that she'd thought about speeding up and losing him, and the one awful moment when he disappeared in the rearview mirror and she thought that she really *had* lost him.

"Why me?" she finally got around to asking him after they'd made love twice and gotten up to drink some wine and fix popcorn, the kids having been put to bed even before she'd gone to the store. They sat across the kitchen table from each other. His left hand held her right one in a tight embrace. She couldn't believe how fast it had happened.

"I didn't choose you. It was just a crossing of life patterns."

"Fate, huh?" She'd always thought that so much crap.

"Essentially, yes. Destined. At any rate, I knew when I saw you."

"Like knowing which Chinese cabbage is going to be the one for you, huh?"

"Well, yes, exactly. We reached for that cabbage at the same time, and it wasn't necessarily the biggest or best one—it was the one we were naturally drawn toward."

"We owe it all to a Chinese cabbage," she had told herself, draining her third glass of wine and nuzzling his neck.

She was still musing on the water-splotched ceiling when the girls came bouncing through, headed for the bathroom.

"Mother," Sherrie, the older, scolded, "why didn't you wake us up? It's almost eight o'clock."

"It's Saturday, Honey, and you two—"

"Who's *that?*" Meg had pulled the sheet back almost to Gene's waist. His marvelously sculpted shoulders and arms, browned from a beach somewhere, she guessed, contrasted so wonderfully with the white sheets and pillowcase.

"Yeah, Mother, who's *he?*" Sherrie moved over to Gene's side of the bed and crouched down to see the details of his face.

"His name's Gene. Let him sleep. Now you two get on into the bathroom and finish whatever you've got to do. We'll be in the kitchen in a few minutes. Scat!" She clapped her hands at them and they chirped off to the bathroom.

"Hey, lover." She nudged him after the bathroom door closed. "Get your clothes on: We've got to fix something to eat." He muttered something sleepy, sighed, and gathered the pillow into his arms. Dottie whirled the sheet back and bit him hard on the buttocks until he sat up, that little-boy grin of his brightening the room.

"Wanna chew on something else?"

"Not right now. Get your clothes on. We have to fix the girls something. And us."

"Yeah, I want to see those girls. If they look as cute as they did in bed last night, you've really got a couple of angels."

"Prettier. Come on."

As they sat together at the kitchen table, looking like any other family at Saturday morning breakfast. Sherrie, maintaining the gravity of an older sister, regarded Gene with reserve. Since the divorce she had turned quite cynical about men in general.

But Meg held nothing back: "How *old* are you?"

"I'm twenty-two," he answered, glancing at Dottie, who, though she did not wince, doubtless let something show in her face.

"Mother's thirty—"

"Would you like some coffee?" Dottie asked him.

"Never touch it. Gives an artificial high. Bad for the body too. Don't drink either, except for a small glass of wine when I'm celebrating something." He smiled at her. "Some orange juice will be fine."

"Are you in college?" Meg continued the interrogation.

"Was. I quit last year, my junior year."

"Why'd you quit?"

"Come on, Meg," Dottie cautioned.

"Aw, it's OK. Really. I just got fed up with people telling me how to think. I was majoring in philosophy, but I came to realize that I understood as much about life as the people who were teaching me and the *great thinkers* in the books they were teaching me out of. There was nothing in those people that made their opinions any more valid than mine. That make sense?"

"I don't know," Meg answered. She pushed a piece of egg white around her plate edge. Sherrie said nothing.

"Well, look, I know that life is nothing more than a natural flow, like a stream moving or the earth changing from spring to summer to fall and on and on. It's not difficult or confusing, life's not, if you just fall into that flow. Just float along with the stream, you know." He bit into another piece of toast and winked at Dottie as Meg mulled it over and Sherrie stared quietly at him.

"Seems like a good way to get drowned." Sherrie was gathering up her plate and silverware. She did not look at him.

"Do you work anywhere?" Meg would not let up.

"I'm a free-lance photographer."

"What does *free-lance* mean?"

"If you're a photographer, where's your stuff?" Sherrie cut in from across the kitchen.

"Back at my apartment. And *free-lance* means that I work for anyone willing to pay for my services." He seemed not to mind the inquiries.

"I thought it meant," Sherrie said, "that you don't have a steady job."

"No, Sherrie, it just means that I am not shackled to a payroll. I'm not forced to sit behind a desk in an office with a whole lot of people I might not like."

Dottie was not certain whether she should shut them up or not, since they were asking questions she had wanted to ask, so she just let them fire away. Before the table was cleared, she had a pretty good composite of her new man.

"Do you think it will work?" she asked him after love that afternoon. The girls were off at a friend's house.

"How do you mean?" He was propped up on an elbow, smiling down at her. She was, as usual, staring at the ceiling.

"Well, you're twenty-two, I'm thirty-three. There's a lot of—"

"Means nothing, nothing at all. Age is never a factor in genuine human relationships. What matters is how strong the bond is that is holding us together."

"Yeah, that worries me too. I mean, a Chinese cabbage isn't a whole lot to have in common." She said it jokingly, but her throat was tightening.

He pulled her to him. "We have a lot more than that in common, a *whole* lot, and we'll have more. Just let things flow, lover, let them flow— especially the juices."

"But the girls . . ."

"Lovely creatures. We'll get along."

"Gene, you aren't—you don't think I'm being too forward asking questions like this so soon, do you? You must be tired of answering questions all day long."

"No, it's fine. You just naturally want to know about me, how I feel about you and all. I don't mind telling you. It's part of an honest relationship. Going back to your question, yes, I do think it will work. I know enough about you already to satisfy myself that I want to stay with you, if you'll have me."

"God." She snuggled up to him, "you're about *all* I want right now."

Somehow what would have sounded absurdly soppy with any other man seemed so reasonable to say to him, so natural. After making love, they lay wrapped together and slept the afternoon away until the chatter of the girls coming through the front door woke them.

Dottie saw little of him the next week—perhaps he was just easing into the relationship, making certain that this was what he wanted—but she didn't dare call. She'd had pushed too many times in the past, forced a man when she should patiently have waited for him to move. Men were like that. When she and Gene got together at her house on Thursday for a salad lunch, she could scarcely conceal her delight at seeing him. Conceal it she did, though, even during their lovemaking after lunch. Late for work, she kissed him goodbye and hurried him off. When she passed him on his bicycle, she lowered the window on the passenger's side to say good-bye, and he yelled for her to call that evening.

She did not call, so he phoned her at work during her lunch hour the next day and invited her to his apartment for an afternoon of *earthly and heavenly delights.* That meant, of course, organic food and lovemaking. She smiled profusely the whole afternoon, ignoring inquiries of fellow workers, and that evening made arrangements for someone to take care of the girls the next day.

Following his directions, Dottie found the apartment at 11:30. He'd said for her to come on in, the door would be unlocked, so she collected herself and entered a man's apartment for the first time in over three years.

Not bad. Not the best section of town, not the nicest duplex she'd seen, but from what she could tell from a cursory assessment, he was neat and reasonable in his tastes, though really there was not much there besides the furniture, which she assumed was furnished. A few photographs hung here and there, a couple of prints, and some sort of photography award. Camera equipment lay in a pile in one corner, and the bicycle was propped against a wall.

She paused long enough to inspect herself in her compact mirror. It took a hell of a lot of effort not to cover over with makeup, but Gene didn't like it. She pinched up some color in her cheeks, smoothed her hair, and was just getting ready to sit down and wait for him when she heard a noise from what looked like a bathroom.

"Gene?" God, she'd assumed he was still out getting groceries.

"Oh . . . Dottie," a muffled voice came back. "Hey, come on in."

She walked over, put her hand on the knob, and, expecting to see her new god shiny and tousled from his shower, swung the door open, and stepped in.

"Oh, my God, Gene," she started, her hand still on the knob, "I thought you said to come in."

He was seated on the commode. One foot shot out and blocked the door so that she couldn't retreat. "I did say come in. Relax."

"Gene, I—"

"Come on, Dottie, relax. We're not strangers, you know." He laid down the book he had been reading and spun some paper off the roll. "Sit down on the edge of the tub. I'll be through in just a second."

"Gene," she said firmly, embarrassment painting her face, "let the door go. Please."

He shrugged and moved his foot. She stepped out into the hallway, caught her breath, and collapsed into the first chair she could find. "My God," was all that she could say.

In another minute or so Gene came out, nude, with that boyish smile on his face, and announced that they could eat first or make love first, whichever she preferred.

Her face was still hot with embarrassment. "I'd like to talk about *this* first."

"About what?" He lowered himself onto the arm of the chair and kissed the top of her head.

"About you telling me to come into the bathroom while you were— while you were sitting on the commode. It would be one thing if you were peeing, but, my God. . . ." She did not look up at him, just kept her eyes fixed on the opposite wall, where a photograph of a graveyard scene hung. A tall, pointed stone rose harsh and white against the sky, its shadow falling like a spear across two children crouched gathering small flowers at its base.

"Aw hell, Dottie, you're getting bad vibes from somewhere, probably from your childhood, and they're contorting your mind. You're associating defecation with something bad, and it's not: It's as natural as breathing, as eating, and people who eat are going to—"

"But that is a *private* thing. It's not like you were taking a shower or something. Or *peeing*. I can handle a man *peeing*."

"Somebody along the way has taught you that it's private. Your parents? How long will their hang-ups rule your life? Let yourself go, girl. You're a grown-up. Get into the flow of life. Everything natural in life is good for you—it's the way Nature intends. He was stroking her hair, punctuating his sentences with kisses.

She pushed him away and, with as firm a voice as she could muster, said, "Gene, whether it's what I was taught or just believe, I will not come into the bathroom when you are on the commode, and I don't want you coming in while I'm using it that way. We have known each other for *hours,* but even if we had been married for decades, I would want some privacy. That smell is the smell of death, and I don't want you associating it with me or me associating it with you." She turned her eyes back to the picture of the grave marker.

"Dottie, it's the smell of life, of the cycle of the living. What you smell is bacteria—"

"I don't care what causes the smell—it's bad and it reminds me of death. It's the smell of mortality. You don't even bother to try to cover it up with anything. You could use a room deodorizer, strike matches, smoke, burn incense, do something to cover it up."

"Why in God's name would I want to cover it up? That's the trouble with this country: Everybody's so ashamed of their bodily functions and smells that they've become *psychotic* worrying about it. Nobody wants to be natural. This psychosis is doing nothing but supporting thousands of businessmen who've built empires on convincing Americans that they smell bad at both ends and every cleavage."

"You know," she said, softening, "I believe that you'd go naked and graze off the roadside and drink from ditches if you thought you could do it without being committed."

"Make it pastures and wild mountain streams and I'd go along with you." He laughed. "Hey, come on, let's eat."

She pulled back. "Gene, please don't think me prudish about this. It's just that I can't so easily break away from what I've come up with."

"No problem." He smiled sweetly. "I'll convert you by and by. I can be patient. Some day you'll be eating nothing but real foods and doing natural things and wondering how in the world you ever did thing differently. You've got a good teacher."

"Maybe, but you'd better go slow."

There was little talk the rest of the afternoon.

The following week Dottie and Gene were inseparable, enjoying what must surely have been the most passionate and blissful relationship that any couple, married or not, could ever know. It was the week of the girls' spring vacation, and she talked Teddy into picking them up on Sunday for the whole week. He had planned to take them on a two-day visit to his folks' house, but her complaints of "female problems" did the trick. A week of paid vacation completed her freedom. Hell, she was entitled to that much of a break. She had earned it—years of bare subsistence with no man—and neither kids nor job would interfere. Gene's job, and she was not yet sure exactly how he made his living, was flexible enough to allow him a week off whenever he wanted.

They stayed at his place one day, hers the next, sleeping late, staying up late, taking in movies, going on long walks and drives, making love twice and sometimes three or four times a day. It was a beautiful, exquisite magic their bodies and minds made, and Dottie was alive again.

"Well, lover," Gene ventured Sunday morning as they lay quietly in his bed with newspapers scattered about, "the girls will be in in another couple of hours, so we've got to get ready for normal life again."

"How normal?" She smiled back, her eyes fixed on the plain white ceiling of his bedroom.

"I don't know. We've got to decide."

"It's moved pretty fast."

"Yeah." He sighed. "But most really good things do. Good movies, parties, vacations, lovemaking—they all just swish right by, leaving you breathless and wishing you could have held onto more."

"The difference is," she said, rolling over to nuzzle his ear, "that this time I'm still holding on," and she grabbed his penis and squeezed. They wrestled around until the inevitable happened again.

Afterwards Gene resumed: "We really do have to decide what we want to come of this."

"What do you *want* to come of it?"

"Well," he said, staring at the ceiling, "I'd frankly like to live with you."

Dottie tried to keep her voice even: "Do you mean marry, for us to get *married?*"

"Maybe in time . . ."

"You just want to *shack?*"

"Well, if we're going to spend all our time together anyway, there's no reason for us to go on keeping up two residences. Moving, for you, would be a real hassle, with all your furniture, but all I've got is a couple of bags and a bicycle."

"Gene, what about the girls? That wouldn't be much of an example."

"See," he said pointedly, turning to face her, "you're speaking your parents' lines again. You're forcing your judgments on the girls, contorting reality, denying them the experiences that are real and wholesome and fundamental. You don't mind shacking, as long as you can hide it beneath surface respectability. Jesus, don't you think they *know* what we're doing?"

Dottie winced at that. "Maybe so, but—"

"No *buts.* Listen, you're not going to fool them, so don't try. Here you've got an opportunity to show them how a genuine human relationship blossoms and matures. They'll be the better for it."

"Yeah, it'll be easier for them to shack when they grow up. I want them—"

"You want them to marry, raise kids, to do what you were taught is the proper thing for a young woman to do—in short, you'd like them to end up like you, dumped out and dumped on after you've lost your usefulness to a man. Come on, Dottie, times have changed. Get into the real world. Marriage is *paper,* an official stamp proving nothing except that you've agreed before a serious state official or patronizing preacher to what you'd live up to or not live up to anyway, with or without the paper. It assures you of nothing but an initial fee and certain property entanglements if you split. When unmarried people break up, they almost always walk away friends. When a married couple split, it's war, because the paper makes it necessary for lawyers to get into it, and when they get involved—"

"OK, OK, Gene, ease up. Enough talk of splitting—hell, we just got together. But please don't rule out marriage. Please."

"Just don't think about it a whole lot."

"Fine, for now. But I do want you to do me this one favor: Let the girls *think* we're married."

"Dottie, you're not going to fool them. Let's just don't say anything unless they ask. And if you do decide to tell them we're married, none of that *Daddy* stuff—I'm Gene to them."

She reached and picked up a section of newspaper. "That's fine."

And Gene he was to them all: to the girls, to Dottie's friends who met him, good ol' Gene, Gene with the disarming smile, with the natural way with people, with the photographic gear and books and bicycle in the corner of her bedroom. Good ol' Gene, who finally agreed, for the sake of the family, to cover at least his loins, to close the bathroom door, to restrain from picking his nose and belching and farting whenever the mood hit him. Not such a bad guy, Dottie mused often to herself—just a wild little boy who needed housebreaking.

He was such a pleasure to come home to at lunch and in the evenings, and he was immeasurable help around the house: cleaning up, fixing meals, repairing things. He was so good with the girls, too, doing little motherly chores like putting bows in their hair and tying their shoelaces and tucking them in at night. And they worshipped him.

What Gene's work schedule was, Dottie wasn't quite sure. He was always there when she left and when she got home. Though she noticed from time to time that a particular camera or bag or tripod had been moved, he never mentioned a job assignment nor volunteered to show her more than a handful of quite ordinary photographs. In fact, he seemed not at all inclined to talk about his work. He brought some money in—just dabs and dashes, she'd have to admit, but he was trying and they were all so happy. Doubtless photographers had artistic temperaments, like painters and poets, so she chose not to quiz him about his work, preferring to concentrate on the luxury of having a good man in the house.

Summer vacation came for the girls, and Gene agreed to stay home with them, saving her the expense of daycare. He took them on his brief and seldom jobs, which the girls, who helped him with his equipment, usually described as "just taking pictures of things"—houses and people and dogs, whatever. The more excursions they went on, the less they talked about his work, so Dottie figured that they were settling nicely into his routine. He'd even started paying them a few dollars along.

"What does he do with his pictures?" she casually asked Sherrie in the kitchen one evening while Gene and Meg were out for groceries.

"Why don't you ask *him?*" Sherrie shot back, with heat.

"Whoa, wait a minute. What's this? I just wondered how he markets his pictures. I haven't seen more than a handful of—"

"I don't ask him about that. I just help him with his stuff."

"Well, you and Meg never talk about his work anymore."

"There's nothing to say. It's just a *job.* Ask *him* about it if you want to know more." Her face glared like a blister.

"Sherrie, don't you raise your voice at me. I'm just interested in his work."

"Then ask *him,*" she returned flatly, obviously closing the conversation.

"I wonder if he'd like to take some family shots. We haven't taken any photographs in a long time, and you girls are growing up so fast. What do you think, Sherrie?"

She whirled and glared at Dottie. "I told you, Goddammit, ask *him!*" She slammed down the plate she was drying, shattering it on the counter, and stormed from the room. Dottie stood looking at the shards of bright blue that radiated out from the central disk of the plate. When the shower started up, she began picking up the pieces of glass. "My God," she said quietly, shaking her head, "what in the world's gotten into her?"

She thought about the scene a long time that night after they had all gone to bed. Sleep was slow coming, as it often was when there was a puzzle in her mind that she just couldn't find the last piece to. Was the crazy kid jealous? Did she have a crush on Gene? That had to be it. The notion was deliciously warm to her as she cuddled against his back.

Still she twisted in the sheets, staring first at the window, where she had last seen the sun, then up to the dark ceiling. She could hear somewhere way off a train blowing at a railway crossing, but the street sounds had died away down, and Gene's breathing had eased into the soft regularity of sleep. She continued staring at the dark ceiling until a lump of something settled cold in her stomach like a stone.

Midmorning Dottie left work without saying anything to anyone. It was past the time for talking. She got into the car and drove to her street, then slowly passed the house, turned the corner, and parked. As she had seen the kids do, she swung aside two boards on the fence that separated her backyard from the lot behind. She didn't know whether it was guilt or fear of what she'd find that gathered in her throat as she crossed the yard and eased up the steps that led to the back door—she knew only that the cold white stone in her stomach had to be dissolved. Her hand trembled as she unlocked the door and entered the morning-silent house.

At first the only sounds that came to her were the slow skip of the kitchen clock as its hand jerked from second to second and the soft rush of air from the ceiling vent. Then somewhere, behind a closed door, she heard one of the girls giggle and Gene's low voice. Dottie stepped into the hallway and listened.

She could hear water splashing. *The bathroom. They are in the bathroom.* She took a step down the hallway toward the bathroom door.

"Meg." Gene's voice rose. "Come on up out of the suds. Be still, Sherrie, leave her alone. Turn a little toward me. You're shading her too much, Sherrie."

"I want to get out," Sherrie said. "I want to get dressed."

"We're about through. Move a little to the left. Meg, just stand up, or get up on your knees. I can't see your—"

"Va-*gina!*" Meg squealed, and there was more giggling and splashing.

Dottie was certain she heard a camera click as she turned and retreated down the hallway as quietly as she could.

"Dear God!" She started up the car and drove away, not back to work, but out the highway to the old dirt road that followed the river in a slack embrace, the way a woman might lie with a man: close but not touching. After a few miles she stopped on a hill overlooking an expansive bend, got out, crossed a sagging barbed wire fence, and walked toward a bluff, beneath which the brown water rolled on forever toward the sea. There, like a little girl worrying out some trivial complexity, her feet dangling over the edge of the bluff high above the river, Dottie sat staring out at the trees, water, and sky until the sun rose high and hot overheard, slid down the opposite side of the sky, and dropped into the woods on the other side. She hardly moved. Barely breathed. If there were an urgency to jump, to tumble down the cliff and into the churning water, she did not acknowledge it. Time and reality seemed to be off somewhere else, in someone else's life. She was one with the river, but not enough to join it. Not yet. The mother in her would not let her yield to the temptation. Not yet. In the soft summer twilight she rose to her feet, took one last look at the dying sun, and started for home.

As she drove, she tried to think of nothing but that brown river sliding off to the sea somewhere far, far away. Oh, God, how sometimes it was that only the fundamental world mattered, that wondrous natural world in which everything worked in harmony, where nothing was right or wrong.

Gene met her at the door. "Damn, lover, where've you been? We've been worried to death. They told us you hadn't been at work since before noon. What's happened? Where have you *been*?"

Dottie just stared at him.

"Yeah, Mother, we fixed cauliflower pizza for lunch," Meg said, reaching out for her. Dottie fended her off.

"Do you want to tell us—" Gene started, but her glare hushed him.

"Mother," Sherrie yelled from the kitchen door, "I've got some of Gene's special vegetable soup going. There's enough for all of us."

Dottie stood in the hallway looking at him, her eyes trying to say what, for the moment, her tongue could not. She knew that if she spoke, her voice would break, her resolve fail, and she would be nothing but pitiful. She stepped into her bedroom.

What happened next must have looked to Gene and the girls like something lifted from a domestic comedy, albeit theirs was not a house of mirth. Dottie walked over to the bicycle, which leaned against the wall across from the bed, guided it down the hallway, slammed it through the doorway onto the front porch, and propelled it into the dimly lit front yard, where it balanced, wobbled briefly, then fell over onto the sidewalk. She opened the camera she assumed he had used that afternoon and stripped out the film, then camera, bags, lights, and tripods followed the bike, each thumping onto the dark lawn. Gene stood mesmerized as his clothes, stuffed into an old pillowcase, sailed off to the edge of the street and tumbled like a clumsy ghost. The girls cowered at the end of the hall.

She took another turn through the bedroom and, finding nothing else of Gene's, stormed into the bathroom, dumping his things—the precious few toiletries a natural man needed—into the matching pillowcase. Making her final stop in the kitchen, she rooted around in the crisper, found what she wanted, a cabbage, dropped it ceremoniously into the pillowcase, then thrust the bundle into Gene's arms.

"There, Goddamn it, don't go hungry, just *go*. Into my life with a cabbage, wham-bam, out of my life with one—it's from California, not China, but it'll do. Now go, pervert, you and your Goddamned cauliflower pizzas!"

He took the pillowcase and backed out of the kitchen and down the hallway to the front porch. "What in God's name, Dottie, what's happened?"

She stopped at the bathroom door. "I was standing about here this morning, just outside your *studio*. I know what you were doing."

"So *that's* it. You mean you're making such a to-do over my taking pictures of the girls?"

"Not just *pictures*, pervert."

"Aw, come on, Dottie. What objection could you have to my taking some shots of those lovely little untarnished bodies, such innocent, natural beauty?"

"Gene," she said evenly, pushing him into the hallway and toward the porch, "you're a Goddamned pervert, and the only reason the police aren't here right now is that I don't want to make it any harder on Meg and Sherrie. But let me tell you what, Mr. *Natural Man,* if one picture of these girls shows up anywhere, I'll file criminal charges against you, and I'll sue you for every damned thing you own, right down to that cabbage. Now get out of my life." She took a book of matches from her purse and, as he stepped out into the darkness, struck one.

He grinned. "That to help light my way?"

"No," she snorted as she closed the door, "I'm going to strike one in every room to rid this house of your stench." And the door slammed to.

A garbage truck banging a dumpster around woke Dottie the next morning, just as the morning light was bringing back the yellow, water-ringed ceiling above her bed. She slipped from between Meg and Sherrie, pulled on her old robe, and with a brave whistle went in to start the coffee.

PART II

The Well

The brassy hot fields of September were at our backs as my grandfather and I stood at the well dipping cool water from a rust-stained galvanized bucket that had just come up from the silver-dollar-size circle of water at the bottom. The surface still danced.

I pointed. "Looks like wind on it, like wind on a little pond."

"Yeah," the old man grunted, "but ain't no wind ever got down there, you can bet."

"It used to look like that when I spit in it or dropped rocks in it," I started, then remembered that it hadn't been so long ago, "back when I was little."

"Yeah, you and all the other young'ns. Rocks and balls and Lord knows what else." He set down the jar he'd been drinking from and leaned over, shading his eyes to see deep. "Bricks, chunks of wood, pine cones, anything you can name y'all throwed down there one time or another."

"Maybe you ought to have a cover over it to keep people from dropping things in." I squinted down beside him. I could see our faces, brick-color smudges in the calming water.

"A well's used too much for that. Nope, not practical. Work you to death."

"How old's the well?" For the first time I felt like knowing something about it, the way any boy at thirteen begins to want to find out about grown-up things that have been in his world all along but hasn't found the time to ask about.

"Older than the house." He lifted his head from the edge of the well and nodded toward the almost paintless house just up the slope. "Of course you know the first house burned, the one my daddy built, and—"

"That's PawPaw Red?"

"Yeah, your great-granddaddy, your daddy's granddaddy. Dead years before you was born. Hell, you know all that, boy."

"Yessir. It's just that I don't see much of you anymore, and Daddy and them don't seem to talk about the family the way they used to."

"Well, nobody said you had to stay away six months at a time, and me out here with your grandmomma by ourselves. Y'all—*you* at least—ought to be able to do better than that. The whole bunch used to come out here at least twice a month, and now we're lucky to see half of you twice a year."

"Four times this year, counting today."

"Yeah, counting today. They come out and drop you off like a stray dog for the weekend and don't even get out and come up on the porch. You just about the only one that still likes to come out here."

"No, sir, they're just busy with opening Momma's new shop and all."

"And tomorrow they'll drive up and swing open the car door for you and—"

"Late Monday, not tomorrow. Monday's Labor Day and I don't have to go to school."

"Well, that's gratifying." He sighed. "They giving you up to me for two and a half days."

I broke away from the subject. "How come the well never filled up with stuff? Rocks and balls and stuff?"

He calmed down and his voice returned to the far-off tone he'd developed as he'd grown too old to work the fields, what my father called "the kind of voice you use when you can't do much but talk anymore."

"Sir? I didn't hear you."

"I said," his voice rose, "because it gets cleaned out."

"How?"

"Somebody goes down there and cleans it out is how."

I swallowed hard. "You mean somebody goes way down there into that water and picks up all that stuff?"

"How else?" He turned and leaned against the rim of the well, facing the overgrown fields. "You figger it cleans itself? You figger God *wills* it?"

"No sir, but who would go down there?"

"Well, I been down there lots of times, back when I was younger. Your daddy used to. Your uncles. Somebody light and young who ain't afraid of the dark and water, somebody . . ."

"Who did it last?"

He squinted toward the fields. "It's been—well, your Uncle Darrell went down . . . hell, I don't know, boy. I hired a nigger back two or three years ago, and he was the last, best I remember."

"You mean a black man went down into that water?"

"Yep. If family won't do it, you take whoever you can get. It ain't likely he'll ever do it again, though. Never seen a nigger shake like he did when he come up out of that well."

"What was it? The cold water?"

"Maybe. Maybe just scared of being down there. You know how niggers are." He shoved his hands deep into his overall pockets and grinned.

"PawPaw—"

"Yeah?"

"Does it need cleaning out now?"

"Probably. No kids around to throw things into it anymore, but stuff blows in. It probably does need it."

"You want *me* to do it?"

"You mean go down there right now?"

"Yessir. I'll go."

He pulled off his shapeless felt hat, ran an age-splotched hand through what colorless hair remained on his head, and smiled down at me. "Tell you what—come spring, if you are still raring, I'll send you down. And I'll pay you ten dollars to do it."

"I'll do it now." I puffed, squaring my shoulders. "For nothing."

"In the spring. That way you'll be able to get out what blows in this winter."

We said nothing more about it. My folks picked me up that Monday afternoon and I didn't get back out there until Christmas, and then only for a day. The family gathered to open presents and eat a traditional meal. Before dark we waved good-bye to the old couple on the porch and headed back home, where the rainbow lights of Christmas and our bright presents waited.

One Saturday morning in March, during spring vacation, the family loaded up and drove out there. The thirty-minute drive from Columbus, just across the state line in Mississippi, always annoyed my father: the up-and-down gravel road, the raw clay banks lining it, the rickety wooden bridges. "No place in the country," he would say, "has remained as backward as Northwest Alabama. God has simply forsaken it." Mother said that the road, the old homeplace, and my grandparents all reminded him too much of what he had come from.

"Just like a bad book he can't seem to put down," she explained once to one of my aunts.

That trip the whole family stayed for three days, not just me and my parents but my uncle and six of my cousins, two belonging to another uncle. For several years it had been an annual ritual to meet out there in the spring and clean up the moribund old house, my grandmother having grown so physically and mentally inept that the old man had to look after even the kitchen. He submitted to the women's scouring hands once a year: The men kept him in the fields or out around the barn or on the porch until the purge was complete. My grandmother pitched right in with the other women as if she'd just remembered to do the things she'd been meaning to do all along.

"Mercy," my grandfather sighed that Monday afternoon after the women's weekend of cleaning, "just look at that junk." He nodded at his old pickup full of trash. "You wouldn't think two people could accumulate all that stuff in a year."

My father stopped puffing on his pipe to say, "Things do stack up." The men and three of us boys were sprawled out across the front porch watching the sun set while the women and girls cooked supper and yammered away about everything *under* that sun. I was sitting next to the old man with my back against the wall. He was slowly rocking in the old cane-bottom chair he had had forever. The others were sitting dangling their legs off the edge of the porch.

It was the way it was always done in good weather. If it was too cold or the rain was blowing up on the porch, we'd go out to the barn and lie around in the loft in the hay and talk. But my father didn't like that as much because he couldn't smoke his pipe up there. Sometimes my grand-father would light up a roll-your-own he made from Prince Albert tobacco, so he preferred the porch too.

It was quiet and peaceful, and the sun had flattened out like the rich yolk of a yard egg in the trees across the road.

"Hey, Poppa," my uncle said, "June and them found something in the attic this morning that we wanted to ask you about."

The old man leaned forward in his chair. "What's that?" He slid his glasses forward on his nose and squinted toward the voice.

"Well. . . ." My uncle grunted and worked something out of his pants pocket, "it looks like some little pieces of gold." He pitched a small match-box to me and I handed it to PawPaw. It felt heavier than a matchbox should, and it rattled.

The old man held the box in his left hand and pushed it open with his little finger. The others moved in from the edge of the porch to see what was in the box. He closed it and handed it to my father.

"What is it, Poppa?" my uncle asked. "Is that gold?"

"It looks like gold." Daddy had opened the box and was stirring the little glittering pieces with his finger.

"It *is* gold." The old man reached and took the box from him and closed it and set it on his knee and looked out across the road toward the woods along the creek. His face seemed tightly drawn to me, older somehow, but I thought it might be the late sun playing tricks.

My uncle reached and got the box, opened it, and picked up a piece, then passed the box on to my father, who took out a piece, and then we all held a little nugget to look at. A real nugget of gold, like you sometimes see in old cowboy movies. I handed the box back to my uncle.

"Y'all don't drop any of this, now. This is real gold." He turned back to the old man. "Poppa, what are you doing with gold out here? Where'd you get it?"

"Yeah, Poppa," Daddy added with urgency, "where in the world did you get gold nuggets like this? Did you find them on the place here?"

My grandfather kept looking across into the woods by the creek. His jaw worked slowly on a piece of tobacco, but no sound came from his lips.

"Poppa," Daddy insisted, "where did this gold come from?"

The old man continued to look into the trees, but his mouth stopped working the tobacco. He still didn't speak.

"Frank, look here." Uncle Don held one of the little pieces of gold up into a stream of light for my father. He'd been examining all that were left in the box. "These aren't nuggets at all. They've been smoothed out in places, like someone's hammered on them, but some're jagged around the sides and bottom. Frank, these are *fillings*. Gold *fillings!*"

"Are you sure?" Daddy took the little nugget and held it between a finger and thumb, then rolled it around in his palm. He moved it back into the sun. "It damned sure *looks* like a filling."

"Hell, I think they *all* are." My uncle was examining one piece at a time. "You boys hand me the rest of it." I passed my little chip of gold to Bobby, who handed it to his father, along with the piece he'd been holding.

"Poppa, where in God's name—" Daddy was right in his face.

His throat congested, PawPaw finally spoke. "What the hell was they doing up in that attic? They wasn't supposed to be up there. Nobody told them to clean up up there."

"Poppa," Uncle Don interrupted, "it doesn't matter why they were up there. Where did those gold fillings *come* from?" He grabbed the old man by the shoulders.

"Don, ease up on him." Daddy pushed my uncle aside and kneeled down beside PawPaw's chair. "Now, Poppa, we have a right to know about this. There's something strange going on when a box of gold fillings turns up in a family. Now, you know about it. Don, get those boys inside, or, hell, out to the barn, somewhere."

The old man raised his hand and motioned all of us together. "Naw, the boys stay. If this has got to be told, they got a right to be in on it too. If you ain't going to let it rest, if you just got to know about something that you have every right to know about but I don't want to talk about, then all right. It ain't gon' do nothing but make things worse, but I'll tell you. If you just got to know."

Daddy turned to me and then looked at my cousins. "You boys get on away from here. Go on. Now!"

PawPaw raised his voice: "I ain't saying another word without them boys get to listen too. It's part of them too, this story is. Them women done dug down and found a family secret, and now I got to explain it."

My father shrugged and motioned us back on the porch. We gathered around him then—the two sons and their sons, the three generations huddled in the dusk—and he began. The sun had dropped into the trees, and the whole stretch of western sky looked like a smear of blood.

"What's in that matchbox is all that's left of more than a pint jar full of gold fillings and jurry. I should of done what I thought about doing a hundred times and throwed the damned stuff down the well, but I never had the nerve. There is some things you just can't get rid of." His face was so grave that no one dared interrupt him.

"Should of dumped it down the well. Something. Instead, I wrapped it up in a bunch of old family stuff and put it in a trunk up there, where I figured nobody would ever find it until me and the old lady was dead and gone. But naw, they had to snoop around and find it. And now you got to know about it."

"Now, Poppa, they were not—" my uncle tried to put in.

PawPaw glared at him and he shut up. "You want to hear about this or what?"

"Yessir," Uncle Don said.

"Then let me talk."

He settled back in his chair and reached into one of his overall pockets and fished out a Prince Albert can and jiggled it until a ready-roll dropped into his hand. He'd always roll up a couple of dozen at a time and stash them in an empty tobacco can until he was ready for one. He kept a little box of matches in there to, which he slid open and took one out of, struck it on the strip on the side, and lit up. Then he put the matches back in the can and snapped it to and put it in his pocket.

"Now. Y'all remember—Frank, Don—that your granddaddy was a constable for years out here, and he run his precinct, his beat, with a tight fist. Didn't nobody mess around with him."

"What's a constable?" one of my cousins asked.

"Sort of like a sheriff," my uncle answered, "now shut up."

"Hell, he had more power than any shurf out here," the old man said, "and didn't nobody—"

"Y'all about ready t'eat?" One of my aunts was leaning out the screen door.

"No," Daddy snapped, "not for at least half an hour." She winced and pulled her head back inside. "Go on, Poppa."

"My daddy was the only law out here for miles and miles, and he run this whole end of the county. He especially had the niggers cowed. *Had* to keep'm cowed in them days, like they need to be cowed now, now that they got *rights* and all."

"Poppa," Daddy cautioned, "you promised that you would not use that term around the boys. This is the mid-seventies, not the mid-forties."

PawPaw didn't even look at him. "My damned house and my damned porch. That's what I've *always* called'm. Can't break some habits. Anyway, they did exactly what he said. Quick. They answered his questions, helped him around the place, just did everything he wanted them to do or they thought he wanted them to do. He didn't treat'm unfair or nothing. He was just firm. And when they worked on the place here, he paid'm. Not much, but he always give'm something for their help."

He cleared his throat and spat over the edge of the porch.

"Well, there was this nigger undertaker over near Slocum that Big Red —which is what they called my daddy, you remember—had had to make professional calls on from time to time, mostly about whiskey that he made in the woods behind his house. One night it turned out to be what it hadn't started out as, and this is where the gold comes in."

He took a long drag on his cigarette, coughed, and continued.

"Big Red was riding past the nigger's house—he undertook the dead right there in what we'd call the *living* room—and decided he'd drop in and see if he could catch Reverend Sam, Sam Johnson, that is, with moonshine."

"A preacher with moonshine?" I asked him.

"Why, hell yes. Ever preacher back in here I ever knew either made it or drunk it or both. Reverend Sam did both.

"He slipped up to a winder and peeped in and seen that nigger gouging fillings out of a corpse's mouth and dropping them little pieces of gold into a pint jar."

"My God, Poppa! Don, we've got to get these boys into the house. You boys get on in there and—"

"Let the boys stay, Frank. Like I done tol' you, they got a right to hear this too. Don, you set still." He shifted his weight over onto his other hip, fished a rectangle of tar-like tobacco out of another pocket, cut a small sliver, and just held it while he returned to his story. "Caught that nigger flat-footed knocking fillings out of that corpse's mouth with a little ball-peen hammer and a ice pick, and the nigger knowed he was caught cold too, the minute Red pounded on the door. He just handed that jar of gold over to Big Red and went to get his coat. Only Red stopped him." The old man paused, stretched, slipped the sliver of tobacco way back in his cheek, and turned toward the screen door to make certain that the women were not standing there listening.

"To cut it short, Big Red take'n all old Sam's gold, nearly a full pint of it that he'd took out of corpses' mouths and stole over the years—there was some jurry in the pile too—only it wasn't all he'd took since he traded some for stuff over in Tuscaloosa at a pawn shop, where didn't nobody ask any questions about where the gold come from. Sam'd take a hammer and beat'm round as he could, so they'd actually look like nuggets, only he must not of done too good a job on some of'm. After he'd got a right smart of'm together, he'd melt the fillings down into a lump and couldn't nobody buying it from the pawn shop know that it come from teeth."

"Poppa, this is incredible," Daddy whispered.

"Take'n that nigger's gold for hisself. And that ain't all. The way he told the nigger, wasn't any way Sam could do nothing with it but keep it, because everybody would know where it had come from, even if he melted it down, and he would make sure that the pawn shops in Tuscaloosa and Birmingham and Columbus wasn't gon' buy from him anymore.

"And where else would a nigger get gold? They had it in their teeth and that was about it, except for a little slick ring now and then that some white woman passed on to one of them or that some maid stole from a white woman.

"Now, what Sam was doing was wrong—I ain't denying it, no more than Red would—but Red figured that if he stopped him from taking the gold out of niggers' mouths, then that gold was gone more surely than it would be if Sam just kept it hid or pawned it off in Tuscaloosa. It would be buried with the corpses. Been a real waste of solid gold. So he got gold fever after that and made sure that ever nigger that died on his beat got channeled through Sam, even got a lot of out-of-county niggers brought in. And he made him take out every gold filling and take every bit of jurry that was gold. Hell, a few times he even made Sam dig people back up and take jurry off—the family would have missed it at the viewing. Paid Sam a little bit along to keep him honest, prolly more than the pawn shop woulda give him for the gold, but it was mostly the threat of what he could do to him that kept Sam going at a fever pitch."

"PawPaw," I broke in, "how did he get away with taking the fillings? Wouldn't the family know?"

"How, boy? How'd they know? Any of y'all ever seen a corpse with his teeth showing?"

"No sir. I've never seen a corpse *period.*"

"Hell, people in a casket ain't *smiling.* They got nothing to smile *about.* He could of took out teeth, tongue, and tonsils and wouldn't nobody of knowed. As for the jurry, he'd take that off just before the casket got closed for good, if he could, or, like I said, dig'm up later."

Daddy was shaking his head in the light of a window. Uncle Don and my cousins just stared in silence at the woods across the road.

"Over fifteen years, right up until old Sam died, Big Red took gold from that nigger. And others."

Uncle Don moved closer to the old man. "Others? There were others?"

Drawing in a deep breath, the old man continued. "Like I said, Big Red got gold fever. He figured if one nigger could fill a pint jar in five years, five niggers could do it in one. That ain't what you call higher math there. It's common sense. So he upped the ante and started paying Sam better, and sure enough, the flow got bigger. Old Sam started a reglar network with other undertakers he knowed. Them that hadn't been stealing started to, wholesaling the stuff—that's the way Big Red put it—to Sam and Sam middle-manning it to Big Red. Once Sam had the other niggers doing it, there wasn't no quitting. He could have told on'm, *ruined'm,* throwed'm in jail forever, or just killed'm. Besides that, even the niggers in other counties knew about Big Red, and if they didn't know what his part in the scheme was, they knowed he was involved and that was enough."

"Poppa." Daddy had moved right up next to PawPaw. "Do you mean my grandfather ran a crime syndicate? And him the *Law?*"

"Get out of my face, boy. I don't even know what a syndicate is—you the one with the education, so you tell me sometime. What they did wasn't any more a crime than most businesses. That was gold that would be in the ground right now, back where it come from and useless to ever-body, or pawned off to some crook in Tuscaloosa. And as for taking it away from them niggers, remember that he *paid*'m, and if it wasn't much, it was more than they could of got for it anyplace else. What could nig-gers do with gold? Like I said, everbody would of knowed where it come from. They could of passed it around among theirselves, but no white man would of took it, knowing it was stole. And you can bet that what they did pawn didn't bring them a hundredth of what it was worth."

Uncle Don sighed. "Nobody would know it was stolen. . . . I just can-not believe that my own flesh and blood would—"

"Don't draw no judgments, boy."

Daddy laid his hand on the old man's knee. "Poppa, how much did it come to? What happened to it?"

"I don't know the answer to them questions. I remember seeing more than a quart jar full of fillings and jurry, only he never knowed I was watch-ing when he had it out. I think he melted it down or beat it out into dif-ferent shapes before he done whatever he done with it."

"You don't know what he did with it?" Daddy asked. "You don't *know?*"

"No. I know he passed it along to somebody over the years, however much there was, until just that little there was left." He paused for a very long time. His jaws moved in rhythm with his rocking while he appeared to gathering strength for what he said next.

"And the ring your momma's wearing."

"What?" Daddy burst out.

Uncle Don grabbed him. "Keep your voice down, Frank. The women might hear." I could see them inside the house pacing, glancing toward the porch, but keeping their distance the way they always did when the men had serious matters on their minds. Dark was beginning to seriously settle, and I never remembered supper being served after dark in *that* house. My grandfather said that habit came from the days before they had electricity —it just saved a little coal oil if they ate before it got dark.

Daddy shoved me toward the door. "Get on in the house." He motioned the other kids to follow me. "Y'all get on in there and eat your supper."

"You heard him," Uncle Don said, pointing for my cousins to follow.

I started off down the hallway, then cut right into the old man's bedroom, opened a window, slid out, and slipped around the house, stopping at the corner of the porch.

". . . and I never spent none of it myself," I could hear PawPaw saying after the brisk flurry of voices quieted. "There wasn't none left anyway, but this little bit. I *never* felt right about it, especially the ring, but Big Red give it to your momma when we got married and I didn't have no idea where it come from until years later, when he told me. Hell, I thought he bought it."

Daddy said something. I think he asked whether she knew where it came from, which I thought was a really dumb question to ask. The wind was blowing through the oak trees and making too much noise for me to follow the conversation well. I couldn't hear the old man's answer, but I knew what it was.

Then Uncle Don's voice rose. "What about the family, Poppa? How much was used on the *family?*"

"Calm down, boy. I told you how I felt about it. I don't like it, I *never* liked it, but it wasn't for me to like or dislike. It was Big Red's business. How much was spent to keep the family going, I don't know. I got money from him lots of times, when things got tough. Ain't no doubt some of it was from that gold. You just got to live with that."

"Damn, Poppa, this is crazy! I don't know how much money for my education came from the mouths of Negroes, and to think my own mother is wearing a ring that came off a black corpse." I could see my father's shadow gesturing in the light from the window.

"What you got against niggers? You been telling me for years how they equal to us and—"

"*Any* corpse!" My father was whispering, but his voice was fierce. "White, Black, Indian, or Chinese. The fact that my mother's wedding band was stolen off *any* corpse is enough to sicken me. Now we don't know how much went to sustain the family and put us through school. Jesus Christ, Don, what in hell do you make of this?"

My uncle's voice was too low for me to hear, but whatever he said, my grandfather shot back, "You might as well shut up about it. There ain't no way of knowing how or when it was spent. Big Red left money—not much, but what there was was in a bank and there wasn't any way of figuring out how much of it, if any, come from that gold."

I could see Daddy's head shadowed on the ground. He was shaking it back and forth, back and forth. He said finally, "I can't stand any more of this, Don. Let's go on inside." His shadow disappeared, Uncle Don's crossed through the light, and then there was the sound of the screen door closing and the heavy creak of the old man's rocker. I eased around the corner of the house and slid up beside him. He didn't seem to notice me.

"Poppa," my mother's voice came through the screen, "are you coming in to supper?"

"I ain't hungry. I'll be d'reckly, Goddamn it. Y'all go on and eat."

"But everything's going to get cold again."

"I'll be in d'reckly, I told you. Now leave me alone."

I leaned and looked through the window. Daddy was at the table and in the hallway Uncle Don was talking to my cousins who had been on the porch with us. The old man just sat, rocking, not chewing his tobacco—not even, from what I could hear, breathing. He was as still as something carved out of stone. When he finally did shift in his seat, he saw me sitting there.

"What you doing out here? You ought to be eating with the others."

"I thought I'd wait on you."

"Get on in there and eat, boy. Now go."

I went. It was the quietest meal I'd ever eaten there. Daddy and Uncle Don just stirred their food around, and I managed only a bite or two of roast. I couldn't keep my eyes off my grandmother's ring. PawPaw never came to the table.

My sleep that night was fitful, even after the murmurings from my parents' room subsided. I knew what they were talking about: He couldn't just not tell her, not since *I* knew about it. Twice I got up and looked out from the second-story window toward the woods where I'd last seen the sun. The sun, the sun. There was something so sane about things on the porch as long as the sun was on us. Then it went down and the shadows came up.

When sleep did come, somewhere deep in the night, I dreamed of long lines of black people coming one by one up onto our porch at home, each with his hand out, the tall and short, pitch black and high yellow, fat and skinny, each with great gaps in his grin, each saying, "Gimme my gold, white folks, gimme my gold." Long before first light I was sitting on the back porch watching the sky in the east and listening to all the birds chirping and chattering and far off the lonesome bark of a fox, waiting for the sun to rise and put an end to that night.

It was a quiet breakfast, after which my father and uncle walked off over into the fields, leaving the women to finish doing whatever had to be done at the house. There seemed to be a sense of urgency as they bustled about with their dust rags and mops. The kids, male and female, fanned out the way they always had, the girls ending up sitting in a circle talking and giggling and the boys off at the barn.

I decided to rummage through the equipment stall, where all the farm tools were kept, hoping to find something I hadn't run across before. As I rounded the corner of the barn, the old man whistled, then motioned me over to the well. With his hat pulled low over his eyes and his scaly-looking arms folded across the lip of the well, he looked like a figure done in stone: the aging farmer pondering the last of the open wells before it drew him in, the two of them disappearing forever from that all-but-forgotten childless land.

"Yessir?" I leaned down to look in under the brim of the hat.

"You ready to go down?"

"Sir?"

"You ready to clean the well out?" He nodded down into the mossy circle of stone.

"Well, PawPaw, I think that the others are about ready to go."

"Ain't no way y'all will be getting away from here before afternoon. You gon' help me?" He raised his head and looked at me, the first time I had seen his eyes since the night before. They were red and tired looking.

"How will I get down there?" The sun was still low, and I could barely see the circle of water at the bottom.

"I'll let you down on the rope. You just stand in the bucket and hold onto the rope. When you get down, pick up all the trash and load it in the bucket and I'll draw it up and dump it. Simple as pie. That water won't even come to your neck."

"Well sir, I—maybe we ought to wait for Daddy and Uncle Don to help."

"Rope won't hold them, but it'll hold *you*. Go on and get your feet in the bucket." He looked down to make sure I was barefooted.

"Hoist your butt up here and dust your feet off. Then step into the bucket."

"All right, I'll go. It's just that, well, they could help you let me down." I'd never doubted his strength before, but now he looked so tired and old.

"Son, I ain't gon' drop you. Now get on in that bucket and I'll crank you down." He unreeled the rope a few feet until the bucket hung at just the right height for me to step in and get a two-handed grip on the rope in a slight crouch.

I jumped up on the lip of the well and rubbed my feet together until most of the dust was gone. Then I leaned and looked down at the little dancing circle.

"PawPaw, I'm scared. That well's deep." But I slung one leg over and dropped a foot into the bucket. The other followed. I closed my eyes and grabbed the rope just below the spool, and before I could think of backing out, he lowered me into that deep dark.

I looked up past the slowly turning spool at the sky, which became a smaller and smaller pale-blue disc as I slipped deeper. Then the bucket smacked into water, tilted, and I fell off to the side, only my tight grip on the rope keeping me from plunging butt first to the bottom. I dangled my feet and eased down the rope until I finally felt the rough stones and God only knew what else at the end of my descent. The water was almost to my armpits.

"You on the bottom, boy?" he yelled down.

"Yessir," I stammered back. The cold water took my breath away.

"Then start loading the bucket. Anything that don't belong down there, put it in the bucket. Give me a tug when it's full and I'll raise it up and dump it. And don't you pee in that water." His laugh sounded far away and yet so strangely forceful echoing down the walls. I looked up. His face, red and heavy, eclipsed the moon-shaped sky.

"Yessir." Then, using my toes to feel out unnatural shapes, I started loading the bucket. There were rocks of all sizes, pieces of brick, a leather glove, a hardball that had practically petrified, beer cans, pinecones, fruit jars. Determined not to get my head underwater, I would wrap my toes around an object and raise it up to my hand, then drop it into the bucket. Sometimes I had to use both feet to clamp onto something big and hang on as hard as I could to the rope, but my hand always slipped when I reached with the other to take the stone or whatever it was from between my feet. Twice the icy water closed over my head.

Each time I put something into the bucket, I looked up to make certain his face was still there. Anything could happen: He could forget me, or die, the walls could crumble in on me, the bottom give way, a snake strike. The loaded bucket could fall and hit me on the head.

He pulled one bucketful up and dumped it, lowered it again. I stumbled around and half filled the second one and tugged for him to take it up. The bucket was just dropping back into reach when my foot felt something, back along the far curve of the casing. I grabbed for the rope, yelled for him to haul me up, and swung my feet into the bucket.

"You got everything?" he bellowed down.

"Yessir, just pull me up. Please *pull me up.*" I felt the first coils collect on the spool as, my eyes, fists, and teeth clenched, I began my ascent on the spinning, creaking rope. I did not open my eyes until I heard him say, "All right, grab the edge, boy, you're up." His big hands hooked me under my arms and swung me over onto the ground. He tried to pull me to him.

"PawPaw, don't, let me go. I'm gon' throw up. I spun away, stumbled to the roots of a big oak just down the slope, and retched until everything inside me was splattered on the ground. The old man stood behind me, his hands in his pockets. I backed up a few feet and rocked back and forth on my knees.

"Scared you that bad, huh?"

I sniffed and wiped my nose and mouth across my arm. "No sir. It wasn't that." My stomach had that awful collapsed feeling, as if giant hands had grabbed it and twisted until everything in it was squeezed out.

"Just scared, Son. Every boy feels that way his first trip down."

I shook my head and sat back against the oak. "No sir, it was *not* being scared." He scooted some dirt and leaves over the puddle of vomit and sat down beside me. The sun was high above the back fields, beating down on the new green that had now replaced the brown-gray fur of winter. There was a scattering of saplings where three years before there had been plowed fields. In another three the woods would be solid to the horizon.

"It was something else—there was something down there, a possum or cat skeleton. I could feel the ribs. But it fell apart, broke up, the bones just. . . ."

He laid his yellow hand on my head. "There's always something down there you can't quite get your hands on. You'd of knowed that if it wasn't your first trip down. You'll know it from now on."

"But what about the water? Can we keep on drinking it?"

"You was drinking it yesdy, and that animal was down there and it didn't kill you. Them bones is as clean as even the sun could make'm. You just forget about it. And don't tell the others. It's just one more thing you got to live with." He was standing above me, his hand on my head, but he wasn't really talking to me. His eyes were off in the distance.

We left the old couple after lunch. They waved and we waved, my uncle's Suburban going off in one direction and our car in another. I watched them sitting on the porch until the towering old gray house fell behind and the spring sky took over.

Time of the Panther

His face contorted by a euphoric grin, the grandfather got into the truck and said simply, "He's back." He said nothing more, did not have to, as they drove the five miles or so back to the farm. He drove and smiled, his eyes on the woods flanking the gravel road as often as he dared direct them there. The boy noticed that the trees had that rust-colored glow they always got when spring was on the way—buds were swollen to the breaking point.

The old man pulled the truck in behind the house and stopped beside the kitchen steps where he always did. "You get the groceries out." He motioned the boy to the pickup bed as he stepped out. "Bring'm and set'm on the porch, then back the truck down to the barn and I'll be down d'rectly to help you unload the feed. Be careful with that truck. Watch that gate and them gate posts. And don't grind the gears."

The boy could hear him talking to the grandmother even before the kitchen screen door closed behind him: "Ludy, he's back. Murle Johnson seen his tracks yesdy morning on his place, and somebody said. . . ."

The gravelly old voice trailed off, but the boy knew what he was telling her: Somebody at the store had told him somebody else in the next county had lost a calf last week. That was all it took—some tracks, a missing calf, the first pulses of wind from the south in March—and the panther was back.

The cat's arrival was as certain as the seasons, yet no one ever knew exactly when it would happen. One day the old men on the great front porch of Dowell's store would be talking politics or weather, with just about as much animation as the two or three sleeping dogs on the porch beside them. Anyone listening just around the corner of the store would hear something like the intermittent buzz of bees, dull and distant, breaking in on the dreams of a noonday napper. The next day, news of the panther would sweep through, and it was like a nest of bees had been flung amongst them, with high-pitched voices and wild gestures. Even the dogs could not rest. To the boy it sounded like the noise of a tent revival. One day he was not there—the next day he was.

The only store for miles, Dowell's was not simply a source of basic commodities for the agricultural community it served, offering goods ranging from fresh meat to plows, but a meeting place for farmers, retired and otherwise, who attended the six-day-a-week social gatherings with far greater enthusiasm than ever they attended church. Then, again, maybe what went on there was a religion in and of itself. The building occupied one corner of the intersection of two farm-to-market roads about twelve miles south of Millport, Alabama. An enormous structure of tin and unpainted wood, the outside walls dotted with dozens of signs advertising everything from motor oil to Rooster Snuff, it was jammed ceiling to floor with sacks, cans, and barrels of food and farm supplies, great coils of ropes and barbed wire, and agricultural equipment of every size and sort. A covered porch ran the entire width of the front of the building, probably sixty feet.

It was there, on that porch, that they began to gather on spring, summer, and autumn mornings, often long before Junior Dowell walked across the road from his little brick house, propped open the doors with Coca-Cola cases, and turned the CLOSED signs around in the windows. The sun still behind the trees, the air faintly chill with the dying breath of night, the first old pickup would wheeze to a stop beside the store, an overalled figure would get out in the early light, then another truck, and the day would begin.

A hard-core cadre of a dozen or so old farmers, alike in their overalls and broken-down field shoes, occupied long-established positions, theirs until they died or became so feeble or crippled that they could no longer show up to claim their places. The boy's grandfather, though still too economically bound to his fields to loll more than two or three hours on the porch, usually very early or very late, nonetheless had a long enough tenure there to claim a seat on the end of one of the long paintless, crudely made benches capable of holding a total of maybe twenty broad-butted men. His initials were carved there as proof of ownership, and if someone happened to be sitting there when the old man walked up, the interloper was shown the initials and asked, sometimes not so politely, to move.

In winter the benches were arranged in a loose square around a large pot-bellied stove in the center of the store, merchandise having been shoved back in whatever disarray to accommodate them. The benches held highest priority. The first day of March, no matter what the weather, they went back to the front porch, and counters and barrels flowed into the void where the benches had been. The stove, too heavy for easy removal, generally stayed fired until mid-March, after which it sat in its place with the lingering sadness of a kitchen closed for the night until the first cold fronts of October stirred the Vulcan back to life again. When the benches went onto the porch, it was an official declaration that spring had come to the country.

It was the early sixties—he was ten and old enough, his father judged, to spend his spring vacations helping out his grandfather on the farm—when the boy first heard the old men discussing the panther. He was sitting on the steps of the store waiting for his grandparents to finish buying the week's supplies when Boyd Pollard slid his pickup to a stop in front, got out, and, even before he had made it to the edge of the porch, said, "Hot damn, he's *back!*"

"Says who?" someone asked.

Pollard stepped onto the end of the porch and squatted to begin council—the old men edged up to him. "My boys was coon hunting last night." He looked from face to face. "And them dogs hit something mighty peculiar just south of that fork on Little Sandy. Run it a mile or so down the bottom and, best the boys could tell, caught up with it."

The boy eased off the steps and down the edge of the porch to a point where he could hear Pollard, about whom everyone was gathered, church-like silent and serious.

"Caught up with that sumbitch. And then there was a bunch of yapping and fighting and them hounds come right back to the boys like they was ready to throw in the tow'l for the night. Hell, one of 'm was tore across the head from one ear to the other and one had a tore-up front leg."

"Coulda been a big coon," came a voice from the crowd.

"Or maybe they got in some bob wahr," someone else said.

"Coulda been either one, but wudn't. Them boys can tell when the dogs is on a possum or a coon, and it wudn't bob wahr done that to'm. That ain't the all of it anyway. They woke me up when they got back home, they was so excited about it, and we all went out on the back porch and listened for awhile. And, so help me God, he squalled off in one of them bottoms. It was *him*."

"You check for tracks?" Will Beasley asked.

"Ain't yet. Don't have to—it was *him*."

On the way back to the farm he told his grandparents what he had heard. The old man grinned as the boy repeated Pollard's story. "Yep, it's about time for him to come back. This the first time you heard about him?"

"Well," the boy answered, looking over at his grandmother, who was staring out at the trees on her side of the truck, "Daddy mentioned something about the story of a big black cat out here, but he didn't say much about it."

"Ain't no story, boy, and it ain't the last time you'll hear about him, not if you keep coming out here in the spring. He comes back ever year about this time."

"You mean nobody's caught him yet?"

"Shoot naw, boy. Ain't nobody even *seen* him up close."

"Then how do they know it's a panther?"

"Well, tracks, for one thing and his scream for another. Half-eat calves, white-eyed hound dogs that won't even get off the porch at night, squawking chickens. Then there's them that's seen him at a distance . . ."

"How big is he?" He could feel his pulse banging away in his neck as he listened to the old man.

"Oh, he's big, boy, *damn* big." The grandmother cut her eyes over when the old man swore, but he kept his eyes ahead or to his side. "Big enough to jump on Billy Camp's mare, which he done one night—she's got the scars to this day, down both sides of her back."

"Where's he come from, PawPaw?"

"God only knows. God only knows where he goes when he goes. But sure as spring he comes back." His grandfather said no more about the panther that day, but the boy could tell that something had changed, that some dark shadow, as thrilling and inevitable as sin, had descended on the hills.

After the old man had finished telling the grandmother everything he'd heard about the panther's return, he walked down to the barn and helped the boy unload sacks of feed. Each year it seemed that his grandfather walked more slowly, worked less, as if he were winding down like an old clock or toy, and each year he himself seemed to grow stronger in will and body until, he'd noticed lately, he could lift as much as the old man and outlast him by half a day.

"I 'spect when we finish here," the grandfather panted, hefting his end of one of the big feed sacks, "that we ought to get them smallest calves in for the night, that cat being back and all. They'll be all right during the day —he don't stir much while the sun's up—but we better put'm up at night."

"You really think that's necessary?" The boy dusted himself off and slid in behind the steering wheel of the truck. His grandfather got in on the passenger's side.

"You think it *ain't?*" the old man grunted. "You can't be too careful. That bastard gets two or three a year around here."

"Aw, come on. There's no proof that—"

He spun his head and glared at the boy. "What the hell you know about it? What you know about that panther, boy? You getting mighty damned big for your britches. Sometimes I wish you had of stayed like you was a few years ago. Just park the truck over there." He motioned to the spot where the truck was always parked, got out, and slammed the door. "Just too Goddamned big for your britches." He muttered as he stormed into the house.

"I don't know anything about any *panther,*" the boy growled, easing the old truck into its customary ruts.

At the dinner table that night the panther was all his grandfather wanted to talk about. Beginning by repeating what Murle Johnson had said, then recalling word for word the porch conversation that morning, he lapsed further and further into his panther lore, retelling stories the boy and grandmother had heard dozens of times before. They sat and listened, she nodding and smiling from time to time, the boy listening halfheartedly and forming his leftover peas into little designs, breaking them up, and reshaping them again.

He finally came out of his reverie and addressed the boy. "Nat."

"Yessir?"

"Tomorrow morning we going over to Murle's bottom and see can we find them tracks. We'll take the dogs with us and maybe the fishing stuff. And a pistol."

The boy scattered his peas and glared at him, gathering strength to challenge. *It is time,* he thought, *it is time.*

"What's the matter?" the old man snapped. "You don't want to go?"

"Go for *what*? *What* tracks?" He felt the muscles hardening in his legs and arms, the anger rising in his face. Then the deference that had not allowed his tongue to serve his mind disappeared as surely as the sun scatters the shadows of night and he spoke quickly: "Daddy says there's no such thing a panther up here in these hills." He met his grandfather's glare as the old woman's head spun toward him. "He says y'all believe in that panther the way kids believe in Santa Claus and the Easter Bunny and the Tooth Fairy. He says y'all like the excitement of believing in a great big black cat yowling and killing calves and slashing up dogs, and you like telling about it at the store. It gives you something to look forward to and to talk about, but there is nothing, *nothing*. There *is . . . no . . . panther!*" He slid back down in the chair from which he had gradually risen as his voice peaked. He stared at his peas, surprised at the strength of his heart as it thrashed in his chest.

The old man spoke quietly, slowly: "That's what my son says, huh?"

"That's what he says, yessir."

"He don't believe in the panther, huh?"

"No sir. He says he hasn't believed those stories since he was younger than me, if he ever did."

"And he don't want you believing them either. That it?" He was sitting with his arms folded across his chest, while the grandmother leaned on her elbows, face cupped in her hands.

"He doesn't think that such superstition is good for young people," the boy continued, but without heat.

"But it's fine for old folks, huh?"

"He says it gives you something to look forward to, that it keeps you from getting so bored with life out here."

"Like Santa Claus or the Easter Bunny or the Tooth Fairy for children?"

"Yessir." He tried to form his peas into a square, but they kept rolling out of formation. "Exactly like them."

"Well, your daddy's got plenty of education—I ought to know since I paid for it—and I guess college-graduated engineers have got to be able to see something laid out right in front of them under bright lights before it's true."

The boy leaned forward in his chair until his face was only inches from the old man's. "He says that if there was a panther in these woods somebody would have seen him up close by now, somebody would have killed him or at least taken a picture, somebody would have brought in some *proof.*" He scattered the peas with his knife. "I've been coming out here for five years now, since I was about ten, and for five spring vacations I've heard about everything there is to hear about that panther, and I have never seen any proof at all, none, and I do not believe in him any more than Daddy believes in flying saucers."

"You believe in God and Satan, don't you?" The old man's face was blister red. "You ever seen *them?*"

"No sir, I have never seen them. Daddy says that God, if he exists, is not what y'all think he is, that if He's anything, He's just all the laws of the universe making things hang together, and that Satan is just your imagination, just a child's boogerman. But I don't want to talk about this." He lowered his eyes but remained standing.

The old man was trembling with rage. He stood leaning with his fists on the table, as if using his body to anchor them so that he could not raise and use them against the boy, who, unblinking, kept his eyes focused on his grandfather's. He said hoarsely, "You better not say nothing else, boy, not *nothing.* This has gone too far already." His eyes bored into the boy's for a few seconds, then he dropped back into his chair, wilted, and stared at his plate. The boy continued to stand, frozen in his posture of defiance, until his grandmother stood and picked up her dishes.

"PawPaw," he tried, "I didn't want to say this—I promise you I didn't."

His grandfather looked up at him. "It's OK, Nat, it's all right. You go on to your room for a few minutes. I got to think."

The boy went to his room, removed his socks, and, leaving the light off, lay down across the bed. Through the open screened window he could see the stars in their distant peace and from somewhere over in the hollows hear the comforting sounds of owls and whippoorwills. He had begun laying out the constellations he could see in his square of sky when the door cracked open and his grandfather said, "Come with me, Nat."

"Sir?"

"I said come with me."

"But it's late, and . . ."

"Get off the bed and come with me."

The boy stood up and pulled on his socks. *If he is going to beat me, I will have to fight back. I can't let him whip me.* He remembered his father's tales of that temper and the belt lashings and the time the old man picked up a piece of stove wood and beat him half to death, just for jumping off a cotton truck. *I may have to just run off into the woods, but he is not going to beat me.*

When he stepped into the kitchen, the old man grabbed his arm and shoved him through the back door onto the porch.

His grandmother's voice came from somewhere behind them. "Willard, wait. You got no right to punish Nat for what his daddy has taught him not to believe. Let him alone, let him go to bed."

"Ludy, you go back to your dishes." He kicked the screen door open. "This is man stuff and don't have nothing to do with you." He stepped out onto the porch and stood beside the boy.

Oh, my God, he is going to beat me. He felt rage gathering in his chest. *I will not take a beating.*

"Now—"

"PawPaw, I—"

"Don't talk, son. *I* am doing the talking. You just listen."

His voice had lost its heat now, so the boy relaxed a little.

"There's some things in this life that you got to learn on your own. Whatever your daddy has come to believe about the panther is his bidness, but he ain't got no right at all telling you what to believe in or what not to believe in, just like I ain't got no right teaching you to believe in the panther or God or Satan or anything else. Have I ever said you got to believe in any of them?"

"No sir." The boy tried to ease away from the old man's grip, which was surprisingly strong on his arm.

"Naw is right. You don't believe in him, though, do you?"

"No sir, if you mean the panther." He hesitated, noticing how the light from the kitchen threw their shadows almost all the way across the yard to the truck. "I'm not sure about the other two."

"OK, then, you won't mind doing what I want you to do."

"What?"

"I want you to go on an errand for me."

"Tonight?"

"Right now." He released the boy's arm and pointed out past the edge of kitchen-light glow toward the dark woods below the barn. "You remember that big flat white rock we found on Little Sandy back last summer, the one with the red veins that looked like they made a big *S*?"

"Yessir, but—"

"We hid it in that old holler stump because we had too much fishing stuff to tote it back, remember?"

"Yessir, I know where we put it, in that old stump, and covered it with leaves to hide it. Why?"

"I want you to go get that rock for me tonight."

"Sir?"

"I want you to go right now and get that rock for me."

"Tonight? Can't it wait—"

"Right now, by God."

"But that is ridiculous," the boy heard himself saying.

"Careful, boy. I'll forgive that, but not another one. Now you get a hatchet out of the toolshed and get some matches and that old flashlight out of the truck—battries ain't all that good, but they'll do." He reached down and picked up the boy's boots, which had been stood just outside the screen door. "Put'm on and go get me that rock."

The boy sat down and pulled on the boots and laced them. He looked up. "You're not going to let me take the truck?"

"Nope. You're going on foot."

"But that's five miles if it's an inch, PawPaw, and it's dark as pitch out there. No moon . . . I can't go through—"

"It's right at three miles, the way we always go. You can make it by midnight if you start now and don't get lost, be back well before first light." He paused and looked at the boy. "And if the *panther* don't eat you. You'll be going through Murle Johnson's bottom to get there."

"Can I take the dogs?" The boy nodded toward the two big hounds slouched against the wall.

"They're staying here. I doubt they'd go anyway, this being panther time and all." He gently pushed the boy off the porch. "Get your stuff and be on your way or you won't get back tonight. Get your jacket out of the truck too."

"What about the shotgun? Can I take it?"

"What for? Ain't nothing gonna bother you. There ain't no panther. Remember?"

"And what if I get lost and don't make it back tonight?" His voice was unsteady voice as he groped in the glove compartment for the matches and flashlight.

"Then build you a fire and spend the night in the woods. Way you got it figured, there's nothing out there can get you. Come on back in the morning. I'll keep you some breakfast in the oven." The old man turned on the porch and went back into the kitchen, already closed for the evening, and flipped off the light. The yard fell into darkness and the boy headed off down toward the barn, whose outline loomed like a great gray pillow against the black trees. As he passed it, his boots making soft little

thuds in the path, he could smell the sweet blend of feed and hay and animals, and in one of the stalls a calf made a soft sound.

He took one of the cattle trails through the woods, hatchet in one hand,
flashlight in the other, dodging from time to time as a vine reached out of
the dark. That part of the trip he could have made even without the light
—the trail was easy. When he came at last to his grandfather's back pasture,
he clicked off the flashlight and took a dead-reckoning angle across it. He
was surprised at how much light the stars gave off in the moonless night.

Reaching the corner of the pasture, he crossed the fence, turned the
light back on, and found the old fishing trail that he and the old man had
made over the years they fished the Little Sandy. Their trips had not been
numerous, and the path was not easily discernible, even in the glow of the
light, though it could be followed.

From that point on, he knew, it was up and down, hollow after hollow,
until the trail dead-ended into Murle Johnson's great meadow, beyond
which lay the bottomlands of the Little Sandy. He dropped into the first
hollow, sliding and stumbling, splashing through the spongy bottom, then
clambered up the other side to a ridge of pines and scattered oaks and fell
headfirst into a deeper hollow studded with hickories and oaks and heavy
with undergrowth.

There the trail seemed simply to disappear, what there had been of it,
swallowed in a tangle of vines and brush along a small stream that he could
not remember being there. In the daylight he knew that he could find it,
but not at night, not with that puny flashlight. He plunged wildly through
the underbrush and up the slope of the ridge before him, knowing that as
long as he ran perpendicular to the hollows he would have to come at last
to Johnson's Meadow, where he could get his bearings and find the path
again. "If I miss that meadow," he panted, laboring to the crest, "if I miss
that damned meadow, I may never get there or back—they may just find
my bones."

But that was panic talking, he assured himself when he made the top
of the ridge and fell to his knees, exhausted and breathless from exertion
and—he did not doubt it—fear. And, hell, he had just barely started the
trip. He turned the flashlight off and sat back against a tree to rest. His
heart lurched along a few minutes, subsiding finally to its steady, predictable pace. And then all was silence, silence and darkness, and the boy
started thinking about the panther. Little animal sounds came from the
hollows on either side, night birds cried out, and a light wind moaned in
the limbs overhead. *What if . . .*

Then he was up and running, like an animal driven, down through the gloom of night trees, which thrust themselves before him as if they knew what they were doing, down into the furious tangle of vines and brush at the bottom of another hollow, through them and over the boggy floor and up the next slope, tearing toward the wide, treeless expanse of Johnson's Meadow. A root or vine, something with dark tentacles, threw him to the ground near the next crest and he tumbled to the side and down the slope, over and over the way he'd seen movie cowboys do when they jumped off trains, until he lay breathless against a tree. His trembling hands still held the hatchet and flashlight.

He scrambled to his feet and started to run again, then realized that he did not know which way he was going, only toward the ridge of the slope he was on. He swept the light across the trees in front of him, found where he had tripped—only a pine root bowed out of the straw—and resumed his assault of the hill. When he reached the top he fell to his knees again and shut off the light. *I am a reasonable person,* he thought, *the son of an engineer, of a scientist, but I am acting like a fool. This is a world of jet planes and atomic bombs and television sets, not gods and devils and ghosts and panthers. I can handle this.*

He resolved then to climb a tree and try to spot Johnson's Meadow. It had to be only a hollow or two over. He had forgotten utterly how many crests he had crossed, how many, indeed, made up the distance between the house and meadow, if he ever knew, if he had ever bothered to count while he tagged along behind the old man. He turned the light on and laid it pointing in the direction he had been moving. *It seems right,* he thought. He selected a hickory tree with branches low enough to latch onto and jumped and caught hold of a lower limb and clawed his way up high enough that he could see the meadow, if it really lay out there, and if he could see it in starlight. *It seems about right.*

And so it was. When the boy reached the top of the tree he looked in the direction he had left the light pointing, and when he blocked out the shaft of light with his arm he could see it, the vague, starlit clearing, beyond the next hollow. *I have been going right, by God, I have.* He shinnied down the tree, picked up his light and hatchet, and, though he knew he was safe, oriented, drove himself like a dogged animal, caught between fear and euphoria, until he burst into the meadow and fell headlong into its deep, damp rye.

He flicked off the light and rested then, gathering second wind, knowing that the worst part was probably behind and the meadow itself, at least a mile across, would be easy going. Little Sandy Bottom lay ahead, and the stump and stone and, he hoped, nothing more. The stream would be almost impossible to miss on the opposite side of the meadow, and the paths up and down it, made by generations of men and animals, would be easy to stay on. He stood, decided the angle he wanted to take, and with the comfortable stride of a long-distance runner crossed the meadow by starlight, the flashlight jammed into a pocket.

The edge of the clearing came all too soon and he stood at the mouth of the path into the hollow where Murle Johnson said he'd seen panther tracks the day before. He took a tentative step onto the trail, stepped back, and switched on the light. Transferring it to his left hand, the hatchet to his right, he lunged off down the trail that led to the belly of the dark hollow.

I do not believe in the panther. I do not believe in Santa Claus and Easter Bunnies and the Tooth Fairy and gods and devils, and I do not believe in a Goddamned panther. I am not a child. He stopped and looked back—the opening to the meadow had closed as resolutely as a set of jaws. *I do not believe.*

Finding Little Sandy was a matter merely of yielding to gravity and letting the path hurl him to the bottom of Johnson's Hollow. He could hear the reassuring ripple of the creek before his light danced across the water where it broke out of a dark pool. Still holding the light and hatchet, he bent over and buried his face in the stream, swishing and snaking his head in and out until all the sting of the night woods was gone, and then he drank, long and satisfyingly, while his heart settled back down.

He refused to think of anything but the smooth white stone as he followed the jerking flashlight beam up the creek path. Twice he tripped on cypress knees and fell onto the slick, leaf-covered trail, but he continued his momentum, forgetting about the mud and clinging vines and his aching toes and shin, and almost sooner than he thought possible found the place.

With believing hands, the boy probed deep into the slippery bowels of the hollow stump, fastened onto the discus-shaped stone, pulled it free, and in the diminishing glow of his flashlight scrubbed it with his shirt sleeve until the red vein burned through the black coating.

This was truth, solid and resolute—a stone occupying space, predictable and real as the universe itself, as undeniable as the stars and the very dirt he stood on. No faith necessary here, no wondering. He hefted the rock, cold and hard, as real as bone, and took it to the edge of the creek and knelt and dipped it into the water and sloshed and rubbed it with his fingers until even in the dark of the hollow he could see in his hands its dull glow. Satisfied, he leaned briefly against the stump, gathering strength, then turned back downstream, rock cradled in his left arm, left hand holding the flashlight against his chest. His right arm, thrust straight out before him and tipped with the hatchet blade, carried him forward down the path toward the end of the steadily failing light beam, toward home.

When he came at last to the place where the trail turned up from the creekbed onto the long slope out of Johnson's Hollow, he laid the flashlight, hatchet, and heavy rock in a neat pile beside the stream and dropped to his knees to wash his face and drink deeply for the trip home. *If it will only go right from here. If only I don't start believing now.* But the thought had only begun to clear from his mind, the last swallow of water halfway down his throat, when he heard from the impenetrable darkness of the woods across the creek the snarl or yowl or whatever it was, a sound that froze him as surely as if he had been doused with cold water from the stream at his knees. He hung in darkness in that awful stasis of incredible fear, which, though it lasts only a split second, seems to linger in an infinite embrace as the body slowly wakens to awareness and stirs its resources for battle or for flight.

And in an instant he was moving, rock and useless flashlight clutched to his left side, the hatchet waving before him as he charged up the slope. On the path or off no longer mattered to him. The safety of the treeless meadow was what he was after, that vast stretch of starlit rye where he could see what was before him and behind, where the sun and cattle would be lolling in a few hours. He fell in the wet leaves and mud, rose and surged again, his eyes closed against the stinging limbs and cobwebs. Time after time the underbrush and roots threw him to his knees, and he clawed up, flailing the hatchet at dark ropes of vines and branches that tried to hold him down.

When he reached the edge of the field, he didn't bother to stop and get his bearings to the other side, not caring so much anymore where he was running as long as he was running away from the thing in the hollow below. *It can't be him,* he kept thinking as he bounded across the meadow, *it can't be him, but it is something.* Somewhere near the middle of the dark sea of grass, legs watery and chest aflame, he plunged forward into the rye, whose cool wet calmed him. His breath came in shallow, inconsequential gasps. *At least here I can make a stand, here I can see him coming for me.* He rose to his knees and faced the line of dark trees behind, hatchet poised.

But nothing came, nothing moved in the grass, and there was no sound but an occasional night bird and the steady drumbeat of his heart. After a while he felt refreshed and reassured that nothing was pursuing, so he stood in the grass and broke into a long stride toward the woods at the other side of the meadow, aiming generally at a place where he might have come out of the woods. Striking the path just right would be difficult, but he would worry about that when he got there. Right now all that mattered was the running, the motion toward something and away, and the hard, undeniable fact of the stone.

Halfway across he stopped, thought a few seconds, then tried to bang the flashlight back to life. All he had to do was get to the edge of the woods and work his way back toward where he entered the meadow. His trail should be clear in the night-wet rye. The flashlight flickered, came to a dull orange glow, then flickered again and went out. *Then I will do without it.* So, flashlight shoved into his back pocket and rock clasped to his chest, he started running again, then slowed to a walk. He tried to see whether the stars gave him enough light to find his trail across the grass, but he could see nothing but the vast sea of grass on all sides.

He ran again, ran simply toward a place in the dark line of woods that looked right. He stopped from time to time and looked back toward where he had come from, to see whether he could judge the right direction to go, but nothing looked right anymore. There was the meadow and the woods surrounding it and that dome of stars, and he was lost, lost.

When finally he reached the woods, he walked along the edge of the field, still trying to spot his trail, to find something familiar, anything that would tell him which way to go. There had to be a field road somewhere, and it would lead him to civilization again, but he had no idea where.

He stood a few minutes looking in the general direction he had come from, then turned and aimed the hatchet before him and lunged into the woods. Sliding and tripping, bulling forward, he made the spongy bottom of the first hollow and churned through thick undergrowth to a point halfway up the other slope, where he collapsed, exertion and what he would have to admit was fear overwhelming him. He curled about the stone and hatchet and with what breath was left cursed the old man with the vilest, fiercest words he could remember. "And I do not," he closed his tirade, "believe in that Goddamned panther!"

He rose then and crossed into another bottom and clambered up the slope on the other side, falling again as he gained the ridge. He lay on his back in darkness, wrestling with his breath until he had calmed enough to think. Through the limbs overhead he could see the familiar constellations in their slow spin toward morning.

I am the son of a scientist, son of an engineer, and I do not believe in gods and ghosts and panthers in twentieth-century Alabama. I believe in natural laws, I know the constellations, I know the distance to the moon, I know what is real and imagined. And I know that if I had to, I could steer myself out of here by the stars.

Then he drew in a deep breath and said aloud, "You stupid shit. That's what you *should* have done. You should have determined your direction by the stars. Look ahead of you and go toward a certain star, then look back at the star you have come from. Remember the stars and steer by them, the way men have for centuries. I have been irrational this whole trip."

He sighed and stood up and turned completely around. "But I did not pick a star to steer by, and it is a fact that I am lost and without a light. The trail is hard to find and follow in the daytime, and I don't even have the moon. If I keep going ridge over ridge, I may hit something I know, I may run across the road, or I may miss the road and end up lost for days in Big Sandy Bottom way to the south." Recalling what the old man had told him so often about panic being the worst enemy of someone lost in the woods, he knelt and laid the rock, hatchet, and flashlight in a neat pile. "No. It is best to build a fire and stay here, and in the morning I will find the path and go on home."

And so he built a fire. Dragging up a heap of dead leaves and pine straw, which readily caught with his first match, the boy added layer upon layer of increasingly larger branches until the flames rose above his head. Hatchet ever at the ready in his free hand, he ventured deeper and deeper into the dark woods in all directions, dragging fallen limbs to his fire, which at times in his distant foraging was merely an unsteady burnish in the high limbs above it. He moved mechanically, mindlessly, not thinking now but *doing*, knowing that it was the only way. When you have thought through to your solution, you set to addressing it through action. In time he had a significant stack of firewood—enough, if he managed well, to hold him until dawn.

He spent the night sitting over the hatchet and rock at the edge of his fire, rising from it only to add fuel. Sounds came and went as the long hours stretched out, eyes appeared and disappeared at the edge of the glow. Possums or coons—he didn't know, didn't care. He tried not to look at them or think about them. Twice he rose to his knees, stirred from a drowse by some sound, and cocked the hatchet to defend himself, but the sound always went away, the eyes seemed to be just passing.

What dreaming there was to interrupt his pitiful little naps turned to the panther. A great black cat would leap toward him from rye grass, a dark shadow would fall from a tree limb, enormous yellow eyes would come closer and closer to his dying fire. And then, uncertain whether he had cried out in fear and awakened himself or some sound had come from beyond his circle of light, he would snap his head up from his chest, raise the hatchet in defiance, and, like a cornered animal set upon by a legion of pursuers, try to focus on what seemed to be the greatest threat—a rustle in the leaves, a pair of curious eyes, an indecipherable cry. But finally there was only the woods, the dark, tall, impenetrable woods on all sides, and overhead the whirling constellations, distorted and confused by the sparks shooting up from his fire. As the night wore on, he slept in longer stretches, comforted by the warm, snapping fire, which he poked to fresh flame and shoved more wood onto each time he awakened.

He wasn't certain what woke him at dawn, whether it was the brightness of the sky or the crescendo of bird sounds, but his eyes opened to the still-warm jumble of log ends that had been his fire and beyond them the hazy, wonderful woods of morning. Above him the sun was just tipping the hickories.

I have made it. The panther did not get me. Then he smiled and muttered, "The panther. That Goddamned panther."

When he rose to his knees, he could not immediately stand, his body soundly beaten and exhausted, but he didn't really have to. Time was on his side now, time and the sun, and there was no need to hurry. He sat back and looked about him in the steadily brightening woods, trying to remember the awful night before, the vines and roots, the brush, the unyielding trees, the jumble of sparks and stars, and the dreaming, the panther mixed and mingled with it all.

Then he stood and followed his clumsy trail back to the meadow, noting when he broke out of the trees the quite visible path across the rye. Judging that the way home was to his right, he walked along the edge of the woods, studying the grass until he found where he had come out of the woods. The rest was easy. Anyone could tell where he had run and fallen and stumbled and slid the night before. He couldn't have left a plainer trail with surveyor flags.

Even before he was quite out of the woods below the barn, the sun warm on his back, he could see the old man standing with his hand shading his eyes at the edge of the calf pen. The boy walked slowly, casually, as if what he cradled in his left arm were nothing more than a loaf of bread he had walked to Dowell's to get, as if he didn't really care when he got home with it, the day being just a nice spring day for walking. The old man saw him and started down the slope toward him.

"Couldn't make it in last night, huh?"

"Could have, probably, but the light went out and I didn't want to get scratched up in the dark."

"My God, boy, you're *all* tore up—"

"Didn't want to get scratched up in the dark and decided to camp. Here's your damned rock." He thrust the stone into the old man's hands when the two of them got close enough for the exchange. "And your hatchet and worthless flashlight." He handed them over like a soldier surrendering his weapons after the war is over and he no longer needs them. They turned and walked toward the house.

"Don't tell your grandma where you was last night—I told her you slept in the barn. When she asks you about the scratches, just tell her you take'n the dogs coon hunting before you went to bed. What you done is between you and me."

"Yessir."

"You hungry?"

"Yessir, PawPaw, real hungry," he answered. As he started up the steps to the kitchen, stopping to look back toward the woods, something—a buzzard or crow, something big and dark—flew across the sun.

J.P. and the Water Tower

"So Daddy told'm," J.P. said, flicking a long ash from his cigarette after nursing it until it seemed to be held up by air and made us nervous to look at, "that we'd paint that water tower and do it for a helluva lot less than they could get anybody else to do it."

"*Y'all* would paint it?" Potts slid down off the porch edge and eased between me and J.P., his mouth hanging open the way it always did when he heard something he couldn't quite believe. "*Y'all* would paint it? J.P., that water tower's . . . it's got to be four hundred feet up."

"Naw it ain't," J.P. said. He reached down and picked up a stick and broke it, his way of getting our attention, as if he didn't already have it, since we knew he could break our backbones just as easily. "It is exactly —" He breathed deep, let his breath out slow. "It is a hunderd and eighty-five feet from the tip of the lightning rod to the ground, as a dead crow would fall."

Potts started again. "You'd be just as dead if you fell a hundred and eighty-five feet or four hundred, just as dead as that crow."

"Which is how come I don't intend to fall." He broke the stick again and again, tossed the pieces out into the driveway, and stood up. "He told'm we'd paint it. He give his word. And, by God, we're gon' paint it, beginning tomorrow morning."

The best we could tell, J.P. was four years or so older than we were, around seventeen, though we never pressed him on his age, or background, or anything else he seemed reluctant to be bothered about. One of the few things we knew for certain was that late on New Year's Eve two years before, a light went on in the old Cox house, which hadn't had a higher life-form than roaches and rats living in it for as long as we could remember, and the next morning, the first day of the year, an old green car was blocked up in front and strange kids had their faces pressed to the windows.

The house was just down the dirt road from us, squatting like some sort of sat-on orange crate, a paintless old derelict dating from just before the First World War. It was as sway-backed as a worn-out field mule turned loose in the pasture to die. A dozen or so families over the years had left it so foul and in need of repair that we kids who haunted the road figured no one would ever live in it again. I'd go in sometimes and lie down on the floor on an old blanket I brought from the house and jerk off while studying a girl on a page torn from the bathing suit or women's underwear section of a Sears catalog. I knew nobody would disturb me in there, so I kept several different pages hidden in a closet. They stayed wrapped in the blanket.

And then the Joneses came: a man and woman and more children than we could learn the names of in a month, ranging from a toddler in saliva-stiff overalls to J.P. The kids were clumped together as if the old man had decided on a family, then against it, then for, then against, then for again. There were three too young for school, four between eight and twelve, and three several years older than we were: two bovine girls and J.P.

Our first encounter with him was not a very pleasant one. Accustomed to having the run of the road and all territory within five miles of it, including front and backyards, we simply nosed our bikes up to the old Cox place the morning after the Joneses moved in and started our appraisal of the new family, beginning with the green Buick, an old rusty leviathan propped up on cement blocks in the driveway with the wheels off and brake shoes removed. Barney Stutts, the most daring of us simply because as youngest member of the gang he had to take more chances to prove himself, had just crawled in behind the wheel to check the mileage and "give'r a feel" when a tall, lean, freckled boy or man—it was hard to tell—rounded the corner of the house with an armload of firewood.

"What you little sonsabitches doing around that car?"

Before we had a chance to answer, J.P. had two of us bleeding on the ground and Barney cowering in the backseat of the Buick, begging him not to swing.

From that inauspicious beginning came a friendship that only time and all the inscrutable forces that always rail against such relationships could, collectively, weaken. I had to sneak around to be with him, since my folks considered him dangerous white trash, but J.P. became for us a hero, a god —pagan, perhaps, but still a god—whose every word and action we lived by. It was he who taught us the meanings of all the terms we'd picked up over the years from older kids and bathroom walls, words that, though not clear in meaning, felt grown-up snapping off our tongues. He showed us how to light cigarettes in heavy wind, how to keep a deep draw of smoke down until we tingled with nicotine. Taught us to dive and jump off a high bridge into the river without breaking something or busting our balls or driving water right up into our brains, which he said he'd known people to do, and they ended up quads. How to fistfight, shoot a pistol, and steal watermelons without leaving traceable tracks in the field. How to drink beer or whiskey and then chew up and swallow green pine needles so your folks couldn't smell it on your breath. What he didn't teach us, we figured that we simply didn't need to know.

There was nothing J.P. did not excel at, from football, baseball, and swimming to carpentry and mechanics. Ah, but so much more than that, J.P., who had made it to the eighth grade and called off his education there, worked part-time at a service station in town and had money of his own and a pistol, a small .22 revolver, which he kept shoved down in one of his hip pockets. We knew that no matter what difficulty we found ourselves in, J.P. could save us, and we clung to him like a shadow.

I especially liked him since he knew what a girl's pussy looked and felt like, and he didn't mind giving me all the details I needed to get a pretty good idea what was behind those panties and bathing suits. He even helped me up in a tree outside the house one night so that I could watch one of his sisters undress. But she was so fat that I didn't see much more than a little blur of dark hair under a real pale belly that hung down like a cow's udder, the same way her boobs did. I saw more naked female flesh on that one girl that night than I would see over the next five years. He asked me one time whether that was my blanket with the Sears pages. He'd found them and hidden them in a shed out back and given them to me later. I guess he figured that was my stuff because of how I was always asking him about pussy, which I did not know a single thing about—only that it was something most boys who hadn't seen one would eagerly give up a nut to lay their eyes on and maybe be willing to die to actually put their peter in.

When he wasn't off in the woods or fields or on the river with us, or working at the service station, J.P. helped his father, a gimpy, ogrelike little man who never had a pleasant word for anyone. Outraged with his lot in life, but too incredibly sorry, white-trash sorry, to do much about it, he'd given several trades a chance—welding, carpentry, shipbuilding during the war, farming—but nothing ever *took*, as they say about salvation when it fails. Nothing ever suited him for long. A housepainter most of the time we knew him, the old man generally worked two full days a week, three if there was a wolf clawing at the door, and lay around the house drunk the rest of the time. We seldom saw him, and when we did, we never got close.

J.P.'s mother did some "sick and shut-in work," which we took to mean that she looked after the ill and elderly for a fee, and one of the hippo girls worked up on the highway at a Dairy Dip, which was the worst place in the world for someone in her general condition to work, being around French fries and milkshakes all the time. The other one managed the younger kids, which amounted to little more than making sure they didn 't starve to death or kill each other. From what we could tell, the Jones family just got by, and that was all.

When J.P. announced that day on the doorstep that his father had contracted to paint the water tower in Steens, we were not so much surprised as awed. And frightened. We knew that whatever role the old man had reserved for himself on that particular job, it would require him to have at least one foot on the ground—J.P. would be the one strung up there with ropes and straps nearly two hundred feet above our heads. As often as we could, we'd be right there in the shadow of that tank, squinting up at him, ready to do his bidding, even if it meant going up the ropes ourselves.

That was on a Sunday in mid-March. When we didn't see J.P. the next three afternoons—he was not at the service station and we didn't see him anywhere around the house, which, out of fear of his father, we rarely went near when J.P. wasn't in sight—we just assumed that the water tank job had started on schedule. We didn't see him at all that week. Though I tried repeatedly to talk Daddy into driving us to Steens, which was too far for a bicycle trip—on a gravel road especially, since it slows you down to turtle speed—he refused, insisting as always that being around *that Jones boy* was bad for us. We resolved that if we couldn't catch J.P. at home that Saturday morning and ride over with him and the old man, we'd pedal the ten or fifteen miles, whatever it was, whatever it took. I knew we'd be damned sick of gravel by the time we got there, and then we'd have to make that long trip back.

Before the sun had cleared the trees Saturday morning, we were easing up the driveway toward J.P.'s house. A ribbon of smoke curled from the kitchen flue—that meant someone was stirring. One of the dogs, his tail wagging in recognition, ran out to meet us. The old Buick was drawn up near the front porch, where someone was sitting with his legs sprawled out onto the steps. A white blanket, or shawl, or something was spread over one leg.

We stopped halfway up the drive. "Is that J.P.?" Potts whispered.

I squinted in the early light. "Looks like him."

"J.P., that *you*?" Barney yelled, running ahead. "Lord, what happened to your *leg*?"

J.P. waited until the three of us were standing before him, our eyes fixed on the long, lumpy cast exiting from his split jeans at the hip and running the length of his right leg. "I fell off that water tower," he answered flatly.

"Aw, God, J.P.," Potts breathed reverently, "aw, God." It sounded almost like a prayer.

"Quit using the Lord's name in vain, Goddamn it," J.P. said.

"Does it hurt?" Stutts reached down to touch the cast.

"Naw," J.P. reassured him. "Itches like a sonofabitch up in there. The onliest way I can scratch is run a piece of baling wahr down in there. You can touch it, maybe write something on it later."

As the sun wormed up out of the trees behind us, we quizzed him about the accident. How'd it happen? Weren't there safety ropes? Did he fall from the very top, or off one of the ladders? Did he hurt anything else? How does it feel to land from a fall like that?

He handled the questions, one at a time, with the assurance of a warrior detailing some grand battle, pausing now and then to adjust the heavy cast on the steps. When he was through, he rose awkwardly to his feet and, with the aid of a crutch, hobbled toward the rear of the house, motioning us to follow. "Come on. I want to show you something."

In the leaning shed behind the house, where nothing had been parked in years, since nobody we'd known who lived on the Cox place drove anything worth keeping out of the weather, sat a red motorcycle. We stood wordless as J.P., like a used-car salesman, pointed out the features of the machine, concluding with, "Naw, it ain't new, but it's been took care of and it's sure better'n what I had before, which was nothing."

"Gimme a ride, J.P.," Barney begged, but Potts and I looked at each other and then at the long, stiff cast and shook our heads.

"Nope," J.P. said sadly, "I can't even crank it very well right now, and the cast drags when I try to ride it, but soon's the cast comes off, I'll ride y'all all over the county."

"Aw, J.P., can't you push it and start it?" Barney would not give up. "Maybe one of us could kick it for you." His eyes dwelled longingly on the bike, strayed to the cast, then eased back to the bike. "Aw, J.P."

"Hey, I'm sorry, but there ain't much I can do about it right now. "Y'all just wait'll my cast is off—"

"Aw shit, J.P." Barney was inconsolable.

"Look, I done told you . . ."

"Naw, J.P., it ain't just that you can't ride us." Barney looked at me, then Potts, and I understood finally what he was trying to say, what I'd been feeling since J.P. told us about the fall, what I guessed Potts was feeling too. "It's just that you . . . ," he tried. "It ain't like you to fall off *nothing*, and here you are, you can't play ball or swim or even crank your motorcycle."

"Yeah, J.P.," Potts picked it up, "how could *you* fall off that water tower?"

On the way back to the house it must have dawned on J.P. what we were feeling: not disappointment over not getting a ride on the motorcycle, but a numbing realization that our own Superman could fall out of the sky and break his leg. Our lanky god, who could climb trees like a monkey and walk logs with the balance of a cat, had clumsily fallen from the ladder of a water tower and was so helpless we had to pace ourselves so that he could keep up. He stood a long while looking at us, the rising sun throwing his shadow across the driveway, then said finally, "All right, all right, Goddamn it, y'all come with me."

"Where y'all going, Jay?" Mrs. Jones yelled from the back porch as we started off across the field behind the house. "You ain't had your breakfast yet."

"I'll eat d'reckly," J.P. yelled back, and we followed him slowly to the edge of the creek that cut across the back corner of the Cox place. He looked over his shoulder toward the house a couple of times, then stopped us. "This is far enough." He swung his cast around and settled onto a stump.

"What is it, J.P.?" Potts asked. "Why'd we come down here?"

"Y'all just set down and shut up and listen, and I better not hear that none of this ever got out. You understand? You ain't to repeat *any* of this. If I hear tell about it from anybody at all, I will know that one of you said something, because the only people that knows is Momma and me and Daddy, and you could cut our balls off and feed'm to the hogs and we wouldn't say nothing. If it gets out, I will find out which one of you squealed, and I will beat your ass to bones and butter. Do you understand me?" He looked at each of us, hard.

"Sure, yeah, J.P.," I assured him, "not a word." The others nodded.

"Everthang but that about your balls being eat by the hogs," Barney said.

"What the fuck are you talking about?"

"You said that you and your momma and daddy knows about it and that if somebody cut off your balls and fed'm to the hogs you wouldn't tell . . ."

"So what the—"

"Your momma has got balls?"

"Stutts, you stupid little shit, I can't worry about ever little detail when I'm trying to explain something to y'all. All right, her *titties,* our *balls.* The point is, the three of us knows, and we ain't gon' tell. Now can I get on with it?"

"But why would a hog eat—"

I looked at him hard. "Barney, shut the hell *up!* Hogs will eat *anything.*"

J.P. looked sternly at us again. "I mean it. If it ever gets out, I'll break your Goddamned little necks."

We nodded again, looking at one another, knowing that this was important: J.P. just didn't talk much, and here he was settling us down like a grandfather drawing the family close for some deep dynastic secret. Well, maybe the grandfather analogy is a little soft. Maybe like a *godfather.*

"Arright, now, listen. I never fell off no water tower. You know I ain't that clumsy."

"But how—"

"Shut up, Potts—I said *listen.* My leg is broke all right, in two places, one above the knee and one below, but I never fell off nothing. Here's what happened." We drew closer as he looked once about him and returned his gaze to the house.

"Daddy contracted to paint that water tower, but he never intended to paint it—he just wanted the contract. He's been paid to paint, let's see, six water towers over here in Missippi and three over in Alabama, and he ain't painted water tower *one* yet. Maybe a little bit up on the legs of a couple, but he ain't never *finished* one."

"I don't see—" Potts tried to break in, but J.P.'s look silenced him.

"He don't play this card till things get real tough, like they are now—it's been a bad winter on us—and then he lays it on the table."

He hesitated, sweeping his eyes about us, letting the mystery swell and deepen, then resumed. "He says it's the only easy money he ever makes, these water tower jobs. House painting ain't for shit."

"How's he do it, J.P.?" he let me ask. "How's he not paint the water towers and still get paid?" It was the question he wanted.

"Well, my daddy may be a little guy and he may drink too much, but he's got guts and brains enough to fill a washtub. Guts anyway. He'll drive around the county we happen to be living in, looking for some little ol' popcorn-fart town, like Steens, that has a ratty-looking water tower that needs painting, one you can't even read the town name on anymore because of rust and bird shit and all the crap that high school kids have painted on it, and he'll ask when they planning on having that sorry-ass water tower painted. He'll start off with somebody at the drugstore or barbershop and sooner or later end up talking with the mayor or a city councilman. Then they'll whine around about how broke the town is and how much they had to pay to have it painted last time, whatever century that might of been in, and what a sorry job the guy did. When Daddy finds out exactly what they paid, he'll make his offer.

"Daddy's bid is always so low and he acts so—well, like he couldn't give a rat's ass whether they accept it or not—that they figure they better grab that fool while they can. So the mayor makes a coupla phone calls and they end up shaking hands. Then Daddy goes out and takes a close look at the water tower."

"J.P.," Potts interrupted, "this don't explain your broke leg."

"Naw, but it will. Just hold onto your balls a little. All right, the next day me and Daddy start in stringing ropes all over the tower, making it look like we got a whole crew of scrapers and painters coming in. Meanwhile, what he's really doing is studying the legs. Some of'm you got to climb up the braces on the legs, but most of'm has got ladders. He goes up the ladder or leg, checking the rivets or bolts, whatever's holding the straps on."

"What straps?" Barney asked.

"The straps, the steps—they're usually just little flat bars of metal riveted or bolted onto the legs to where you can climb the tower. They got to have a way to get up there, just like they got to have some way to get down. Sometimes they're welded, but he ain't run across but one like that."

"He's making sure the steps are on good, huh?" I think Potts asked.

"Naw. Naw. He's looking for one that's *loose*. And if he don't find one, he's got to loosen one hisself. I seen him one time, up north of here, just outside Tupelo, work three nights hand-runnin' trying to worry a rivet out, but he done it."

"But why's he—"

"Hang on, Goddamn it, Potts. I'm doing the telling here. You just listen. Arright, once he finds or gets a strap loose, he's set up to play his card. Me and him'll go home that night and then get up real early the next morning and get to the water tower long before anybody else is stirring, and even if anybody's out that early, it's too dark for'm to see what we're doing. We get the car up close as we can, and I help drag him over to the bottom of the ladder."

"*Drag* him over?" I asked. "What's wrong with him?"

"Hell, his leg is broke."

Potts gave him his old now-that-don't-make-a-lick-of-sense look. "How'd he break his *leg?*"

"Well, just before we go into town that morning, I drive the car over one of his legs, whichever one he figures can take it best. He just lays down in front of one of the wheels and I drive over one of his legs. Sometimes I have to do it twice if it don't break the first time."

A silence settled on our little group, each of us looking at the other, then at J.P. Finally Barney moaned, "Aw, God, J.P."

J.P. gave him a look.

"You drive that big old car over your daddy's *leg?*" Potts was standing there with his mouth open.

"Let me finish. OK, with his leg fresh broke, we go on into town, and I help him to the bottom of the ladder and lay him out like he's done fell. Then at the first sign of life in town, I run up the street yelling that my daddy's fell off the water tower and broke hisself up bad. I bang on doors and holler for a doctor. In no time at all half the town's around the bottom of that tower, and people are trying to help Daddy, and me pointing up at that catty-wampus strap and yelling about the ladder being broke.

"Daddy's usually got his leg in a cast by lunchtime, so he walks, the best he can, right down the middle of main street to the mayor's office, swearing all the time about that defective ladder. By the time he's through raving and waving his crutch around and threatening to sue the town, the mayor's ready to give him just about anything to shut him up and get rid of him. Daddy gets the contract money and generally walks away with damages, or at least the promise of'm, and ain't no doctor yet had the gall to ask for a penny. The town always pays—they don't want to get sued."

"But what about painting the tower?" I asked.

"Hell, Daddy never intended to paint no water tower. He just tells'm that he wouldn't be caught dead climbing around on something as dangerous as that old tower and that they ought to just go ahead and tear it down before it hurts somebody else."

"He gets all that money and don't even have to paint the tower . . . ," Potts whispered. His eyes were wide with wonder.

"He figures the broke leg is worth the labor of painting a water tower. We ain't painted one yet, and we ain't come away with less than the contract money but once. Over in Louisiana, in some little old French-sounding town not far from the state line, the mayor give Daddy a ten-dollar bill and told him to go ahead and sue—the town didn't have shit they could lose anyhow, except maybe the tower, which he could have if he could tote it off. Then there was one time just northwest of Aberdeen that a doctor said the broke leg looked like it had been run over by a car, but he finally give in and said it *could* of been broke in a fall, mainly because he couldn't believe that anybody would be stupid enough to let somebody drive over their leg with a car.

"But one time we got the contract money, which was five hundred dollars, and two thousand for damages. That's the best it's ever come out. God, we lived good that year."

"How long's he been doing it?" Barney asked him, grinning, his eyes shining the way they always did when he was immensely impressed.

"Since I been old enough to reach the pedal and see over the steering wheel at the same time."

"You mean ever time y'all pulled that, you had to drive the car over your daddy's leg?" I asked.

"Yep, all but one." He pointed to his cast. We all looked down at it.

"You mean—" I leaned down over to touch it.

"You ever noticed how crippled he is? In both legs? They's a pin in one of'm over a foot long, the other one's just barely hanging together. When he take'n that Steens job, he done it without thinking things out. We talked it over and decided it wasn't worth him maybe not walking again, but he'd already give his word, shook on it, and we needed the money bad, so we had to go thoo with it."

"Give his *word*? But, J.P."

"That's right, Potts, he give his word, he contracted to paint the water tower, and there wasn't nothing to do but go ahead and do it."

Potts persisted: "But if he wasn't going to paint it anyway . . ."

"That ain't the Goddamned point. It was a matter of honor with him. He's a lot of bad things, my daddy is, but being dishonorable ain't one of'm."

Barney pointed to the cast. "So he made you let him break your leg?"

"Naw, I volunteered. It was the only thing to do. That, or maybe actually paint that water tower, which neither one of us has got any idea how to do."

"You mean you just laid down in the driveway and let him drive that big old Buick over your leg?" Barney's voice was just above a whisper.

"Twice. But not in the driveway. We done it down the road, to where the others wouldn't see. Like I said, Momma knows about it, but the kids don't. He figures they wouldn't understand. He drove it over my calf, but it didn't feel broke to me, so he backed up and come across above the knee. I heard it snap that time. When the doctor set my leg, he found out that it was broke twice, above *and* below the knee, which made it even better. Daddy figures we got a few hundred more for that double break."

"Lord, J.P." Barney slowly shook his head as he looked at the cast.

J.P. gave him a hard look. "I have told you about taking the Lord's name in vain."

"How much did y'all get altogether?" Potts asked.

"Well, the contract money come to something over four hundred and they sending us a check for twelve-hundred more. And they paid the doctor bill."

"And all you're getting is a motorcycle?"

"Potts, what you understand about right and wrong wouldn't fill the end of a fucking rubber. I'm talking *fam-i-ly*. I let him break my leg because he was planning to have his leg broke again until I talked him out of it. He would of let me mash one of them gamey legs of his for the family, and he was ready to do it, knowing he might not ever walk again."

"God, J.P." Potts's reverent utterance echoed over and over as we walked slowly behind him back to the house. I doubt that we would have noticed if he had reversed the two deities. I tried to step where J.P. did, my tennis shoe settling loosely into his boot print the way my hand always seemed to drop into one of my father's gloves. I looked back and saw that Potts and Barney were doing the same thing. On one side of our trail there was a confusion of tracks, punctuated now and then with cast-peg and crutch depressions—on the other, one big boot print after another, straight and deliberate, cluttered with the treads of our shoes.

The Day J.P. Saved the South

On a Monday morning in 1962, the fall James Meredith brought Mississippi to the point of mania by enrolling at Ole Miss, we sprawled on the high shoulder of Highway 45 North just outside Columbus and watched the federalized National Guard units heading toward Oxford: boys from towns to the south—Meridian, Macon, Lauderdale—in long olive-drab strings of jeeps and trucks and trailers rolling to the north and the showdown we'd dreamed for years would come. Some of us nearly high school age, some much younger, we were charged with a patriotic fervor we found heartening and at the same time frightening, as so many emotions at that age are. We waved and yelled and swung our Confederate flags. Pale faces grinned from the open ends of troop trucks, hands waved back, and an occasional rebel flag whipped from an antenna.

"The goverment may think them boys are Federals now," Billy Stevens observed, "but when the bullets start flying, they'll be hitting niggers and yankee agitators, bet your ass. Them's Rebel troops there, by God, and if they didn't figure they was going up there to help the South, they wouldn't be going at all."

"Reckon they got real bullets?" Barney Stutts's eyes were wide with excitement.

"I expect so," somebody behind me said. We all nodded.

"I still don't see why they're going up there," Potts continued. "If the goverment figures them boys there are going to pertect that nigger from them Ole Miss boys, they're crazy."

"I guess they're more worried about outside agitators stirring up things," I answered, "yankees and them Northern niggers down here to egg Meredith on. They figure folks from Ole Miss and Oxford are going to raise hell."

Barney swelled. "And you can bet, by God, that they're right—they'll hang that nigger and all his agitator friends."

"Boy, it's gon' be exciting," a small voice came from behind.

The next morning word spread that the Columbus unit was mobilized and would be moving out before dark. We were gathered outside the cyclone fence surrounding the armory by noon—excitement having built to the point that our teachers simply threw up their hands and said that those who needed to go on home could go for the afternoon—watching the trucks being loaded with racks of M-1's and carbines, duffel bags, tents, and kitchen gear. An air of nervous excitement pervaded the compound: Officers shouted commands and enlisted men scurried about, swearing and laughing, joking about Negroes and Northern agitators and the federal government.

We knew several of the younger soldiers, fellows just a few years older than we were, two or three just out of high school. J.P. was one of them. He hadn't been in the Guard but about a month—he was afraid he was going to be drafted, he said. Besides, he made some extra money. We yelled at him a few times, but he ignored us, dogged as everybody was by the officers, who knew that for the unit to be on the road by dark some real ass kicking had to be done. Finally, during a lull in the loading, J.P. walked over to where we clung to the fence, a cigarette dangling cockily from the corner of his mouth.

"What you little shits doing up here?" He pushed the brim of his steel helmet up at a jaunty angle.

"What you wearing your steel pot for, J.P.?" Potts asked him. "Figger you gon' get shot at by a nigger?"

"Never know. The officers said get used to wearing the damn things. Hell, did y'all know that somebody shot at one of the Guard colyums just outside Oxford yesterday? They never seen who it was—got everybody nervous."

"Boy, J.P.," Stutts stammered, "I wish we could go with y'all."

"Naw, this ain't the same thing as going swimming or fishing—this is serious stuff. You ain't big enough to *tote* a M-1, much less shoot one."

"Y'all got real bullets, J.P.?" somebody asked.

"Yeah. I seen some boxes of ammo in the back of one of the trucks. We going loaded for bear."

"You mean coons, don't you?" Potts asked.

"Yeah, coons."

"Hot damn," Stutts sputtered, "real bullets in them M-1's. I hope you get you a nigger."

"Well, I ain't shooting nothing *but* niggers or yankees, no matter what the goverment or the officers say—bet yer ass on that."

"How's it feel to be a bluebelly, J.P.?" Potts ribbed.

"How do you figure it'd feel getting your asshole kicked up around your neck, you little fart?"

"Just kidding, J.P., you know I was just kidding."

"Well, Goddamn it, don't—this ain't to be kidded about."

"Hey, Jones," a sergeant bellowed, "get your ass in that kitchen and help them boys get them stoves loaded."

"Yeah, OK, I'm coming."

"Hey, J.P.," Potts said, "that's old Sam Sturgis, works at the county dump. You gon' let him order you around?"

"He's a sergeant, and I ain't. When we get back and outta uniform, let him try. Well, look, I better get on over there. You little shits take it easy and keep the home fars a-burning. We'll get this over with real quick and be back." He turned and double-timed through one of the big armory doors, and we sat down at the edge of the fence to while away the afternoon. We wanted to be there to wave them off when they started north. Judging by the crowd that was gathering, lots of other folks had the same thing in mind.

Just before the last of the sun skipped off the courthouse roof, the lead jeep left the main gate, followed by a column of other jeeps and troops trucks, tankers, trailers, and an ambulance.

"Can you see J.P.?" someone shouted at me as we loped alongside the convoy, which roared up the street to the square, took a hard left, and strung on out Main to Highway 45 North.

"Not yet," I said breathlessly, elbowing ahead of the others, struggling to get through the thickening crowd of townspeople so I could be on the courthouse corner when the troop trucks passed. It seemed the whole town was there, shouting, waving, whipping rebel flags in the charged evening air.

"There he is!" Potts panted as he and the others caught up at the corner. "There's ol' J.P."

He was pointing to a troop truck just turning onto Main. All the guys in the truck were waving and yelling, so I couldn't tell for certain whether I had seen J.P. or not. I pretended that I had.

"Hot damn, ol' J.P.'s going off to war, the lucky bastard."

Stutts was beside himself, dancing on one foot, then the other, with saliva stringing out of the corners of his mouth.

"Yeah, them lucky bastards," someone else said. In the fading light the trailing National Guard ambulance disappeared off toward the highway. A sobering silence settled on the crowd as we watched our warriors heading north. Not one of us would have dared suggest that the collective feeling was anything less than the pride and fear our predecessors must have felt a hundred years before when the boys in gray rode off toward the dusky north and whatever fate awaited.

J. P. Jones had long been a hero of ours, probably as much as anything else because he was a successful high school dropout with a job and pistol of his own, which he carried in a hip pocket wherever he went. Besides, he was the best athlete we'd ever known.

He never played on the school football teams because the coaches couldn't do a thing with him, but he could catch a football better than anyone else I ever knew and throw one better than most college quarterbacks: Those big freckled hands were made for a football. And if anybody ever threw a baseball harder, we never knew about it. Nobody ever hit one of his pitches—nobody that we ever knew of—unless J.P. wanted it hit to see what the fielders could do with it.

He lived half a mile or so down the gravel road from our house, down Sand Road that is, which looked like its name suggested it ought to look. Most of the kids down Sand Road were tough and poor—J.P. was just the toughest and the poorest. He was several years older than the rest of us who hung around together, but he spent a lot of time with us since there was nobody else his age in the neighborhood. Oh, there was Herbert Newell, but he was an indisputable queer. After J.P. had beaten him up twice, he said the *dicksucker* liked it so much he wasn't about to do it again.

Daddy told me emphatically not to hang around with J.P., which just added to the mystique, of course.

"That boy's bigger'n y'all and mean, and I don't want you having nothing to do with him," he told me periodically.

"You can look in that boy's face and just see meanness working away—the pure-dee devil," my mother added.

Grandmother, my mother's mother, who lived with us, always had something to tack on: "His folks ain't nothing but no-counts neither. Plumb trash. His daddy dranks and smokes like a freight train, and ain't none of them never seen the inside of a church more than twice in their life, if that much. Lard asses, his momma and them two girls. Sorry is whut they are. Trash. Ever day of their life. Dog dookey sorry."

"Momma . . ." It was Mother cautioning her about using bad language in front of me. Oh, bad language *really* bothered me. Yes indeed, right to my spiritual core.

Now, grandmother was what bothered me. I mean, there were things about her that would just drive me crazy. If I ever needed to curb a hard-on in church or some other inappropriate place, all I'd have to do was think about her, and it would shrivel like a snail in a handful of salt. Things like this: She would use a term like *dookey* or *dooky* or however the hell it is spelled—it's not in a dictionary—when she just might as well have said *shit,* since you can mix them up in a pile and you can't tell one from the other. Then I'd think about this: What can be sorry about dog shit, since dogs have to shit like every other living thing, one way or another? Birds shit, bugs shit, the pretty girl in class that you know you are never gonna get to kiss, much less see naked, has to shit. You take a load on, you gonna lay a load off—a little lighter maybe, but you gonna offload. This is natural law I'm talking about here. Only ghosts get a pass, but they don't *eat.* I just thought that *shit* got a bad rap, being as it was so natural. There were all kinds of things she said that didn't make sense. Like not giving a dead rat's ass about something. How does a dead rat's ass—or a *live* rat's ass— figure into anything? But I always just bit both my lips, almost to the bleeding point, to keep from saying something that would get me in trouble with Daddy.

"He sure can play ball" was my usual retort, depending on Daddy's mood. Sometimes he just wasn't in the mood to discuss things like that, and I knew that one word more than he wanted would result in the *flap, flap, flap* of the Bible Belt coming off and then *my* ass was dead.

"Ain't nobody arguing that," Daddy always said, when he was in a debating mood, "but he ain't going nowhere with it because they don't have professional ball teams in the penitentiary, which is where he's headed faster'n any freight you ever saw."

"Him and his daddy," Grandmother helped. "And prolly that sorry-ass momma, who you can just bet steals stuff from them sick and shut-ins she works for."

God, she was a mean woman. I'll bet the undertaker took two extra hours to make her face look pleasant enough for viewing, like anybody'd want to see her, unless it was one of us kids, who'd have been damned happy to see her in a casket.

"And maybe them twin cows he calls his sisters. I bet you anythang that the one that works at the Dairy Dip steals ice cream by the gallon. Onliest reason she ain't been caught is she's got it inside her when she leaves."

I just glared at her. She was, after all, talking about the only girl I'd ever seen naked.

"You just keep away from him," Mother warned.

So I did stay away from J.P. just as long as I possibly could, usually about a full day. I'd be comfortably sprawled out on the front porch or lying on the ridge of the chickenhouse with my .22 to kill rats when somebody down the road would come running up, yelling, "Here comes J.P.!" That would do it. I'd check to see whether anyone in the house had me in sight, and if they didn't, I'd fall in with the troupe panting at his heels. Whether we went off into Jim Ward's pasture to play ball or struck off across the fields to the river didn't matter: We were with J.P., and all was well with the world.

No one ever managed to figure out what the J.P. stood for. He certainly never volunteered an explanation, and none of us—not even Potts—dared ask him.

"Maybe it stands for John Paul," I ventured one evening while I was sitting on the back porch with the family shelling peas, "you know, John Paul Jones."

"Could, I reckon," Daddy said, "but there ain't nothing special in that. Maybe it's James Peter or Joseph Phillip. . . . "

"None of them names," Grandmother piped. "All them's Bible names, and none of his folks ever read it."

"I don't remember no Phillip in the Bible," I said. Then: "Naw, Daddy —I mean, maybe he's named after John Paul Jones."

"Who's that?" Grandmother asked.

"Yeah," Daddy said, "we supposed to know who that is? He a politician?"

"Aw, y'all don't know nothing about history. John Paul Jones was a naval hero in the Revolutionary War."

"That the Silver War?" Grandmother asked.

"*Civil!*" I slammed my handful of unshelled peas down into the bowl. "You have never got that right in your entire life. It is the *Civil* War, not the *Silver* War!"

"Quit yelling at Momma like that," Daddy said.

"She ain't *your* momma. Why you keep calling her Momma when she's *Mother's* momma?"

"At's what I've always called her."

"And you call Momma Momma and *your* momma Momma too. Sometimes it gets confusing is all."

"How can it be confusing, since my actual momma ain't here but your momma's momma is? Who would I be calling Momma but her?"

"Sometimes you call Mother Momma too. That's how it gets confusing. You call three people Momma, and I'm always supposed to know which one you're talking about?"

"Well, I don't give a dead rat's ass—"

Mother interrupted to turn the heat down. "So you are talking about the War Between the States?"

"Aw, God, y'all are so d-d-d-d. . . ." I wasn't stuttering. My mouth was just trying really hard to keep from saying *dumb.*

"Don't you swear, boy," Daddy snapped. "It's been a long time since we was in school, and we can't remember everthang. Now what war you talking about?"

"The American Revolution, the war we fought to get free from England, to throw off the yoke of George."

"What yoke?" Grandmother asked.

Then Daddy: "George who?"

I started to turn and look at her but I just couldn't—it was too much like looking into a bucket with nothing in it. You're expecting apples or peaches or maybe some kind of nuts, but it's just a bucket full of nothing. You know that feeling? So I let the yoke business go. "Just George, *King* George," I said to the dark yard, where lightning bugs were zipping around all over the place. "He didn't have a last name—that I know of. He was the third or fourth George, but I don't remember which." I swear to God that I never understood how the three of them lived as long as they did. Nature just usually won't let mistakes like that go long without correction. It's a thousand and twelve wonders I turned out even *half* sane.

"And didn't nonna them have last names?" The old lady shook her head. She was behind me, but the light from the kitchen threw her shadow out into the yard. "Them are strange people over there. How in the Lord's name can you keep everybody straight without they got last names?"

"His name don't matter. But John Paul Jones *did* have a last name and he was an officer in *our* Navy, and he was a hero. He said something like 'Damn the torpedoes, run right over'm' or *thoo*'m,' something like that. Everybody remembers that."

"Stop cussing," Daddy said. "I don' told you about that."

"But—"

"I don't remember nothing like that," Grandmother mumbled. "Never heard that in my life. And why," she continued, "would that pair of heathern name the boy after somebody famous, especially since neither one of them has got more years of school than they got real teeth?" She pushed her glasses way back on the bridge of her nose the way she always did when she wanted to look somebody in the eyes and get a straight answer.

"Like you got . . . ," I started, then thought better of it. I'd already pushed my luck with Daddy. "Well, maybe somebody in his family was in the Navy, maybe somebody real important."

"The closest that trash has ever been to water is the Luxapalila," Grandmother shot back. "And you can bet that wudn't to be *baptized.*"

"Yeah," Mother followed, "and the onliest boat any of them has been in was one loaded with moonshine or something they stole that they was hauling from one bank to the other."

I bristled. "For all *y'all* know, his folks came over on the *Mayflower* with the rest of the Pilgrims."

Grandmother snorted. "If they was on that boat, they was chained or in cages down in the belly with the goats and sheeps and chickens, and you can bet they wasn't turnt aloose until everybody else got off their belongings. That bunch woulda stole everbody *blind* and probably took them animals."

I didn't say anything else, just set to my bucket of peas with a vengeance. I never in my whole life could argue successfully with those three, set as they were in their ways. And me already with more education than the three of them put together and probably with more teeth.

When the Guard unit returned in mid-November, we were there, of course, waiting to welcome the boys home. They seemed glad to be back. Except for a few days and nights of tension, the whole trip for them had been mildly boring.

Sam Blevins summarized the mobilization: "We camped on a hill this side of Oxford, about ten miles out. Had a regular camp, like any other bivouac—slept in tents, ate Army chow, crapped in trenches, and set around on our butts. Never seen no action a-tall. Wudn't nothing but backup troops, in case things got bad and we was needed."

"Y'all get any real bullets?" Stutts asked. We had cornered Blevins at his truck when we couldn't find J.P., who apparently slipped off somehow and avoided having to help unload. Blevins drove a delivery truck for one of the big furniture stores in town.

"Shit naw, we didn't get no ammo. We never even got M-1's except when we was on guard duty, M-1's and bayonets and no bullets. J.P. had real bullets, though." He knew that would get our attention.

I looked him in the eye. "J.P. had real bullets?"

"Hell, he take'n that damn pistol with him—of course he had ammo for it. He carried that pistol in his hind pocket the whole time."

"Jesus," Potts whispered with adulation. "He carried that pistol the whole time y'all was up there?"

"Yep. Said if we got attacked, he wudn't going to be caught standing in line waiting for a rifle and bullets."

"He never used it, did he?" Bobby Shelton asked.

"Naw—never seen nothing to use it on. But he would of." Blevins threw his duffel bag into the back of his pickup and got in to leave. "Gotta get on home. Got pussy waiting on me. You boys behave yerselves."

"We *bein'* hayve," Potts said.

"Hot damn, that J.P." was all I could say, "that damn J.P."

After laying out of school a while, J.P. took a job at George Studdard's Gulf station just off the square, pumping gas, changing oil, greasing cars, cleaning up, doing all the things that George and Buddy Yeager, his mechanic, wouldn't do unless traffic got so heavy that they had to. He worked from noon until ten o'clock six days a week, then walked or rode his bicycle the five miles home or hitched a ride with somebody. Had a motorcycle for a while, but he tore it up in a wreck.

It wasn't much of a job, J.P. admitted, but it sure as hell beat school. He said he reckoned if he could hang around long enough, someday he'd own that station, or one like it. Then he'd close off a portion of the garage and put in a sandwich shop and serve the kind of sandwiches that people really go for, the kind they eat at home—you know, like grilled cheese, pimento cheese, tomato, fried egg, egg salad, tuna salad, pineapple, banana, baloney, Spam, sardine, peanut butter and jelly, even straight mayonnaise sandwiches. What he called the *sandwiches of the people*. Hamburgers and hotdogs too. Gonna call it J.P.'s Home-Grown Sandwiches. Said he'd get filthy rich. J.P. always did have a dream.

In the summer of '63, a year after the mobilization, he was still working at the Gulf station: same duties, same pay, same hours. The only difference was that from time to time George would have to be off somewhere, and Buddy would be out for the day or on a wrecker call, and J.P. would be left in charge of the station.

"Yep, I'm the boss." He'd swell out his chest and rare back in George's chair, prop his feet on the Coke box. He'd let us do little things, unimportant things, like pick up oil cans or sweep the office out or hose down the pump island. We loved it, and two or three afternoons a week we'd walk to the station right after school and hang around just as long as we could before we had to get on home, often as not having to walk the entire distance out to Sand Road. Some Friday or Saturday nights we'd talk our folks into letting us ride our bikes to the movies, and we'd go by the station and ride out with J.P. afterwards. All he had for transportation was a bicycle too, but he talked a lot about saving his change and buying another motorcycle, which he pronounced *motorsickle* or called a *motorbike*.

"Why ain't you ever bought a car?" I asked him one night while we were striding out away from the lights of town.

"Not me. I see enough of them thangs at the station. I wouldn't be saving nothing if I had a car. Since I tore up my motorbike—that asshole that run over me ain't paid up yet—I ain't really cared about vehicles. I'll just keep walking and riding my bicycle. Keeps me lean and mean." He patted the bulge in his pocket. "Gonna get me another motorbike, though."

The July Sunday it happened, J.P. wasn't even supposed to be working. He never worked on Sunday. It wasn't anything religious, since he was about as religious as your average hog. Things were just slow at the station on Sundays, so usually George let Buddy and J.P. off. Sunday was our one good day with him. Just as soon as we'd gotten home from church—something we escaped only if we were deathly ill—and eaten and changed clothes, we were out to find J.P. It was either football or basketball the cooler months or baseball or fooling around on the river in the summer. What else could there have been in those days for us?

That particular Sunday we passed J.P. on the way home from church. He had a lunch bag and was striding out toward town like he was madder than hell.

"There's that sorry-ass Jones boy," Daddy pointed out.

"Prolly going to steal something," Grandmother said. She muttered something about dog dookey. . . .

"Or gamble and drink beer," Mother added. It was like all three of them had to say something about J.P. every time *one* of them said something, like they were parts of a chorus. And it was always in that order: Daddy sang bass, Grandmother sang tenor, then Mother would join right in there. It irritated the shit out of me, but I just crossed my eyes and held my breath until I almost passed out, which was one way of dealing with it.

When his folks told us after we'd eaten that George had called him in to work, four of us kids decided to go up and spend the afternoon with J.P. Sunday without him just wouldn't be Sunday.

When we got to the station a little over an hour later, J.P. was characteristically sprawled in that chair, feet up on the Coke box, an old G.E. oscillating fan beating back the sheen of sweat that would have been on his face in an instant without that current of air. It was a dreadfully hot day, high humidity, full sun, and not so much as a random breeze. J.P. used George's key to the box and got us a Coke each and we sat on the concrete office floor in range of the fan sweep, content to wear out the afternoon. It was probably as cool a place as there was in the county— outside that spring-fed Cold Hole or down on the river, which was where we would all have been, J.P. concluded, if George hadn't called him in.

"He sick or what, J.P.?" Potts asked.

"Naw, he ain't sick. He's off farting around at the drag races. They opened that new track over there near Gordo. If I was gon' open up a new drag-racing track, it sure as hell wouldn't be at Gordo, which sounds like one of them big lumps women get on their necks. Here I am working on Sunday for almost nothing and him out jacking around at them Goddamned races at *Gordo*—there won't be four cars in here the whole afternoon, and two of them won't want no gas. Just need to piss or something."

"Where is Gordo at anyhow?" I asked him.

He shrugged. "Damn if I know. On 82 somewhere between here and Tuscaloosa. The track is right near Bad Luck Creek, George said, which is another reason I wouldn't want to go there." He dropped his feet to the floor. "Gordo, my ass. Good mind to shut this place down and go on to the river."

He flung his head back to clear the sandy-red hair from his eyes. His lean, freckled jaw worked on a chew of Beechnut, stored it in a ball a few seconds while he primed and spat into an open-top oil can, switched it to the other side, then commenced working on it again. He had his feet back on the Coke box. Times like those, when we knew he was pondering, we didn't dare interrupt him, though collectively we wanted to say, "Do it, J.P., lock the place up and let's go swimming."

Potts pointed up the street and jolted us from a half-hour-long stretch of drowsy silence. "There comes one with a arm out and up like he's coming in here. A big old green car, Oldsmobile or something."

J.P. craned his neck and looked up the street. "That arm don't mean nothing but the winder's down. Niggers, sure's shit," he muttered, though the car was yet half a block away. "I'd a knowed that without the arm. Look at how the sprangs is broke down. They'll wedge the whole tribe in a car, enough weight to bust the tars on a quarter-ton truck."

"Maybe they just turning onto Market," I suggested.

"Naw, they coming in here. Bet your ass on it."

"It's niggers all right," Potts announced as the long, low sedan turned onto the station apron and eased up to the island, "a whole pack of'm."

"Goddamn yankee niggers," J.P. grunted. He dropped his chair to all fours and lowered his feet. "Illinois tag. Must be seven or eight in there." He didn't get up, just sat there with his feet flat on the floor, going after the cud of Beechnut with his right jaw. We stirred uneasily as the doors of the car opened and they got out: four from the back, three from the front, five males and two females, all adult. One of the women was tall and skinny, the other tall and heavy, I mean water buffalo heavy. The men were just, just niggers—they all looked pretty much the same, like everybody said. They were just standing around the island, stretching and talking.

"J.P., you going out there or not?" Barney asked as they milled around the island. "It looks like they want some gas."

"Naw. I ain't moving. They coming to me or else."

One of the men, the one who'd been driving, walked back around to the driver's side, leaned through the window, and blew the horn.

"Well, if that ain't the Goddamndest thing I ever heard of," J.P. snorted, getting to his feet. "Brassy bastards." In two of his incredibly long strides he was standing in the doorway. "What y'all mean, blowing that horn on Sunday, the Sabbath, the Lord's day?"

The driver had popped the hood. He looked over at J.P. "You pumping gas?"

"I 'spect I am," J.P. shot back. "How much you want?"

"Just top it up. And check the oil."

"You mean *fill* it up?" He still didn't move from the doorway.

"Of course I mean fill it—what else would I mean?"

We'd never heard blacks talking to whites that way before, so we edged in behind J.P. to see what he would do.

"You pump it yourself," J.P. said, "if you want it that bad. And check your own Goddamned oil. But I want the money in advance."

"That is absurd." One of the men walked toward us. "How we gon' know how much gas it will hold?"

"I don't *care* how much it will hold. You figger it out. But you ain't getting gas without you pay me first, and you gon' pump it yourself."

The men, all dressed in dark Sunday clothes, including coats and ties, and drenched with sweat, moved together for a short conference. They were obviously agitated, and the driver seemed especially impatient just to get on down the road.

One of the women, the big one, had waddled over into the shade of the station canopy.

"What'd y'all decide?" J.P. asked them.

"Well, er uh," the driver said, taking out his billfold and removing two crinkled dollar bills, "we'll just take two dollars worf and be off. We do need—"

"I thought you said you wanted to fill it up," J.P. flared. He took a step out of the doorway toward the man.

"Two dollars worf will be enough to get us on to Meridian with what we already got in the tank. But we—one of the ladies there—would like to use yo' bafroom. She somewhat discomfitted."

J.P. took the two bills and pointed toward the end of the station. "They's a colored restroom around back. She can use that." He stuck the money into his shirt pocket and returned to his chair. "And you remember that all you got coming is two dollars worth of gas. I'll be watching that dial."

"Thank you," the driver said, "that will be fine." He walked over to the group and spoke briefly with them, pointing to the end of the station. The fat woman, who'd been under the canopy, walked back over to the group and then glared at the office and mumbled something. Then she and the thin one went on around the end of the building while the driver pumped his gas and the others spoke softly. One took out a package of cigarettes and a match folder.

J.P. jumped to his feet and yelled through the doorway. "Hey, y'all get on away from that island with them damn cigarettes! You can't strike no match where they's gas! You'll blow this place to hell!" They moved on out to the edge of the apron, and J.P. returned to seat and his Beechnut, his eyes on the pump dial.

The doorway darkened, and I looked up to see the fat woman standing there, arms crossed. "They ain't no do' on dat bafroom. Ain't no privacy. Ain't no stall. Ain't nothing. Mind if I use one of them inside?"

J.P. got up. "That's y'all's restroom. Can't nobody see in to where anybody'd be setting on the commode—besides, they's bushes all over the place, blocking it from the street."

"That place is a *hogpen!* Got flies everwhere, big ol' green flies. There ain't even no toilet paper in there, just some paper tals."

"That's all I was told to put in there. You coulda got corncobs. Now y'all use it if you want to or hold it in till you get to Meridian—it ain't no skin off me. Like it or lump it. But if you do use it, be sure to flush. Been too many people just used it and walked off. That's why it's so messy. And why they's flies. It was a Nee-gro tore that door off one day too, and that ain't none of my fault." He shoved past her to make certain the driver had not gone over his two dollars.

The skinny woman had already returned to the car and gotten in. The driver was closing the hood while the other four males were washing their faces and hands at the water hose.

"Y'all about ready t'go?" the driver asked. He looked over at the fat woman.

"I 'spect so," one of the males answered.

"Hey, Mattie, you ready?" one of them yelled to the fat one, who was still standing by the door glowering at us and J.P.

"I be right along, after I get me some water. Go somewhere else to use d'bafroom." She started through the doorway toward the water fountain, which was clearly labeled *White Only.* J.P. stepped between her and the fountain, his freckled fists clenched to the white-knuckle point.

"Can't you read, nigger?" He reached over and wrapped his huge right hand around the knob. "You go out there and use the hose, like the others, if you want water."

She pushed out her lips and glared at him. "Now, you listen to me, white boy. We been traveling more than twenty-four hours, we all hot and tired and ready to be in Meridian. I been done had about all yo' shit I'm gon' take. Ain't no skinny-ass Missippi white boy gon' call me a *nigger* and tell me I can't have no water with it right in front of me. Now, you move out t'way!" Almost as tall as J.P.—who was over six feet—and weighing perhaps twice as much, she flung an arm out and elbowed him to the side. We cowered in the corner of the office.

J.P. took two steps back, then lunged and swung his right fist just as she was ducking her mouth down to meet the stream of water. I was directly behind him and couldn't see the whole thing, but I saw his enormous freckled fist arch way around and come across to where I guessed her head was. There was a flat smack and the woman stumbled to the doorway, her face a shapeless mass of astonishment and outrage.

The four of us flushed like quail from the corner of the office and headed for the garage area. Potts, just in front of me, with Stutts and Jimmy Simmons just behind, had almost reached the opening when J.P., who had followed up his roundhouse with a leap to the doorway in pursuit of the woman, careened across the office past the water cooler and into the shelves of oil and additives, candy, and chewing gum. He flattened Stutts and fell back over him, I stumbled over the two of them, and all three of us were showered with the contents of the shelves. I had little more than time enough to roll off J.P. and catch a glimpse of Potts and Simmons inching back into the corner behind the desk before the big woman loomed over us, hands on her hips. Stutts was grunting and squirming to get out from under J.P., whose face was bright red on the side next to me. He was trying to get his pistol out.

"Get up, white trash boy!" she bellowed. "Get y'self up so I can knock yo' ass off again." From where I lay she looked like a gathering June thunderstorm ready to mow down a county, her eyes flashing red, her enormous belly heaving. "Get yo' Goddamned self *up!*" She took another step toward J.P., who was still flat against the floor, pinning Stutts.

What happened then was simply too fast for the human eye to follow. We talked about it for years and some of it never did come clear. J.P. had just managed to get the pistol unpocketed and pointed toward her when the black woman whipped it from his hand and we heard five or six loud pops. Pieces of the ceiling splattered all over us, the black woman fell forward onto J.P. and Stutts, oil cans and gum packages flew like buckshot across the office, and the doorway filled with black faces. I rolled until I was out the garage door and under the grease rack, and Stutts and Potts dove behind the desk.

"Hell," Stutts said later, after the crowd had left and the sheriff had gotten his paperwork done, "I was under J.P. and all that oil and fanbelts and shit, so I couldn't see nothing, couldn't hear nothing but a bunch of pistol shots and them niggers yelling."

"All I know is," Barney said, "when I looked over the desk and seen that nigger woman holding J.P.'s pistol, I figgered it was all over, she was gon' kill all of us."

"You reckon she was aiming at that water fountain, J.P.," I asked, "or at you?"

"I don't know. She sure put two holes in it, though."

"Ruined the damned thing," George lamented. "Got water a inch deep all over the place." He'd come on up to the station as soon as word of the trouble got to him. "Ceiling's got two holes in it. Wonder somebody didn't get killed with all them bullets flying around in here."

"How'n hell did she get that pistol away from you, boy?" some old man who stayed on after the main crowd left asked J.P.

"She just flat take'n it away from me, like I told the shurf. Hell, she landed on me and nearly knocked me out. Must've weighed three hunderd pounds."

"Just ruined my Goddamn fountain," George grieved.

"You reckon the Highway Patrol will catch them sonsabitches?" J.P. asked George. "They got my gun."

George shook his head. "I doubt it. They take'n a back road to Meridian prolly, and y'all didn't get no tag number anyhow."

"We pretty well described them to the sheriff, though, Illinois tag and all," Stutts put in.

"Bullshit!" George snorted. "A carload of niggers in a green car with wore-out springs on Sunday in this state. That ain't hardly what you'd call narrowing the field down a whole lot. Hell naw, they won't catch them bastards. And me out a water fountain and a ceiling to patch and most of my candy and gum waterlogged, and the whole town talking about it. I believe I'll just close down on Sunday from now on."

"Tell you what, though," the old man said, grinning, as he started out the door, "you got yerself on the map today. They ort to put one of them fancy signs out front—a historical marker, you know. And you got yerself a hero in thatere boy there." He pointed to J.P. "We got to have more like him, boys willing to stand up for what they know is right."

"At's a fact, Mr. Studdard," Potts added. "You got to remember this, no matter what else happened," he continued with such gravity that J.P. and George stopped picking up gum and candy and looked at him. "Just this: She never got no water out of that fountain. At least not to drink."

That night I was sitting with the folks on the front porch trying to get cool enough to go inside to go to sleep. The crickets were playing "Dixie" in my ears, and off in the distance lightning scooted around.

"I still can't believe that you was up there with all that violence going on," Daddy was saying.

"Yessir," I swelled, "I was there."

"I'll tell you this," he continued, "niggers is getting out of hand these days. They got the idear they can just run over us now."

"Well," I said, "J.P. and Stutts sure got run over by one."

"You coulda been shot," Mother said.

Grandmother, who'd been silent up to that point, stopped rocking and cleared her throat, like she just realized that she had missed her turn. It was a signal for the rest of us to quiet down and yield to the voice of experience. She took her glasses off and laid them in her lap.

"You gon' say something, Momma?" Daddy asked, knowing full well that when Grandmother took her glasses off like that, even God had better listen.

"All's I know is," she sighed, "the South is going to need a bunch of young men like that John Paul Jones in the years to come. If we gon' survive these times, we got to have more young men like him, heroes willing to take a position on the thangs that matter."

I nodded on the dark steps as the far cloudbanks heaved and flashed, rolled and flashed.

The Hands of John Merchant

Any time I'm back over that way—which is not often, since I've come
back to Texas, where I should have been all along—I drive along the beach
road and look out over the Gulf toward the islands, which, when the sun
is high enough, give off a little glare so that you can tell exactly where they
are without actually seeing them. Like an aura, you might say. It's ghostly.
And if I let myself, in those brief glimpses before I have to turn my eyes
back to the road, it's not so hard to imagine that I see ol' John Merchant
reaching a hand up to me from out of that green water, cupping it toward
me, with bright red and yellow spices slipping out between his curled fingers like sand, and I can smell the spices so distinctly that my nose burns
and my eyes haze over. And I can't wait to get back to Texas.

So here John Merchant was again, his skillet almost red hot and smoking,
spices singing on the air, while just outside the screen door evening was
softening into night.

   I was slouched over his kitchen table working on my fifth or sixth beer
of the evening and feeling it from head to bladder while he prepared our
dinner, redfish we'd caught in the surf at Petit Bois Island the weekend
before. The broad fillets and a few odd little nuggets lay on a piece of waxed
paper at the end of the table, and an assortment of spices trailed out in a
long line of jar lids like something for a witch's broth, carefully measured
out, mostly reds and blacks, some greens and yellows. It would all be
dumped together in a bowl when he was ready to roll the fillets and throw

them into that hot skillet, where they'd sizzle and pop until the smoke that rose from them would take John completely, and his feet and hairy legs would drop out of that cloud like some sort of very human god just touching down to earth.

Then his lean, sun-darkened hands would reach out and whisk up the fillets in one run, like a card dealer, and sooner than I could focus on the flurry of fingers the spices were gone and the skillet shrieked and smoke billowed up until finally I could see him only from the ankles down, just a great cloud with two hairy feet.

This was the way it usually went. Most Saturdays we'd get up early and make a run to the islands, spend most of the day thrashing the surf, and come back in and feast. And if we didn't catch anything to eat, we'd just drink beer and get drunk as coots and sprawl out on the floor of his living room or den or wherever and sleep it off—without dinner. It was a point of honor with him, a little less with me. If we didn't catch fish he wouldn't touch a solid thing, just beer or whiskey, and not eat until the next day, but likely as not, I'd wake up during the night hungry enough to eat the linoleum tiles I was stretched out on and crawl to the refrigerator and graze through the bottom shelves—cheese or left-over meat or lettuce or a jar of olives. Hell, it didn't matter as long as it filled the hole in my stomach enough to let me sleep through till dawn, when I knew he'd get up and fix a manly breakfast.

John wasn't married—*had* been but wasn't when I knew him back then. His wife ran off with somebody very different from him, which was the way he wanted it, he said. If she'd grabbed on to somebody just like him, he would have taken it hard and probably tracked down and killed both of them. It was that honor thing again. The overweight used-car salesman with his gold necklaces and polyester leisure pants, over which his belly hung like a double scoop of ice cream spilling over the edge of its cone on a hot summer day, was exactly what she needed, he figured, and he could live with the image of her bearing up under him night after night like a terrible smothering dream. It was better imagining that than shooting her, he said, and spending the rest of his life in prison.

He lived in a drab little house at the end of a drab little street in Gautier, Mississippi, about three miles from a trailer I shared with a couple of dogs, which I was fairly confident would never abandon me for a used-car salesman, and even if they did I'd just get two more. Dogs are easier to come by than women and a hell of a lot less expense and trouble to get *and* keep satisfied. And you can have as many as you want and not have to worry about them killing each other in a jealous rage. Don't have to listen to'm bitching or fretting over makeup. All that shit.

We worked at the big shipyard in Pascagoula, in the electrical department, pulling cable mostly, since neither one of us had been there long enough to work our way up to anything better. We were academic dropouts from the University of Texas waiting around for some sort of easy life that just never seemed to show up. He'd talked me into coming to Mississippi with him, since he'd grown up there, but there wasn't much light work around. John had tried his hand at reporting at a Coast newspaper for awhile, and I substitute taught in math in area high schools and did some night security work at a mall, but all that was meaningless and didn't pay enough to live on. Not a year after we moved over there he knocked this waitress up and married her and stayed married long enough for their trailer to turn green. When she left him, me and John had a one-beer discussion about going back to Texas and finishing school. A six-pack or so later we had decided on the shipyard. Next day we bought some rugged clothes and hard-nose boots and went to work.

Weekends, we fished. Seriously. Like it was a religion. If the weather didn't lay us in, we took off on Saturday morning in John's sixteen footer, the only thing he kept from the marriage, and stayed at the islands all day, sometimes spending the night out there and sleeping on the beach. We ate what we caught. You can catch fish if you know you're going without food if you don't.

This was one of those Saturdays, though, when the weather threatened early, blowing like a sonofabitch from the east with low white clouds trundling along under darker ones, and you don't want to get caught out there in a sixteen footer in heavy weather. We already had the beer iced down and the rods stowed when John said he reckoned we'd better wait, so we unloaded the ice chest and spent the day lounging around watching baseball on the tube and drinking beer. Now the only thing between us and a hell of a meal of blackened fish was John's magic with the spices and that skillet. There was a big bowl of salad on the table already, but the fish was what mattered. Jesus, what he could do with those spices.

After a few minutes in the thick smoke he dipped down and out of the cloud and said, "They're about done. You wanna eat outside?"

"That, or we're gonna have to eat on the floor, where we can see what we're eating and where there's air."

"Arright, you get that bottle of red wine out of the refrigerator and the salad and a couple of plates and glasses and silverware, and, shit, some napkins—you know what to get—and I'll meet you on the porch."

Half an hour later, high on the earlier beer and half a gallon of cheap red wine, we finished the last of the fish and studied the weather, which seemed to have washed out over the Gulf like a faded flag.

"I guess we should have gone out," John said.

"Yeah, but we'd have missed out on this miracle you've wrought here, Sir John. You dropped down out of that cloud like God Hisself and broke fish with me, enough for the multitudes, and turned beer into wine. You're even better at turning beer into piss."

"For a fact." He sighed and leaned back in his chair. A crusty piece of fillet lay on his plate.

I pointed to the piece of fish. "You gon' finish that?"

"Naw. You want to eat it?"

"Nope. Just thought I'd package it up and send it over to Ethiopia for some poor starving sonofabitch." I reached over and speared it with my fork.

"Uh-*hunnnh*," he said.

Now, John Merchant was one of those folks of few words. He just never talked much. But when he used that *Uh-hunnnh* as a lead-in, something was coming, something big, something significant.

I held the piece of fish on my fork, balanced it between the plate and my mouth. "What? What is it, John?"

"Well, I was just thinking that most folks believe that all you can blacken is redfish or snapper, but fact is, you can blacken almost anything. It's the spices, of course, and the hot skillet. I'll just bet you could season anything that swims or walks or crawls or just lies flat on the highway and fry it like this and you'd like it just the same. Like barbecue. You can barbecue any Goddamned thing in the world and it tastes good. Rat or snake or squid or—hell, like I say, *anything*. That's what barbecue sauce and deep-fat frying is all about. Making even the worst piece of meat you can come up with taste good."

I finished off the piece of fish and picked up the glass of wine and sipped. "You reckon, huh?"

"Well, back at UT there was this wormy little guy—a business major, marketing, I believe, short and stringy and mousy looking—and a bunch of the jocks in a sociology class got to where they picked at him regularly. Just for the pure hell of it, meanness, because he never done anything to'm.

Except he made some remark the second week about athletics and athletes being the bane of American society, setting all the wrong role models and stultifying the American mind, establishing a ridiculous value system, and ball clubs paying millions to people with minds like mites.

"Hell, they set in on him like bad yard dogs. They'd do things like track in dog shit and step on his foot, you know, high school stuff, put Elmer's glue in his books and paste the pages together, goofy stuff. Whisper, 'Hey, faggot.' All silly, juvenile stuff, but they really kept on him and didn't let up all semester.

"And he never said a word back, just kept on with his studies. And just to show these ol' boys there were no hard feelings, he invited them to a party at his apartment the afternoon before their exam. Now, they wouldn't have gone to any party of his, of course, except that there wasn't any way *he* could be a threat to them and, after all, he said he'd have a keg of beer, and then everybody wanted to know how to get there.

"What he did was, he got with a medical-student friend of his and the two of them slipped into the anatomy room one night and pulled out this ol' fat gal that had died of natural causes—or, hell, *un*natural, whatever —and cut a big thick flank steak off each thigh, underneath, where it wouldn't be missed for awhile. Folded the skin back around and tucked it, you know."

"Jesus Christ, John, what kind of shit is this you're—"

"Ol' Gerald sliced up and marinated the meat for a couple of days to take out the taste of any kind of preservative. Barbecued strips of that fat woman's thighs and fed'm to that gaggle of jocks. They shot the beer and wolfed that fat woman and said it was the best meat they'd ever had any-where, tasty and tender and juicy, and wondered what it was, but he never said a word except that the meat was a rare delicacy, and rare it certainly was.

"News of a mutilated cadaver hit print two days later—they found out sooner than I'd have thought—and the little business major sent a copy of the article and a letter to every one of them football players telling them that he hoped they enjoyed the barbecue. That made them cannibals, you know, which is one of the few things you can't just offhand accuse jocks of being, so all they could do was try to keep it quiet. And they sure as hell wasn't going to bother him, since anybody who'd break in the anatomy room and whack on a cadaver might be dangerous. Bet you this much, though—I'll bet every time they've had barbecue since that night they been reminded. . . . "

I downed the last of my wine and stared at my plate. "What's your story got to do with this fish?"

"Nothing, nothing, only how do you know what you've just eaten?" His eyes were glittering like sun on a sea rod. The wine soothed my burning tongue.

"The only reason you think what you ate was fish is that you saw me get something out of the freezer and take it to the stove," John said. "But you didn't see *what* I got out. I could have thrown anything into those spices and blackened it. It's all in the hands, and in the spices. And you don't have any earthly notion what's in the spices. Might be ground-up frogs or bat wings or dog shit or anything."

I smiled. "I'd know redfish from dog shit, even fried."

"You think I'm kidding." He tilted his glass back, swallowed deep, and looked away at the moon, just coming up over the edge of the Gulf. "There's more things in Heav'n and Earth, Horatio . . ."

"Bullshit, John—"

"You never noticed any difference, did you?"

"Any difference in *what?*"

He was smiling, a secret, dark smile. "Well, I've told you I could blacken anything and it'd taste good. The theory's just been tested."

"Bullshit, John." I stared down at my bread-polished plate. "Just bull-shit." I was thinking about a slice of fat-woman's thigh, barbecued and served with beer. "Besides, I never did anything to you."

"Those fat-woman thigh strips didn't hurt the jocks. They enjoyed them and came away kinda liking ol' Gerald, I'd say. Probably the best piece of woman they'll ever get. A good joke's a good joke, even if the one playing it is the only one that knows about it."

The fat moon crept up higher in the sky as I sat leaned back in my chair, smashed on beer and wine, looking over at John. The grin on his face told me he was lying. But who could be sure with John Merchant?

He drowned in the Gulf the very next day during a squall when the last thing I saw of him was his two big hands reaching up out of the tumbling sea toward me while I clung to the side of his small boat, unable to turn loose to extend a hand or throw him a line. The joke was that I never knew he couldn't swim. In all the time I knew him he never told me.

They pulled his body out just inside the cut between Horn and Petit Bois almost a week later, after he'd probably washed way out and come back in with the tide. And I was there. After the Coast Guard picked me up and they checked me out at the hospital, I came right back out and borrowed a boat and helped them search, eating when I had to and sleeping in snatches until on the sixth day someone spotted him riding the currents in the channel.

He was dreadfully bloated and a strange purple and white color, like a blow-up toy that kids punch on, and all kinds of fish had been at him. I wouldn't have known him but for his shirt and pants, and his hands. Everything on him was swollen like a balloon, but his hands—somehow they looked the same, same color and shape, his fingers curled like they were reaching up for my hands or down to pick up fillets.

I live in Galveston now, but I stay away from the Gulf. I have tried to blacken fish since, but I can never get the spices right. I get close enough, though, and the spices and beer and smoke always take me back to John Merchant and that evening when he may or may not have played a big trick on me. Who could know what thing with wings or fins or scaly legs he had waved his dark hands across and transformed with magic spices and fire and served me with blood-red wine?

Crows

I grew up hating crows. I can't explain it for sure, but anytime I saw those glossy black bastards, my blood picked up temperature and speed and I hurried home to get a rifle or shotgun and nail as many as I could before they got out of range. For a fact, if one settled anywhere on my father's property, small as it was, he was asking for a killing, usually a single .22 shot through the head.

Maybe it was the fact that my folks were always filling me with notions that crows were agents of the Devil and were sent to earth to torment decent people who had a hard enough time getting along without being bothered by those noisy black bastards that seemed to multiply like mosquitoes or flies, or that they were trained by Gypsies to swoop through windows and seize jewelry and wallets and watches, anything that glittered and might have value. Once my mother told me about a baby being killed by a crow—sailed right through an open window and landed in the crib, pecked through the soft spot on the infant's head, gobbled up his brains while the poor little thing was shrieking away, but his momma was vacuuming and didn't hear him. Came to check on him later and found the skull hollowed out like a coconut shell and the crow just laboring into flight off the sill, so full of baby brains that he barely cleared the clothesline where the poor little thing's diapers were drying. And they'd peck out a baby's eyes in a heartbeat if you left one unguarded outside, zip down there and in two strokes leave two hollowed out places where the eyes had been. I never got names or anything, but I didn't have any reason not to believe what I was told.

There were stories of crows attacking horses and cows, dogs and cats, and chickens. Even a rooster had to watch himself when they descended into the chicken yard to help themselves to feed. Face-to-face a rooster could take one on, but crows always tried sneak attacks and would hammer a rooster senseless from behind, knock him silly, then peck his head off. I never saw this happen, but I heard tell. They'd eat dead things, too, which to my way of thinking made them no better than buzzards.

And they would simply devastate a garden. I mean, eat all the tomatoes and squash and what have you, then peck on all the stuff they couldn't get down, just for pure-dee spite. Why, I've seen watermelon patches where not a single melon went untouched, and cantaloupes, which were softer— well, they didn't stand a chance against those savage beaks.

So, there wasn't much chance that I could have grown up not hating crows. All the Christian charity I could summon simply wouldn't allow them a place in my heart. I remember thinking one time that Noah had to bear some of the blame, since he must have had a couple of them roosting on the ark. I just wondered how anything else on the boat survived, given the hell crows could visit on other creatures.

I cannot tell you how many crows I killed growing up, but it was plenty. I even hooked one one time with a piece of fatback on a fishhook. There was flock messing around in the garden, so I baited and cast way out into the backyard, then stood just inside the door with my rod ready. A brazen one finally got tired of vegetables and got a whiff of the meat—I guess that's how he noticed it—and fluttered up and over to the fatback. He strutted up and studied it a few seconds. Crows are awfully smart and very suspicious, you know. Then he reached down and pecked the end of the meat, satisfied himself that it was safe, snatched it and slugged it down, and started sashaying back to the garden, just chattering away like he was rubbing it in about how much better fatback was than tomatoes.

About that time I kicked the door open and set the hook, and off he went. Lord, what a fight! I've caught redfish and snapper and bluefish and sand sharks and every kind of trash fish imaginable, but nothing ever gave me the battle that crow did. All he could do was fly in circles, of course, like a control-line airplane, except when he'd try a new tactic and fly straight across above me, only to get yanked back into the circle again when the line played out. Once I got the idea that he was going to attack me, but he never did it. He just flew slower and slower and finally landed. I tied the line off to a peach tree and went in and got my .22 and put him out of his misery. I almost felt sorry for that one, but I couldn't quite coax up the emotion—I just hated crows too much.

The most serious dent I ever made in the local population came when my father bought a crow-calling record and portable player, which we set up in a pine thicket way back on what we called the Marshall place, a few miles north of the house. The record had the sounds of crows fighting and raising hell with an owl or something, and when we got it going, the air was suddenly full of crows. They were all over the place, wheeling in among the pines and out, some landing and looking. Then we unlimbered the shotguns and for the next minute or so the only sound was our twelve gauges. We dropped just over twenty before they caught on to the ambush and headed for other places.

In time, of course, as girls came along and my mind turned to other things, my war with the crows seemed a little less important and we settled into a kind of uneasy peace. Until Fort Jackson.

Three days after I graduated from high school, I was on the way to Fort Jackson, South Carolina, to begin a short stint with the regular Army: eight weeks of basic followed by sixteen weeks of advanced training, then eight years in the National Guard and Army Reserve. It was a plan lots of college-bound kids opted for in those days. I could have taken my chances with the draft board with no wars going on, but I wanted a car and wanted to start to college—though Army pay was a pittance, I'd be able to save it all.

So, for a while, I forgot about crows. But not for long. One afternoon I was struggling through the barbed-wire obstacle course, on my back, pushing with my feet and wiggling with my butt and shoulders to get from one end to the other, dragging along my M-1, with barbed wire snagging my fatigues and scraping across my helmet, machine gun rounds snapping a couple of feet above me, and tubs of explosives blowing sand all over us soldiers under the wire, when I happened to open my eyes and see a whole congregation of crows lazily flapping over the range, the rattle of machine guns and the explosions no more to them than a chorus of crickets.

It was amazing to me at the time, though lying in the barracks late, after everyone else was snoring away, I theorized that they were smart enough to know that the machine guns and grenades and explosives were not directed at them. They were used to it. Acclimated. And it burned me up. I wanted to slap a clip in an M-1 and let them have it the next time a flock went over, but I knew better. So I formed another uneasy truce with crows and went on with my training.

A week after basic training was over, a sergeant came into the barracks one evening and announced that the brass needed a volunteer to fire the battalion cannon at Retreat each day. The catch was that he'd have to be there to fire it on weekends too. Well, hell, I never went anywhere on weekends anyway, since I was saving every penny for college, so I said sure, I'd do it. It would get me out of KP and deadeningly dull guard duty at some ammo site or motor pool. Besides, I'd seen that cannon fired before, and I rather liked the idea of being the one to actually yank the lanyard. I also had lodged in my head the fact that one of my forebears, Edmund Ruffin, a Southern plantation owner, was given the honor of touching off the opening shot of the Civil War when he yanked the lanyard on a cannon and fired on Fort Sumter over in Charleston.

The cannon, a French-made 75 mm field artillery piece that resembled a 105 howitzer but had a longer barrel, was aimed harmlessly off toward a small park and adjoining golf course across a paved road from the barracks I stayed in.

In no time at all I had the routine down: Each evening I requested a shell at the HQ supply hut a few minutes before time to fire, just before sundown, and walked to the cannon, opened the breech, slid in the bright brass shell (a blank, of course), closed the breech, and waited for the last note of the bugle call. When it came, I yanked the lanyard, the cannon boomed out its message that day was done, and another recruit lowered the flag. After firing, I removed the spent shell, which I returned to HQ when I picked up my live round the next day, and the flag man and I policed up the paper wadding, which sometimes sailed well into the park across the road. The final step was to open the breech, untie a ramrod from the side of the cannon and run a brush through the bore, then a plain rag, then an oily rag. Then I'd clean up and oil the breech face, and that was it.

The shell I fired had a reduced powder charge in the base, capped with wadding, leaving between the wadding and lip a space of several inches where, in a regular shell, the explosive round would be seated and crimped. It seemed to me such a terrible waste of space. Often I thought about how many ounces of shot might be packed into that shell, what it could do to a flock of ducks, what a magnificent shotgun it would have made. I had read stories of big four-gauge and six-gauge punt cannons that folks in Louisiana used to fire into ducks and geese. A shell probably held a quarter pound of shot. They strapped those monsters to their punts, barrel pointed along the longitudinal axis of the boat, then poled silently through the bayou until they spotted a large feeding or roosting raft on the water, aimed the boat toward them, touched off a round, and loaded the boat with birds. That was serious hunting.

On the fort the only ducks I knew anything about were some broadback white waddlers down on the pond at the edge of the golf course, and they could have been taken with a stick or a rock by anyone seriously after meat. Not much sport in that.

But, ah, the crows, the *crows*. Most evenings a great flock of them came and cavorted in the pines across from the barracks, zipping in and out, cawing, and it happened that one of the trees they lit in was not far out of line with my cannon. I studied the situation.

I figured South Carolina crows weren't a hell of a lot different from those in Mississippi. They certainly looked the same, spoke the same language. It seemed to me that they lit in that tree simply to irritate me, knowing how I felt about them and their Mississippi cousins but knowing as well that there was nothing I could do to them. Like most people, crows are smart enough to be spiteful.

The cannon was heavy, its massive breech and barrel bolted to a steel carriage, but it sat on wheels like any other field artillery piece, so one evening after cleaning up the wadding from firing, I sat down on one of the legs of the carriage—they formed the tongue for hauling the gun, and when you got it in position for firing, you spread the legs and the flanged ends dug in to lessen recoil—and calculated that with only a small amount of leveraged nudging at the tail end with a two-by-four I could bring the gun into proper alignment with the tree the crows congregated in. The movement would be so slight that no officer would notice it, especially if I took care to scrub out the marks on the concrete pad where the wheels had been sitting. I could have adjusted the barrel with the windage screw, but someone might notice that it was no longer perpendicular to the axle. Didn't want to take a chance. I would also have to elevate the angle of the barrel to aim at the top third of the pine, a slight adjustment done with a simple wheel.

Late one Friday evening, well after firing, when almost everyone was gone from the barracks, I slipped out and rummaged around beneath the steps until I found a two-by-four of suitable length in a pile of lumber left over from some framing for a new floor furnace. Holding the board down by my side, I stiff-legged it over to the cannon and sat down on a leg and waited until full dark, then crouched, removed the recoil chocks behind the wheels (little recoil with those blanks, so the chocks did the trick), and with the two-by-four worked the legs around to bring the barrel in approximate alignment with the trunk of the pine. It moved with difficulty, but it moved. The screw of the elevation wheel was gunked with olive drab paint and took some effort, but I chipped away as much of the paint as I could with my bayonet and then, using it for leverage, I managed finally to make enough revolutions until the cannon was aimed about forty feet up the tree.

After stashing the board, I filled my steel helmet with hot soapy water and set to work scrubbing the wheel and chock marks off the pad. I had all but finished when a voice came out of the gloom.

"Well, now, aren't you the industrious one?" A flashlight played over the cannon and pad.

I knew the voice. It was a second lieutenant checking the area before retiring. Always friendly, he was simple enough to have been trapped in grade for over five years, so he was of no great concern to me.

"Why aren't you in town like all the other hardlegs?"

"Saving my money, Sir." You have to tack that *Sir* on, even if it's a *hog* with bars, because it is not the hog but the bars that count.

"What else do you do here? I mean, son, most of the boys just want to get away from here as far as they can and still manage to get back early Monday morning. Whiskey and pussy and stuff like that is what they are interested in. You ain't into that?"

"Nossir. In fact, I am doing some writing and some reading."

"What kind of stuff you read?"

"Eliot, Frost, Jeffers."

"I have heard of Frost and Jefferson. Thomas, I guess you mean. But Elyut who?"

Now, what the hell do you say in answer to that when your presumed superior has asked it? Thomas Jefferson, my ass. I said the only thing I could: "Thomas Stearns Eliot. T. S. Eliot."

"What'd he write?"

Well, once you realize the depth of the pond you're fishing in, you relax a little—I mean, you know pretty much what kind of fish you are dealing with. "Torrid romance novels, all sex and violence, incest and rape and sodomy, lots of really kinky fucking, stuff like that. Excuse the language, Sir."

"Hmmm. Well, sounds like my kind of guy."

"It's a woman, sir. Victorian. They sometimes had names that sounded masculine. Like George Eliot, you know."

"George Eliot was a woman? And she wrote shit like that?"

"Do you know George Eliot's work, Sir?"

After a long pause he said, "No, but, I mean, with a name like George and all."

"That was her pen name. She wrote some stunning novels, like *Silas Marner, Middlemarch*. Her real name was Mary Ann—"

Then he swapped subjects on me, which an officer, if not a gentleman, has the right to do: "Well, you are doing a fine job with that cannon. You will go a long way in this Army."

I sat back on my heels and wiped my cheek with the back of my hand. "Well, I love my gun, Sir. I just thought the pad might need to be cleaned."

In the reflected glow of the flashlight I saw the officer shake his head and tip a salute with two fingers, like a Boy Scout. "You keep up the good work, son, and keep on with that reading, even if it *is* trash." I returned the salute and the lieutenant walked on past me and disappeared around the corner of the barracks.

The next morning I hitched a ride into town to a hardware store and bought two boxes of shotgun shells, twelve gauge, number sixes, hitched back with them, and while everybody was away doing whatever they did on the weekends, I cut open the shells and emptied the shot into my canteen cup and poured them into a boot sock. Then I dug out the wadding and poured the powder from each of the shells into the canteen cup and emptied that into another sock. The two boxes yielded over four pounds of number sixes and I don't know how much powder. I stashed the socks under my pillow, then took a folding shovel and crawled under the barracks and buried the boxes and shotgun hulls.

Now, crows are persistent as well as smart. A crow hunter I knew back in Mississippi observed that they can count up to five. "Four men with guns goes into a thicket, and four comes out, and crows'll fly in. Five men with guns goes in and four comes out, won't no crow fly in there. Six goes in and five comes out and crows'll fly in there. You take a pencil and set that down on paper, and you come up with the fact that crows can count to five." I figured that put crows on roughly the same math-achievement level as the hunter.

They knew, for a fact, that my *boom* each day would do them no harm, and though they usually flew off in a chorus of caws when the gun fired, just as quickly they settled back into the pine, almost as if they were daring me to harm them. Cackling, cawing sonsabitches. It was a game for them, and they enjoyed it. How otherwise account for their derision as they flocked into the tree just a few minutes before I fired each day, chattering among themselves as if to say, "Hey, Mississippi boy, we like your toy. Yo great big gun don't skeer us none." When I was through picking up the wadding, they flew off, jeering all the way out of hearing. But I doubted that were they smart enough to notice a fifteen-degree horizontal and twenty-degree vertical adjustment of the cannon, or if they noticed, they would not surmise the reason behind the fine tuning. Most *people* wouldn't have figured it out. That's what I was counting on.

All the next week I fired in the new position. No one said a word. No one noticed. The crows flew into the pine well before sunset, had their noisy powwow, scattered when I fired, circled a bit, then returned to it.

That Friday evening the flag man, an older boy from Tennessee who had to stay on the post on the weekends because he'd sassed a policeman in town and got reported, did notice that a piece of wadding wedged high in the tree. "I ain't never seen that happen before. How you rekkin it done that?"

"No telling," I said. "Genetics maybe."

"Genetics?"

"Yeah, that's a law that has to do with the turning of the Earth on its axis in late summer. The wind'll blow it out. Don't worry about it."

It is so easy to be a smartass among people who don't have any notion what you're talking about. I could have told him any lie under the sun about how that wadding got up there, and he would have swallowed—breech, carriage, and barrel. He was an RA, that is Regular Army, as opposed to us NGs, the *college boys.*

Saturday evening the post was pretty much dead. Everybody was off somewhere. Manning HQ, as he did most weekends, was a lone and ever lonesome clerk, a mouth-breathing corporal by the name of Billy Droit (called Malla behind his back, even though half the recruits who used the name didn't know what was funny about it—neither did Droit). He had nowhere at all to go and no one to go there with. I went in to check out my shell fifteen minutes or so before time to fire.

Droit looked up from some manual he'd been studying and sighed. "You early." His teeth were dry, the color of Octagon soap, which the Army used in those days for scrubbing down the heads.

I looked at my watch. "A minute or two."

"Y'ont yer shell?" He got two, maybe three, syllables out of *shell.*

"No, I came to see if I could sign out a woman until late tomorrow. You got a real pretty blond or brunette back there about—"

"Very funny," he said. "I'll get yer shell."

"I appreciate it. Asshole." I said the last part under my breath, not that I was afraid of him. I just didn't know when I might need him for something besides a damned artillery shell.

He went into a backroom and returned with the round wrapped in a plain white rag. Droit took tiny, deliberate steps and handed it to me, cradled like a sacred relic. "I often wondered what one of these summitches would do if you was to drop it."

"Wouldn't do anything," I said, "unless the primer landed on a nail or something. If it did, it would do the same thing it does in the cannon and it would do it right in your face. I 'spect that for the rest of what you had left of eternity, if you had *any* left, you'd be picking paper out of the holes in your head and not be hearing much of anything but the sound of the sea."

"Then you best not drop it."

"Don't intend to." I clamped the shell like a football under one arm and walked back out to the cannon. Droit had returned to his manual. He was studying to be an officer. Oh, yeah. . . .

Out at the cannon, with my back to HQ, I used my bayonet to pry the wadding out of the shell and dumped the shotgun powder in with the base charge. Then I forced a bar of soap onto the fine brass lip and cut a perfect wad, which I pushed down with the handle of my bayonet until it bottomed against the powder. I really had no idea what all that powder would do, but it *was* a fucking cannon, after all, and ought to be able to take a little overcharge. Then I stuck the open end of the other sock into the shell and poured in the shot and pressed another bar of soap against the end, forming a closing wad. All the while the pine was riotous with crows.

Then I heard the voice of the flag man, who'd walked up on me. "What in the hell you done put in that shell?"

It was a nice rhyme, but I ignored him and kneaded the soap with my fingers to make a tight seal. I slid the round into the chamber. My companion stood there watching, slackjawed, until I told him to get back to the flagpole.

"Go on," I said. "Get ready to lower the flag."

He just stood there.

"It's none of your business. The gun is my concern. The fucking flag is yours. Now go on and get ready to lower it."

He just stared at me, unmoving, like he couldn't believe what he'd just seen.

"Loading and firing the cannon is my job, Goddamn it, and lowering the flag is yours. Now go get ready to *lower the fucking flag*."

He turned around and walked over to the flagpole.

When the last bugle note sounded, I yanked the lanyard. The sound the cannon made was a little louder than usual and the barrel definitely twitched a little more, but my eyes were on the pine, where something that looked like a hurricane gust tore through it: One violent *whoom* and the tree canopy just seemed to shatter, then stilled, while black feathers and crows, clusters of needles, and pieces of bark rained down all around it. What was left of the flock didn't even bother to caw—they were distant specks against the evening sky before the last feathers landed.

"Holy sheeeeuuuuut," the flag man said, clutching the unfolded flag to his chest. "Holy—"

"Just hush and let's go. I'll swab the bore and pick everything up later." I led him away to the barracks.

When we got inside, he turned and whispered to me, "I don't know what you just done, but you and me both know it's gotta be against regulations. You just blowed the shit out of a whole bunch of birds. You know that? With a cannon. A Goddamned *Army* cannon!"

"Crows," I said. "Don't insult the bird kingdom. And what I did was *my* business, none of yours."

"I just hope to hell that Droit wasn't watching."

"Fuck Droit."

"If anybody asts who was with you this evening, you'll just have to say you done it by yourself, because I wasn't even on this post. I was over at

Myrtle Beach—I was back in *Florida*—and I'll have a whole bunch of girls lined up to testify where I was at."

"Fine," I said. "Lay it all on me. You weren't even here. Girls, my ass. More like cows and sheep—like to see *them* testify. *Moooooooooooooooo. Baaaaaaaaaaaaaaaaaaaa.* Go on and fold the fucking flag."

I went upstairs and surveyed the damage from a window. I counted at least eight black spots among green clumps of pine needles at the base of the tree, and far off on the golf course a crow flapped along the ground toward the woods that bordered the pond. I could see one little group of golfers going about their business at a distant hole. The sound of a retreat cannon was nothing to them—they heard it every day.

After dark I slipped out and across the street and counted my crows. There were nine dead ones plus the injured one, which had probably made the woods—foxes would make quick work of him. I loaded needles and limbs and wadding and dead crows into an old duffle bag and lugged it to the edge of the pond, where I pitched the birds out into the water and scattered the pine twigs along the shore. Turtles would make fast work of the crows. I took the wadding and disposed of it as usual.

When I returned to the barracks, I retrieved my two-by-four and inched the cannon to its original position, chocked it, and cranked the elevation wheel until the barrel was back where it had been. After swabbing the bore, I went in and showered and crawled onto my bunk and lay there a long time staring up at the ceiling, most gratified. Then I read a little from Eliot and finally drifted off. That night I dreamed of war, great cannons rumbling, and dark birds falling from the sky.

Hunters

The three Indian hunters, two barely teens, one much older, stood quietly on the slope of a hill leading down onto the plain and studied at some distance the scene before them. Far across a rolling stretch of grass a wagon sat near the mouth of a wooded draw formed over millennia by water cutting down from the plateau behind it, its trees and shrubs sustained by the spring that issued from somewhere up near the point where its sharply defined flanks joined the mesa. Near the wagon stood horses tethered to a rope strung between two trees, and between them and the wagon five men moved about a fire. At the periphery of the encampment large reddish lumps lay in the grass.

"Do you find it strange, my young hunters, that we have found them the way they say that they find us, by following the circling birds?" The older Indian spoke quietly, as if fearing that even at such a great distance the buffalo hunters would hear him. "They attract more birds than we because they leave more for them to eat than we do. They take the hides and tongues and perhaps a few cuts of flank or hump meat and leave the rest to the birds and beasts—more, even, than *they* can eat. Much of it corrupts and seeps into the ground, a waste. See the dark green spots of grass where in years past they have melted in the sun like grease?" He pointed. In all directions there were bones.

"Who *are* they?" the one on his right asked, leaning forward on his horse and squinting.

"They are buffalo hunters, white men, and they have found what we have not," the older hunter answered.

The other young hunter shook his head. "How have they found buffalo when we could not?"

"The buffalo are becoming scarce," said the older hunter, Wolfkiller. "There was a time when there were seas of them, when we would not have had to come so far for them, when the whole village would turn out for the hunt, but now. . . ." He shook his head. "Now we have to ride for days to find even small herds. These are the ones we have been trailing. The wonder is that the white hunters have found them first. I think that they have had very good luck."

"What are they doing, butchering them?" Yellow Feather asked. Of the two boys he was the leaner, lighter of complexion, almost tawny, and his muscles were more pronounced.

"Butchering?" He shook his head slowly. "No, no. They are skinning them. The skinners ride in the wagon, following the hunters. When they kill buffalo, the skinners take the hides and perhaps cut off a few choice pieces for food, leaving the rest for the birds." Wolfkiller pointed to the ring of vultures spinning high above the camp. "You cannot see from here, but they have staked the hides out for drying. Soon they will roll them up and load them into the wagon and try to find another herd."

Young Buffalo, the shorter, heavier boy, spoke: "Wolfkiller, I am hungry. We have not eaten fresh meat for days. Would they let us have some from what they have killed?" He grimaced and licked his lips. "Only a little?"

The older Indian studied the question a few seconds. "I do not know. They are strange people, the white hunters, unpredictable, and I know little about them. They are best avoided. Yet—" He rubbed his stomach. "Yet I too am hungry, and what they have killed will merely rot on the plain. We will ride closer and see whether they are hostile. If they do not threaten us, perhaps we may ride in and ask." He pointed to the short bows balanced across the necks of their horses. "We will leave our weapons here and ride in slowly, and we shall see."

Yellow Feather turned quickly to him. "I do not like going in unarmed."

"They will not let us ride in armed. We will do as I say."

Wolfkiller held out his hands on either side and the young hunters reluctantly proffered their bows. The older hunter joined his bow with theirs and leaned over and dropped them gently to the ground. Then the three of them urged their horses slowly toward the dark gash of the draw, against which the wagon stood starkly white. The white hunters continued with their work, bending and straightening, clumping and separating, unaware of the Indians dropping down out of the sun.

Wolfkiller held his hands out and stopped. "They have seen us." They were now very near the beginning of the grassy flat, perhaps five hundred paces from the wagon. The two young hunters crowded up to him. The white men had stopped their work and gathered close to the fire, their faces turned toward the sun, which slowly fell toward the hills behind the Indians.

"Shall we ride closer?" Yellow Feather asked.

"No," Wolfkiller answered. "We must see what they do."

"Do you fear the men?" Young Buffalo was turned, looking back toward the spot where Wolfkiller had dropped their bows.

"I fear them, yes, but I have nothing but contempt for them."

"You do not fear them. You fear their guns," suggested Yellow Feather.

"I do not fear their guns. A rifle or a handgun may be used for good or bad purposes, or it may lie wrapped in oiled skins all a man's life and *never* be used. It has no evil except as a man directs it. No, I do not fear the long rifles you see leaning against the wagon—I fear the men who would as soon use those rifles against us as against a buffalo or deer. If they killed us for food, it would be one thing. They kill us only because we are here, because they can see us, because we are not one of them. They think of us as animals, no better than a four-legged creature."

"They will allow us to ride down to ask for meat?" Young Buffalo asked.

"I do not know," Wolfkiller answered. "But soon we will know. One of them has picked up his rifle, the one with the dark coat. We will go no closer until we receive a peaceful sign from them."

"We have done nothing to alarm him," the Yellow Feather answered. "He can see that we are no threat, even at this distance. The sun is not in his eyes."

"No. And he is using a long glass. He knows who we are and that we are unarmed. With their guns they would not fear us even if we *were* armed. The bow is for close-range fighting. We will go no closer." He raised his arms and held them straight out on either side, palms up, to indicate that they were without weapons.

Yellow Feather snorted. "How will we ask for meat from here? We must ride closer."

"No, no, young blood. Even from here the man is dangerous. You see that he is propping his rifle across the front of the wagon. We would do better to ride on."

"At this distance we are in no danger, surely," Yellow Feather said, looking impatiently at his leader. "Why—"

The roar of the great rifle reached them an instant before the bullet hit, thumping like an arrow striking an inflated bladder. Wolfkiller lurched forward, an astonished look on his face, and tumbled from his horse. The two younger Indians wheeled their ponies about and thrashed them directly away from the hunters toward a grassy hump and over it, slowing only when they could not see the wagon.

"We must go back," Yellow Feather panted, reining his horse. "We must help him."

Young Buffalo stopped his horse alongside. "Wolfkiller died before he struck the ground. The long rifle was true. The bullet went in here." He jabbed his chest with his thumb. "We can do nothing for him."

"We cannot leave him. That we cannot do. It would be a great shame upon us to leave him."

Young Buffalo scanned the ridge that lay between them and the hunters. "Then we will wait until the sun has set, when they cannot see us. There is no shame in that. There would be greater shame for another of us to die on a foolish mission, perhaps both of us."

"There is wisdom in what you say. We must go back to see that the hunters have not come to claim the body, to take his hair. Some say that the white men earn a bounty on our scalps."

"They do not know how many of us there are and how we are armed. They would want only his horse." Wolfkiller's horse stood with them, his sides heaving. "Still, we must be certain." Young Buffalo dismounted and tied his horse to a small tree, then caught Wolfkiller's horse and did the same. "Come."

Yellow Feather remained mounted. "Get back on your horse. If they have come up the slope they have not come afoot. If they catch us on foot while they are mounted, we will have no chance. It may be that they are in pursuit, though I do not think so. We are gone, and that is all that matters to them."

Young Buffalo remounted and joined Yellow Feather in a slow stalk to a point where, rising on hands and knees on their horses, they could just see over the hump. They looked, then turned their horses and trotted back to the tree where Wolfkiller's horse was tied. Yellow Feather spoke first.

"I cannot believe that even as Wolfkiller lies dead from their rifle, killed for doing nothing more than standing and watching from a great distance, they are going about their affairs as if nothing has happened. Does killing another man mean nothing more than that to them? Like killing a dog or a snake? They are tending hides! And Wolfkiller lies dead from one of their bullets."

"It is as Wolfkiller said—we are only animals to them. They do not care about us. The one who fired on us, did you mark where he was?" Young Buffalo asked.

"Yes. He sits in the wagon watching, with his rifle ready. I saw him. And the others are working away as they did before. As long as they have the long rifles, they do not fear us."

"We must wait, then, until the sun is gone and recover Wolfkiller's body. They care nothing for us. Only that we are gone. They will not disturb Wolfkiller's body—it means nothing to them. No more than if they had killed a dog or a snake. He is no more than a skinned buffalo to them, fit only for the birds."

"Young Buffalo, there is something wrong in this."

"We are doing what is wise. What our elders would do. What Wolfkiller would do if one of us lay dead out there."

"That I do not believe," Yellow Feather said. He rubbed his horse's neck as he spoke, the two of them still mounted and ready to ride if the hunters appeared. "Wolfkiller would avenge one of us."

Young Buffalo shook his head. "No. Wisdom says no. We cannot ride against so many men so well armed. They would kill us before we were close enough to fire our arrows."

"If we rode straight in, yes. If we followed this ridge to the back side of the draw and attacked from the trees above them, we could pin them down and shoot them one by one. They would be within easy range of our arrows."

"Yellow Feather, they have the wagon for cover, and horses for escape. They have long rifles, which reach much farther than our arrows. And the short guns that shoot many times before reloading. We would have no chance against so many so well armed. It would make more dead. And they have food and water. We can not starve them out."

"We must avenge, Young Buffalo."

"I say it would be foolish to try."

"At least we should ask advice. That would be honorable. We cannot simply wait until dark and carry Wolfkiller's body back to camp. Eyes of

Stone will know what to do. If he thinks vengeance is proper, then we must act. If we take the body back and the hunters leave while we are gone, we may not catch them before they are with more of their kind and vengeance is impossible."

Young Buffalo studied his face. Behind his friend's back only half a sun sat on the hills. "What do you suggest then? We are not wise enough and strong enough to act on our own. We are boys. What would you have us do?"

Yellow Feather held out his hand. "Give me your arrows."

"I do not understand."

"You will. Hand me your arrows." Young Buffalo removed his quiver and passed it to Yellow Feather. "Thank you. When I have recovered Wolf-killer's arrows, I will have enough, I think." He stared stonily at his friend. "We are not boys."

"What will you do, Yellow Feather?"

"It is what *we* will do. You must ride to Eyes of Stone and report all of this. He will know what to do. If he thinks vengeance is proper and reasonable, he will return with you with more of the hunting party. And with the rifle. He will know how to do this." He remained quiet a few seconds, then said, "We are not boys."

"And what will you do?"

"I shall recover our bows and ride out in a wide circle and slip into the trees above them and hold them under fire until you return."

"But, Yellow Feather, we could not possibly return until long after dark. How will you keep them from leaving?"

"They will not leave the safety of the wagon. They have food and water and weapons with them. It would be foolish of them to try to move in the dark when they do not know how many of us lie waiting for them."

It was agreed then. Young Buffalo would ride to the hunting chief and ask his orders while Yellow Feather held the buffalo hunters under siege. They clasped hands and parted, Young Buffalo toward the falling sun and Yellow Feather to the trail where they had crossed the hilltop. They left Wolfkiller's horse tied to the tree. Young Buffalo leaned low on his horse and thrust his heels into the animal's flanks and within a hundred paces was over another rise and out of sight, flying toward his chief.

After tracking back to the bows on hands and knees, lifting his eyes from time to time to see that the hunter was not taking aim at him, Yellow Feather returned to his horse and rode along the back side of ridge of the hill and crossed the stretch of plain out of sight of the hunters. In a little while he was at the top of the slope that formed the right side of the draw that led to where the men were camped. He noticed with gratitude that the right slope was steeper and higher and had more trees than the other, making it possible for him to work his way with good cover to within striking distance of the wagon. He tied his horse high on the slope, just out of sight of the hunters, but close enough so that if he had to retreat he could do so quickly.

With his skin of water and a length of dried bison in one hand, Wolf-killer's bow and three quivers of arrows in the other, he began his descent, tree to tree, bush to bush, outcropping to outcropping, until he reached the ledge of stone he had kept his eyes fixed on. A clump of cedar grew an arm's length out from it and shielded the ledge from view below. He had carefully noted the wagon's position as he dropped into the draw, so he knew that he had to be within range now. Flat on his belly, he inched forward until he could see the hunters and their wagon through the canopy of the cedar.

The wagon was parked just out from a clump of yaupon, twenty paces or so from the spring that began somewhere at the head of the draw and pooled briefly before disappearing into the grassy plain. Even in the late light he could see clearly that the pool was muddy and faintly tinged with red, where the hunters had washed their arms and hands after skinning the buffalo. Over two dozen carcasses lay like blisters in the dropping sun. The men had stretched out and staked the hides around the wagon, flesh side up, to dry. Yellow Feather could hear the drone of flies that splotched the pink skins.

Their work for the day apparently done, the skinners, two older men and a boy, sat in a circle before a large fire roasting what looked like buffalo tongues. One hunter sat with them, but the one who had shot Wolf-killer stood vigil near the wagon. He would study the plain and hills for a little while, then look back at the circle of men. Laughing and joking, they passed a bottle about, each of them taking a long drink and handing it to the next. From time to time the hunter leaned and whispered something to the young skinner and they laughed and jostled with each other, once falling back in a heap, the hunter pinning the boy's arms to the ground and rubbing his great hairy face against what looked like hairless cheeks.

The two older skinners seemed less concerned with their rollicking comrades than with the hillside where Wolfkiller's body lay in the grass. One of them tended the meat but kept his eyes on the hill. The other watched in one direction a few minutes, then in another, as if uncertain where trouble would come from if it came. Their horses and mules, six in all, were tied to a rope strung between two small trees a few paces from the wagon. The men had gathered grass and piled it before the animals for fodder.

Yellow Feather studied the scene until he knew where the strength and weakness of his enemies lay. Their fire was very near the wagon, where they would go for immediate protection if trouble came, but they had tied the horses too far away to offer fast and safe escape, and the wagon was much too far from the cover of the brush and trees of the draw. The two hunters had their rifles at hand, and the older skinners wore handguns. Perhaps there were other weapons in the wagon, and certainly extra ammunition. Their strength lay in numbers and arms, their weakness in the location of the wagon. A barrage of arrows from above would drive them into and under the wagon, where Yellow Feather could keep them besieged until the others came. There would be no way for the men to know the numbers of their enemy or precisely where they fired their arrows from. When the hunting party arrived, if Eyes of Stone saw wisdom in vengeance and ordered an attack, they would spread out and shoot their arrows from many directions, and if they brought embers or a fire drill, burning the wagon would be easy. For now Yellow Feather had merely to wait and watch.

The young Indian knew little of white men. The village he grew up in was never in one place for more than a few months, moving with the buffalo and the seasons and avoiding white men, especially the blue soldiers, at all costs. Whites were the cruel ones, men who brought disease and death, men whose rifles spoke a deadly language from hundreds of paces, men whose crazy water made the best of warriors dizzy and helpless with stupor.

On one of his first outings, when he and two of his young friends had accompanied a hunting party to manage the horses in camp, he had watched blue-coated soldiers riding along a river valley as the hunters spied from trees along the ridge. The hunting chief motioned his men to move off quietly, and they left the soldiers to their scout. Yellow Feather did not know why the chief had decided not to attack, but he was disappointed that he had not witnessed a battle—he did not doubt that the hunters would win.

The chief and two of his closest warriors carried flintlock rifles, which they handled quite well, though the boy knew that in a close-quarter battle, which the Indians always tried to arrange, a dozen arrows could be flung with accuracy at the enemy before a man could fire a rifle twice. In open landscape at long distances soldiers with their rifles were deadly—at close range the bow was superior.

Beyond that one occasion most of what he knew of white men he had heard as the old men spoke of trading with them or warriors boasted of attacking cabins and wagons and, quite infrequently, skirmishing with the blue soldiers. Two white children and a white woman were brought into camp one fall, but before the first snow they had been bartered to Mexican traders for cloth and blankets and trinkets. They had been kept well hidden in a lodge at the far end of camp, so he had seen little of them. Their skin was very fair, like something kept out of the sun, and their hair was lighter of color and not straight. He had noticed among the many war trophies strung up about the village that the scalps of white people always stood out starkly among the Indian scalps, whose straight, dark hair looked more like that of a horse's mane or tail.

Soon darkness settled on the camp, and what little light there was came from the fire. The hunter who had been wrestling with the young skinner had pulled the boy into a sitting position and wrapped his legs around him, leaning and whispering, the two of them laughing, while the other hunter looked on. He seemed displeased. One of the older skinners continued to watch the horizon while the other cooked, glancing up from time to time at the hills.

Yellow Feather sipped from his skin and chewed a piece of dried buffalo as he studied the camp. When the others arrived there would be no time for drinking and eating. The smell of cooking tongue drafting up the slope of the draw had aroused his hunger, but mixed with it was the taint of the carcasses and the corrupt odor of excrement where the white men had relieved themselves in the bushes without bothering to cover their droppings. His hunger gained the upper hand and he ate.

Just as the camp settled into a dusky twilight, the hunter who had been playing with the young skinner pulled the boy to his feet and led him to the wagon. He said something to the others, who laughed, and pushed the boy into the rear of the wagon and forward beneath the canvas-covered foresection, where they disappeared.

It was only then that Yellow Feather understood. While Wolfkiller, who had been like a father to him and taught him all a young warrior and hunter needed to know, lay dead on the hillside, these strange, bearded men who had killed him laughed and ate and drank and violated their very natures as if they had killed only a snake or a dog. He now understood, and a great tide of anger welled in him. He laid down the strip of buffalo meat and plugged his water skin. With Young Buffalo's and Wolfkiller's arrows he had nearly six dozen. He lined out a row of them on the ledge before him.

His first arrow penetrated the canvas cover of the wagon, the second landed between the two skinners at the fire, and the third dropped beside the hunter keeping watch. Accuracy was not his purpose—he wanted only to frighten and confuse. He fired his next volley at their animals, the first and second arrows striking the earth, the third catching one of the horses in the flank. The animal reared and plunged and sent the others into such a frenzy that their collective lunge against the rope broke over the small tree it was tied to and in one great dusty sweep they threw their weight against the other tree and the limb to which the end of the rope was tied gave way. Yellow Feather watched them gallop abreast, dragging the tree and branches with them until the knot disappeared over the nearest hill to the west.

The hunters and skinners were under the wagon now. He had seen the hunter who had been with the young skinner roll over the side and crawl under with the others, the naked boy following soon after. Whether either had been struck by an arrow he wasn't certain. One rifle still lay beside the fire. That meant that they had one rifle and at least two handguns to defend themselves. Other weapons and extra ammunition were probably in the wagon, but they would not come from beneath unless desperate. Yellow Feather had them where he wanted them.

Darkness would soon join them as his enemy. There would be a partial moon, but the day had not been altogether cloudless and he had little knowledge of the ways of weather. If the sky clouded, the men would be able to enter the wagon, take whatever provisions they needed, and assume defensive positions near the spring. Any attack against them then would very difficult. He had to keep them cowed so that even in the dark they would dare not move from their cover.

He watched intently as the camp grew darker. When one of them raised his head to look, Yellow Feather flung an arrow, again hoping not to hit such a small target at that distance but rather to keep the men frightened and beneath the wagon. The hunters could not see him through the cedar branches, but one of them fired several times when an arrow struck the earth or clattered off the wagon. He shot wildly, not once kicking up dirt near Yellow Feather or whizzing a bullet through the cedar. It was obvious from the loud reports that the rifle he was firing was of large caliber and from the number of shots fired that the men had plenty of ammunition. That was not good. If they could reach the other rifle, things would become much worse.

Darkness finally fell completely, but the quarter moon, obscured only by an occasional cloud, threw enough light on the camp that Yellow Feather could see clearly when a dark head or arm or leg broke the outline of the wagon. As his arrow supply dwindled to only a dozen or so, he began throwing large stones down the slope to unnerve the men. He discovered that due to his height he could throw smaller stones as far as the wagon itself, so periodically he pelted the camp. It was absurdly like childhood battles he had fought with Young Buffalo and the other boys he had grown up with. There was exhilaration in the siege now, and Yellow Feather could barely refrain from yelping every time a stone bounced off the wagon. His tongue remained quiet—better that the men not know where their attackers were and how few.

How long he lay there watching and listening, occasionally throwing stones and twice firing arrows, he could only guess, though he knew from the slow slide of the moon that it was a great while. There had been no motion about the wagon since he began throwing stones, and though once he heard boards splitting and popping, there had been no noise since. The men must have decided that there was no way of fighting back in the night, that it would be better to wait for daylight, when their guns could find targets. There would be no sleep for them, though—Yellow Feather had a strong arm and more stones than he could throw in a lifetime.

He had just bounced a stone off something in the rear of the wagon, setting off a loud clang, when he heard from off down the ridge toward the hillside where Wolfkiller's body lay a familiar bird call. Young Buffalo was back. Yellow Feather returned the call and listened. From across the draw, somewhere above the camp, came another bird call, then another from out on the plain between the camp and the hills. Eyes of Stone's hunters had surrounded the camp.

"Well, my young warrior," a voice came out of the dark behind him, "you have done well with only a handful of arrows . . . and a few hundred stones."

Yellow Feather drew back from the ledge and sat up. A dark shape rose before him. "Eyes of Stone, I am glad you are here."

"We have been here for some time." The chief dropped to his knees and crawled up beside him. "As you heard, we are all about their camp. Young Buffalo is out there." He motioned toward the plain. "We have Wolfkiller's body in keeping, and now we will deal with these animals."

"They have no horses, and I think that they have only one rifle among them. Another lies out by the fire, and there may be others in the wagon, but they have only one with them."

Eyes of Stone patted him on the shoulder. "We have their horses and mules. They were tangled up in the rope that held them, wrapped so tightly together that we had to cut them loose. They are tied in the hills."

"Did you bring fire?" Yellow Feather asked, "and the rifle?"

"Yes, of course. We have embers and the rifle. Tomorrow we shall have two more rifles, at least, one of which shall be yours, unless these men are luckier than I think. You go back into the trees and sleep. I will watch and wake you at dawn. We are starting fires in a ring about the camp to let the white men know that we are all around them."

"The hunters will shoot at the fires," Yellow Feather answered.

"No one will be near the fires except to add fuel as they die out. Let them waste their ammunition. It will be easier for us at dawn. Go and take your rest. You have done very well." The chief pushed Yellow Feather toward the trees behind the ledge. "When the time is right for us to move, I will wake you. Go and take your rest."

His sleep was a troubled plain, crossed time after time by great hairy men with long rifles racing with the buffalo. One bearded man rode near the edge of the herd, naked, and before him, just out of his reach, ran Young Buffalo, his feet bleeding from the stony ground, his shrieks echoing across the hills. Yellow Feather stood high on a ridge overlooking the cascading herd and the naked hunter and threw white stone after white stone, each falling short of his friend's pursuer. Each time he woke from fear, he looked about at the ring of fires and, comforted, settled back into sleep, only to stand once again high above the buffalo and hunters, absurdly throwing stones at a naked, bearded man thundering down on his friend.

"Awake, my young warrior." Eyes of Stone was shaking him. In the smoky first light birds were twittering all around. Beside his chief crouched half a dozen hunters like himself, but older, each bristling with weapons and heavily streaked with charcoal across arms and face. One held a charred branch out to him. "Paint your face and arms, Yellow Feather. Soon we will be at war." He accepted the branch and drew the burned end down his cheeks, across his forehead, then down his arms.

"I wish we had colors," he said as he finished with the branch. "Reds and yellows, white."

Eyes of Stone patted his head. "When we left we were hunting for buffalo. Buffalo are not impressed by war paint. This will do for now." He grasped the younger Indian's hand and pulled him to his feet. "The sun will soon be up and we will strike. Here—you might need these." He held out a handful of fresh arrows.

Yellow Feather took the arrows. "I am glad for these. I had only a few left."

The chief laughed. "But many stones."

"How did you know about the stones?"

"You nearly hit Flying Bird with one. He had crawled close to the wagon to observe the men when something struck the earth behind him. His heart almost stopped."

"I was afraid to use all my arrows."

"You did well. But no more talk. We must strike." The chief motioned for the hunters to follow him. The Indians crept out to the ledge behind the cedar and looked down on the camp, where in the light of dawn nothing moved. The men were huddled beneath the wagon with low barricades of earth and stone and buffalo skins thrown up between the wheels and at the ends.

Eyes of Stone spoke. "They have built a fortress. In the night they must have pulled skins from the wagon. Doubtless they broke through the bottom. They have more ammunition now, maybe more guns, more water, more food. And certainly they have more stones, if the battle should come to it." He grinned at Yellow Feather. "Strong Hand. Here." A powerfully built hunter dropped down beside his chief. "Go get the fire arrows." He held up his spread hand. "This many. Soak them well in oil. Bring a burning branch with you."

The hunter nodded and slipped up into the trees, where Yellow Feather had seen a fire burning in the dark. In a short time he was back with five arrows, their tips wrapped with oil-soaked strips of deerskin. He handed the arrows to Eyes of Stone, who laid them out on the ledge before him, then passed the branch to the chief, who gathered a clutch of dry grass, laid the smoking end in the little nest, and blew on the stick until the grass flamed.

Eyes of Stone raised his face to the morning sky and uttered a series of short yelps, sounds Yellow Feather had never heard before, then set an arrow tip aflame and launched the fiery missile down the slope, where it struck the side of the wagon and bounced off harmlessly into the dirt. The second landed just beneath the end of the wagon and a flurry of sand quickly put it out. The next two dropped into the bed at the rear, and the last landed on the canopy. Soon the entire wagon was burning.

The first man to break from beneath the flames was one of the skinners, an older man, balding and slender. His pants leg was smoking. He started toward the spring pool in a crouching run, waving a large black handgun before him, but before he had made half the distance to the pool, the air was whistling with arrows, two of which struck him in the back. A third hit his left leg, just below the knee, and a fourth struck him at the base of his skull. As he fell to his knees, the second older skinner scurried out of the smoke and fire and ran for the spring, only to meet a barrage of arrows. He dropped beside his companion, who was now writhing on his side, tearing at the arrow lodged in his neck.

The boy burst out next, fully dressed, followed by the hunter who had taken him into the wagon the night before. Firing blindly at the trees of the draw with his handgun, the boy was two strides past the fallen skinners when a hail of arrows felled him. The hunter behind him spun wildly about, looking for a target for his handgun, while the second hunter rose from the billowing wagon, the long rifle in his hand. Eyes of Stone shouted commands, and a rush of arrows spiraled down onto the first, and he fell beside the boy. The hunter with the rifle stood, brushed out a flame on his shirt, and turned slowly with his rifle to his shoulder, but no arrows came. He dropped to his knees and swung the rifle from slope to slope, looking for a target, but there was none.

Silence settled on the camp. Only the crackling of the burning wagon disturbed the morning, the column of smoke rising almost straight into the air. From time to time there were small pops when ammunition exploded. The lone hunter sat back on his heels waiting for the arrows to come, and when none did he rose to his feet and stalked slowly toward the spring. A staggered row of arrows fell at his feet, between him and the water. Another row fell behind. Eyes of Stone stood up on the ledge and shouted down at the hairy man standing among his dead and dying companions. He could not have known what the Indian was saying, but neither could he have confused the tone of triumph. He shouted back and raised the rifle, but the whistling arrows that fell at his feet weakened his boast. He lowered his weapon and stood looking toward the cedar behind which Eyes of Stone stood.

The chief turned to Yellow Feather. "He is for you and Young Buffalo to do with as you wish. But do not let him die quickly." He lifted his face to the sun and uttered a series of yelps, whereupon the Indian hunters advanced from trees and brush and rocks toward the lone white hunter. Broken Hand approached him first, motioning with his bow for the hunter to drop his rifle to the ground. When the man hesitated, the Indian swept his hand in a broad arc to show how many hunters surrounded him, all with bows drawn tight.

Whether hoping for mercy or weary of the fight and ready to accept whatever fate his captors intended, the bearded man dropped his rifle to the ground and fell to his knees weeping. The ring of Indians closed, joined by others from the plain until the full hunting party surrounded him. Broken Hand stepped forward and pricked the man's shoulder with his arrow tip. "Is this the one who killed Wolfkiller?" he asked Young Buffalo, who was standing just behind, peering around the warrior at the white man.

"Yes, he shot Wolfkiller." The younger Indian leaped from behind Broken Hand and struck the white hunter savagely with his bow. The man drew back and lowered his head and wept, muttering something that they could not understand.

Yellow Feather and Eyes of Stone approached from across the draw, followed by a band of young hunters, all with arrows drawn. Had the man made a menacing gesture, half a hundred arrows would have filled his body before he fell dead to the ground. "Broken Hand," Eyes of Stone said, "lash him securely and pull your hunters back. Gather the firearms and ammunition and anything else of value and carry everything back to camp. This man's rifle—" He motioned to the sobbing hunter. "This man's rifle belongs to Yellow Feather."

The chief turned to the hunters behind him. "Be certain to take all the skins, but take no meat from the dead animals. The white men sometimes sprinkle poison on them so that we cannot eat the meat. Take what meat they have salted or dried and leave the rest for the birds and beasts. Let us hope that our other hunters have been more successful than we have been. Surely these cannot have been all the buffalo on the plain." He swept his arm toward the swollen carcasses that lay near the burned-out wagon. "Young Buffalo and Yellow Feather and I will finish here." He motioned for the young hunters who had been with him to join the others. "Leave Wolfkiller's body and his horse. We will bring them with us." He pointed toward the dead white men. "You know what to do with them."

Broken Hand gave his orders and as he tied the white hunter with strips of buffalo skin the Indians rummaged through the camp, dumping their spoils into the fresh buffalo hides. Young Buffalo and Yellow Feather could not see what was happening to the bodies of the white men, but they knew from the whoops and yelps that the warriors were taking scalps and mutilating the corpses. When they had finished with the camp, they split into their hunting units and returned to their horses. The three remaining Indians watched as the hunters rode off toward the hills.

Eyes of Stone turned to the Yellow Feather and Young Buffalo. "He is yours now, and you must punish him as you please. He must die, though I would urge you to be slow about it—he must suffer greatly for what he has done. If you wish me to assist you, I shall do so gladly."

The two younger Indians looked at each other, then at the white hunter, who was slumped forward on his knees weeping and crying out in his strange language. "No," Yellow Feather said to his chief. "Young Buffalo and I will punish him, and you may be comforted that he will die in anguish. When we have finished, we will join you."

"You must bring his hair." He glanced at the sun. "Take your time, but before dark falls again join us at the fork of the big river. We shall meet with the other hunting party and see how they have done, then return to the village. I trust that they have found buffalo." He mounted his horse and turned toward the hills. "I shall take care of Wolfkiller and his horse. You have your duty."

When their chief was gone, the two boys stood in silence staring at the white man before them. His filthy face was streaked with tears, and he worked constantly at the leather thongs that bound his arms behind him. He was on his knees, buttocks resting on his calves. They would not let him lie down. When he tried to roll over onto his side, Young Buffalo grabbed him by his hair and righted him, as one might a grass-stuffed toy.

"They kill, we kill. What is the difference?" Young Buffalo asked. He stood with an arrow still nocked in the bowstring, the bow slightly drawn, as if fearing that the hunter might break his bonds and spring upon them.

"The difference is that we kill because we must—they kill for the sake of killing."

"I cannot kill him," Young Buffalo said. "I have never killed a man. I cannot do it."

"You have never killed a buffalo either, but you would do it if you had the chance."

"That is different. This is a man." He nodded toward the slumped hunter.

"Not much different," Yellow Feather answered. "He has almost as much hair as a buffalo. He is no less an animal than a buffalo. I would not eat an animal so filthy." He suddenly reached out and grabbed the man's hair, rolling it into a tight knot with his fist. The hunter grimaced and moaned. Yellow Feather released him and smelled his hand. "Smell it. He stinks like death itself, worse than dung. He smells worse than the dead buffalo out there."

Young Buffalo shook his head. "He is a man. A hunter, a warrior."

Yellow Feather sneered. "He is a coward and a beast, and he weeps and moans like a baby. If you will not kill him, I will." Before his companion could answer he unsheathed his knife and neatly sliced the white man's right ear away, then his left, holding the moaning man's head steady by the hair with his other hand. "But I will do it slowly. Now the beast without ears will be the beast without a nose as well."

The white hunter's head was thrown back, his twisted, streaming face to the sky, while his teeth ground in pain, and from deep in his throat came a sound so alien that Yellow Feather's hand, poised with the knife, stopped in its downward arc. The boy could not take the nose. He dropped his hands to his sides and stared at his bleeding enemy, who seemed for that one moment to be like any trapped and suffering animal that needed simply to be killed. He turned and looked at Young Buffalo. "We must punish him more."

"Then you will have to do it," his friend said. "I cannot. You say that we are not boys, but I am yet a boy, I fear. I can kill a rabbit or a deer, and maybe a man, but I cannot do it like this." He would not look at the white hunter.

"Eyes of Stone says he must die slowly, painfully, for what he has done. We cannot disobey our chief." He had not raised the knife again.

Young Buffalo shook his head. "I cannot do it."

"Take out your knife!" he commanded. "You must take his nose and I will gouge out his eyes and cut off his tongue and then cut off his eggs and put them in his mouth. But you must take the nose."

"I cannot."

Yellow Feather took a step toward his friend and raised the knife until it pointed at his throat. "You will do your part. We are no longer *boys*. Now we are *warriors* and you will do your part in this. Eyes of Stone has commanded."

Young Buffalo shook his head. Yellow Feather took another step and thrust the knife straight out before him until it was no more than inches from the other Indian's throat. Young Buffalo held his bow down, arrow tip toward the ground. He made no move to raise it. He stared into his friend's eyes. "If it has come to this, then you must kill me. I am not ready to do these things. In time, perhaps, but I am not ready. I am a boy. *We* are boys."

"You must do this. It is our duty. And we are not *boys*! We are *warriors!*"

"Yellow Feather, he has suffered long enough. He is our enemy and he must die, but I cannot kill him. I cannot cut on him."

"This is a great shame that you are bringing on us. This is our chance to prove that we are not boys any longer. We are warriors. We must prove ourselves." Yellow Feather was pleading now, his hand with the knife dropped back down to his side. He wept openly and settled to his knees. "I cannot take his nose either, or gouge out his eyes." The white man continued to stare into the sky, raising his muffled cry to whatever god might listen.

"I do not know what to do, Young Buffalo," the boy said. But just as the last word was out he was aware of his friend's arrow tip rising, the sound of a strained bow, and the slap of bowstring as the arrow leaped. When he spun on his knees and looked at the hunter, the man was in the same position, head thrown back, but now his eyes were different, the sounds from his throat different. From a small red puckered spot in the haired flesh of his chest a brief trickle of blood spiraled down. The arrow was sticking halfway out of his back. The man rocked gently a few seconds, then fell back onto his bound arms, eyes fixed on the sky.

Darkness was beginning to settle when they topped the last hill before the valley where the river forked. Yellow Feather could see smoke from the campfires hugging the river bottom. The two Indians had not spoken in many miles, each deep in his thoughts. Yellow Feather reined his horse and motioned for Young Buffalo to do the same.

"We will tell Eyes of Stone that he suffered greatly," he said to his friend. As he spoke his eyes fell on the scalp dangling from his pommel, its bright-blood interior dry now from hours of wind and sun. In his mind's eye could still see the naked body of the hunter, as pale as buffalo kidney fat, stretched into a cross shape, his testicles stuffed into his mouth, his noseless and eyeless face ready for the meat-eating sun of tomorrow.

"I think that he did suffer," Young Buffalo said, easing up alongside. His hands were still stained deeply with blood. Like Yellow Feather he had three streaks of his enemy's blood on each cheek. "I think that he is not the only one who has suffered today."

Yellow Feather looked at him. Young Buffalo's face seemed harder, darker in the dying light, and as he looked into his companion's eyes, he understood.

The two warriors dropped over the hill and descended into the river flats and the deep shadows of evening.